Fall and Rise of the Macas

Fall and Rise of the Macas

Chronicles of the Maca VI

Mari Collier

Published 2016 by Creativia

Book design by Creativia (www.creativia.org)

Cover art by http://www.thecovercollection.com/

http://www.maricollier.com/

Contents

Chapter 1

Contact

Jarvis, Maca of Ayran, Captain of Flight, stirred at the sound of Captain Tamar's words coming into his quarters. "We are closing in on the attackers," brought him to his feet. He finished dressing and ran through the short corridor into the Command Center.

He clenched and unclench his huge hands, easing the tenseness of all those years of searching for an enemy that they knew were out there. His dark eyes swept over his staff as he ran in and slammed his bulk into the commander's chair. His straight, dark hair was swept back and heavy, black eyebrows softened the wide angled face cut by a huge wedge of a nose. His thick, sensuous lips curled in a triumphant smile. His facial features were supported by a wide, corded neck blending into the slope of his shoulders. His whole body gave promise of vicious fighting, but now he was stilled as he focused on the screen showing the approaching craft.

Jarvis never cared if his crew hated his decision to remain these extra five years in space searching for Draygons. They had known this would be a long mission in a Thalian spaceship designed to find and close with an attacking ship. Over the ten years of this mission their enthusiasm for a fight had dimmed, but Jarvis persisted.

At five minutes before twelve hundred hours the message had come through the Communication's audio. The De'Chin's language was auto-translated into Thalian. "Urgent! We are under attack by unknown beings. Respond. This is our exploratory outpost at system Twenty-five on the Quadrant charts. Respond. This is urgent!"

He had squelched any reply the staff person at the communications station was ready to send. Lasa, a Tri from Don protested.

"They need assistance."

"Aye, and they shall have it, but whoever the attackers are, they shall nay ken we are coming."

Now Jarvis turned to Captain Tamar, Lad of Don, and snapped out his orders. "Take us in."

Lillie, Lady of Don and Betron, his Communications and Recording Director, sat to his right, her dark head bowed over the screen. He heard her mutter, "Here it comes."

All were staring at the screen. Jarvis looked at the shape and the numbers running at the top of the screen and worked his portion of the panel to settle his ship slightly lower and to the left. The alien's craft was round, unlike the oval shaped spaceships in the Justine League.

"Steady, Warriors. Nay misses."

"They will try to fire first." Lillie was muttering.

"Aye, when we close." Jarvis's response was clipped as his attention was on the screen and the number coordinates massing in his mind. He sensed, rather saw the ship shift to his left and he redirected the first blast.

The alien returned fire and both ships wobbled as they moved closer. Again and again his wide fingers struck the blast panel, their bodies rocking with the ship's sway. The alien ship tilted and shifted downward toward the planet and Jarvis followed.

"Back off," Lillie pointed at the screen. "They have a craft below us and are firing upward."

Jarvis saw the alien ship turning and moving toward them.

Tamar's frantic voice advised, "We must go up."

"'That tis what they want," and Jarvis swept his ship lower and to the left. His eyes danced as the beam from Dragon's grounded fighter caught its own ship. He swung his craft around and Tamar had to grasp at the arms of his chair to keep from tumbling out. Jarvis leveled the craft and fired again. Elation surged through him as the alien vessel spiraled downward and once more his fingers worked the panel blasting the ship into debris that turned into burning bands as they entered the atmosphere of the asteroid. He swooped down and blasted the fighter that was beginning to rise.

"Lillie, run the scanners. We need to determine where the rest of their fighters are."

"Ye pilot recklessly." She smiled at him, her brown eyes gleaming and then bent over the screen.

Jarvis leaned backward and swiveled the chair. "Damage?" He noticed Tamar helping Lasa up.

Lasa gave both a sickly smile and scanned her section. "Nay damage here, but the Supply Sector took a hit. All systems are operational."

Jarvis nodded and connected to Engineering. "Are we battle ready? We need to take out any low flight fighters and ground installations."

"Aye, Captain, Nay damage here except minor shaking of our teeth. All shields are intact again."

He swung back to the screen. Lillie had the locations of grounded fighters and their coordinates in batches of numbers. The crew could hear his words on the Command channel.

"Three fighters coming upward," Lillie could not help adding unnecessary words. "Mayhap they think we are damaged to send such insects after us."

"Do ye wish to capture them?" Tamar asked.

"Nay, I wish to check their abilities." Jarvis eyes were lit with hard beams of light. The fighters were swift, but lacked the fire power of the mother ship and one by one the bolts from the Thalians' ship made them disintegrate.

"Shall I take it down for ye?" asked Tamar.

"And be blown into the Darkness?" Contempt was beginning to build in Jarvis. He swallowed and turned to Lillie.

"Lillie, keep the scans going. We'll cruise for a closer look. Tamar, when anything shows, I want degrees for blasting."

"Captain, there could be De'Chins alive," protested Tamar. "Ye canna destroy the base without cause. The Justine League has certain standards."

"The League can discuss standards for centuries," he snapped as he completed the maneuver to orbit.

Lasa's next words stopped any fight. "Captain, the Director of Supplies reports a disaster area."

Jarvis punched the communicator. "Kahli, what tis wrong?"

"The shaking and turning has tumbled some of our tanks. Sodium and hydro trays were dumped. There tis metal in the walls. Mayhap the shields shifted. The engineering crew tis on their way to do the repair if possible. We may go on short rations ere we return to Thalia if we canna pick up supplies and bios off the asteroid below."

Jarvis suppressed a grin. Kahli, Lad of Don, did nay believe in failure. He simply totaled the obstacles and calculated ways to circumvent them.

"If ye were thinking of blowing up this place, dinna." Kahli's sharp voice continued. "Besides the bios, I will need fresh water. We have been away too long."

"Aye." Jarvis conceded. He needed his crew intact when they returned and he needed to ken more about the enemy. It had been the excitement of battle. The space attack forty years ago when on a probe had been a blow to his pride. He was nay sure whether it was his fighting skills, the technology, or Daniel's

4

starpath skills that had mapped the way home that enabled him to make it to Brendon and then back to Thalia. Some had speculated the attack had been lost beings from another part of the universe. Now he could prove them wrong. The Justines had not approved the building of space fighters, but since Thalia controlled the Justine League, it mattered nay.

Lillie nudged him. She had everything displayed on screen: ship locations, hot spots, and where all the beings were.

"Good," he grunted not bothering with thanks.

"There are still three fighters grounded," she said. "A ground cruiser tis there, but I canna determine whether they belong to the De'Chins or the attackers."

He took the ship in on her coordinates and blasted. In battle, he expected no favors and granted nay. Thrice he held the key down and then looked at his Recording Director.

"All tis logged."

Jarvis could almost hear the crew relax.

"Do we land now?" asked Tamar.

"Nay in this ship. I'll take warriors in fighters and the cruiser. Ye are to remain in orbit. There may be more fighters stalking for an intruder. Ye are to head for Thalia if things go wrong. If ye are swarmed, send messages to the closest planet or mining exploration colony."

"Lillie, ye continue to look for ground cruisers or hidden mining camps. I dinna like surprises."

"Jarvis, ye need me there to record the events, and I am a Warrior." Her voice was as direct as her eyes.

Jarvis studied her six-foot five frame, the same as his though not as wide or muscular. She was, however, the Guardian of Flight's lassie, a descendent of the Great LouElla.

"Besides, Rade can scan as well as I can. He tis awake and chomping for something to do."

"Aye," he conceded. "Ye will attend."

Chapter 2

The Enemy

The asteroid was a cold and dreary; a barren rocky outpost of sand dunes shifted by fierce winds that screamed through the rock canyons. From high above, scanty moisture dripped to feed what few life forms existed before evaporating away in the open. Any falling water that might hit the sand disappeared. Any warmth at midday vanished within two hours. The De'Chins had claimed this desolate place to mine for the depleted mineral and ore supplies on their home planet. There were two known inhabited outposts.

A quick survey of the landscape turned up the aliens' fighters and the De'Chins' outposts. The De'Chin vessels and one of the outposts were melted into lumps of odd angles and twisted metal. Jarvis remained wary. He set his fighter down and walked with Lillie and Pillar, Captain of Troopers.

"There should be ground cruisers, De'Chin, or the attackers. Where are they?"

Jarvis answered Pillar's question. "They are waiting to draw us into a trap." he turned towards Pillar. "Would the De'Chins have started another outpost and nay had time to install the power source?"

"Aye, there could be another either for a new mining shaft or for defense." Their voices buzzed in their ears through the protective helmets. "I would have another fighter underground. It would be essential for survival. It could even be used for a retreat to their home planet with the right two people and a starpath finder."

"Aye, have your troopers shield for battle. Ye will take a quick turn in the fighter, but nay hover if ye find them. Ye can order those above to fire."

"Captain, if ye stay afoot, request to do the same. All Captains are trained to observe from a fighter."

Jarvis grinned at the man. Pillar was a true Thalian Warrior. The arena would seem tame after today. "Where would ye say the probable location tis?"

"They would situate it like the other outposts for mining. That means set into a canyon with protecting ledges and/or walls as a buffer against the winds."

Jarvis nodded and contacted the waiting troopers. "All advance, except the five chosen to remain in our ships. Captain Beni, take one of the fighters and locate any life forms and relay the coordinates. They should be within a five mile radius. We'll check the other outposts till ye tell us different. Just execute a fly over and dinna hover; nay do ye attack. Keep an eye out for any hidden fighter."

"Aye, Captain," said Beni and she ran toward her fighter.

They waited in the cold sand swirling up to their knees as they watched the fighter move along the base of the foothills, then move higher until it was a spec sweeping under the clouds. They were fifteen men and women waiting for a battle they had trained and trained for but didn't expect in their four hundred year life span since the peace imposed by Thalia was now almost one hundred years in effect. The winds swirled the sand upward, then shifted the grit and dust downward. Over the howling wind, someone could be heard muttering on the com line, "I wonder if they breathe this piss naturally."

Their weapons were ready, set to drop any known being, but not kill. The Guardian of Flight had given orders that prisoners be taken if contact made. The Justine League would need a live De'Chin to prove Thalia was nay the attacker. Ten minutes later, Captain Beni's scouting message sounded in their ears.

"Captain Jarvis, life forms three miles to your right. A deliberate cloaking cover has been designed over the area. There are two types of beings: four are De'Chins, the other ten are nay recorded. One fighter tis under rock cover and two ground cruisers are there. One of the cruisers tis the De'Chins'. Ye could drop a party just above them."

"They would use the fighter if we dropped too low. Will they be able to see us as we approach?"

"Aye, Captain. If ye try to go straight at them, the wind twill sweep the sand in a different direction and give a clear view for a while."

Jarvis looked at Pillar. "Any suggestions?"

Pillar, once a Tri from Don, had worked his way through the Army ranks after it opened for men. In truth, most of his crew were of Tri origin, nay House. Thalia's Houses had been depleted during the Justine Wars, and the imposed Sisterhood rule had completed the decimation.

Pillar pointed upward, his dark eyes shaded by a helmet. "We move into the foothills here, work up and around, and then down."

"They will be expecting us."

"Aye, but once we're out of sight, we break into two parties. One group will take a twenty minute lead, climb higher and then descend."

"They could be using field scanners."

Pillar shrugged his broad shoulders and grinned. "Tis a chance we will have to risk."

Jarvis nodded and was disappointed when Lillie was drawn to proceed with the first group. He did nay wish to explain to his

Guardian of Flight how his darling lassie was killed. Ye worry too much, he reminded himself. Lillie tis a Don Warrior.

Pillar left with his six people and the rest marked time. Silence was maintained. After twenty minutes Jarvis signaled with his fist to proceed.

They were sweltering in the protective suits by the time they reached their objective. Rivulets of water ran down their chests, backs, and legs, and was flicked up and recycled through the condenser and dripped into an expandable pouch. Jarvis led them down to an outcropping that protected the canyon outpost to wait for Pillar to start the attack.

Every head jerked when the roar of a fighter echoed against the sides of the stone outcroppings. Jarvis set his weapon to full fire and stood as the fighter started to rise upward and raked its side. The fighter wobbled as fire from the Thalian fighter raked downward.

I need to commend Beni, thought Jarvis as the fighter flopped over and burst into flame. A tall, brown clad being jumped out of the fighter's door and onto the sand. It didn't look like the being had on protective suiting. There was a clear helmet, or at least a plas-like helmet, but it was split. No sound reached them and the being rolled over and over, and then lay still, twitching a brown clad, muscular leg.

"Move out!" Jarvis reset his weapon to stun, and they descended to the last of the boulders to rejoin Pillar or for a retaliating volley from inside the outpost. An uneasy quiet descended over the group and the fire still consuming what was left of the fighter spread a blue-gray sheen through the dust laden air.

Jarvis studied the being on the ground. What skin showed through the torn material seemed to be brown. The face covered by the transparent plas-like helmet had an elongated jaw, a less imposing nose than his, and the eyeteeth seemed fang like. Inch long, honed nails protruded from the one extended hand. There was a backpack with tubing running to the helmet. This group of beings needed their air supply. He couldn't tell what color the eyes were, a condition he didn't deem important. Nay but the beings on Brendon, the slavies of Ayana, or the Laird's Earth had any eye coloring other than brown.

Pillar's voice boomed over the com and down to the outpost. "We dinna wish to destroy. We will take prisoners and arrange for an eventual return to your home base. It tis your choosing." Whether the new beings could ken Thalian was nay important. The De'Chins would ken.

It was a De'Chin's voice that answered in a high, rapid yapping sound to their ears. "We thought you were more of them. We held this outpost. You are welcome to enter."

Pillar did the expected. Weapons went to full fire and flames hit the outpost and surrounding fortifications. The rock ledge above the opening came crashing down.

"I'm afraid it's a swabbing operation now." Jarvis's voice on the com was slightly apologetic. "Advance with caution. It tis possible for them to survive if they are deep enough inside." He nodded at his group and the formed into a unit of twos. They bent low and used the fallen rock for cover and stopped at the last line of stones.

Jarvis noted that Pillar had similarly divided his group for moving downward. Corded muscles bunched and tightened as they waited for a response from the jumbled opening. Pillar's group was almost even with them when a blond haired De'Chin female crawled out of the rubble. Her face was cut and bleeding. Blond fuzz covered her gashed arms where dark red was oozing out. She was naked, no protective clothing or plas helm. Her teats on her four mammary glands were torn and she was so dazed she did nay call out. She simply crawled towards them on all fours, gasping and struggling for breath.

"Shall we call in another fighter?" asked Lillie while recording everything on her crystals.

"Nay yet, as this could be but a ruse."

Once he had answered, Jarvis continued to watch the De'Chin. The wind was lifting the woman's hair. He realized everyone was as fascinated by her struggle as he was and not watching the opening, and he shifted his view to the outpost. The De'Chin had emerged from the side where a portion of the roof was supported by a half-melted beam.

"She will make it," someone grunted over the line.

Jura, a trooper from Ayran reached out and dragged the De'Chin behind the protective rocks.

A brown, plas helmeted being leaped from the opening, his weapon trained on them as Jarvis and Pillar let loose their stun bolts. The alien's yell stopped at mid-crescendo and he crashed onto the rocks as flames spurted from someone's weapon. Pillar could attend to the trooper who had nay reset the fire power. It was a beautiful strike, except this one was useless as a hostage or prisoner. The full beam had sheared off the being's arm holding the weapon and part of his head. What was left of the being was stretched out on the rocks, an odd caricature of a muscular being.

Pillar's voice was in his ear and he caught the motion of someone ducking down inside the outpost. "Captain Jarvis, there are more inside. Do we fire or attack?"

"What information from the lass?"

"There tis nay but babble. We are sharing our air, but she keeps begging us nay to hurt her or bed her."

"Fire, your weapons at full force."

The flames shot out and stones and wood melted together to form an impassable barrier. They could see the rock vibrating as though those caught inside were firing their own weapons.

Jarvis eyed the stunned being lying by the fighter and exposed to fire and considered the possibility that it still lived. He gauged the distance. It was worth the risk. He motioned the others to remain hidden and swung over the rocks. Twenty strides brought him alongside the being and he bent, hefted the being over his shoulder, and charged back to the others through the shifting sands. The weight was like two hundred and forty pounds or a bit more.

"Move out," commanded Jarvis and they filed out away from the fighter. Then he punched the com for Beni in the fighter.

"Take out the rest of the outpost." They felt, rather than heard the vibrations from their fighter's blast completely destroying the outpost.

"We can slow down now," said Pillar.

It was Jarvis's turn to share his air with the De'Chin female and the group stopped.

"Pick up now." Jarvis gave the command after retrieving his air. He kept the other being on his shoulder afraid that the sand would cover the being's nose or mouth in this open area and having his one prisoner dead was nay to his liking.

* * *

Jarvis and Kahli sat hunkered down beside the runnel. "The water tis metallic," was Kahli's comment and he pushed the small analyzer back in his carrying bag. "The bios here are ill and nay worth the bother. They all contain lead and Gar kens how many other metals. We have nay the water to spare for cleansing."

Beneath his helmet, Kahli's ruddy face was twisted in disapproval. His slim hand reached down and savagely crumpled the sand clod. Always slender in youth, he had remained so at coming of age.

"Will we make it back to Thalia?"

Kahli looked at Jarvis and nodded. "Aye, we will, but it will be rationing and somewhere we must find a place to stop and replenish our bios. Do we head for the De'Chin's planet first?"

"Nay, tis out of the way and would add two months' time to our return."

Kahli rocked back and forth on his heels. He turned back toward Jarvis. "Our first stop tis where? The Justine Refuge?"

Jarvis grimaced. "Nay, they would insist on keeping the prisoner for questioning. It tis for Thalia to decide his fate."

Kahli nodded and used his fingers to trace a pattern in the sand. "That means our first stop tis Brendon."

"Aye, how does the Supply Director feel about that?"

Kahli grunted and stood, then flung his arms wide. "I dinna care. We two at least ken going hungry. The rest may nay."

"Ye would mention that." Jarvis stood. "Kahli, how bad?"

Kahli shrugged. "The temperature may nay be comfortable in all areas. Once ye make your announcement for our return and first destination, I'll distribute the last of the brew. There tis nay water enough to continue making more.

"Thalians without their brew? Man, ye are cruel."

"There tis more," Kahli's grim voice continued. "There will be but a shower every other day, mayhap we will need to cut that to once a week."

Jarvis heard the blasphemy with wide eyes. "Their tempers will shorten."

"Mine tis already short. Do ye ken how long it has been since I've bedded Lania?"

Jarvis had no answer. Of course he knew. Lania was Kahli's counselor to be. They had announced their intent to Walk the Circle at the earliest possible age. She was a Director's lassie from the Laird of Don's home. They had met when the Laird took Kahli off the Ab list to anger the old Martin. Lania had been his true love then and remained so in his heart. Jarvis brushed such matters aside. "For Gar's sake Kahli, ye have been bedding."

Kahli turned to him, fury lashing the brown-red skin of an Ab born even redder.

"Aye, I bed because I am Thalian. Do ye ken the guilt that gnaws at me when the vows are broken; the anger that rises when I ken that Lania tis driven to act the same?" He clenched his fists and drew in a deep breath.

"Jarvis," and he forced his voice lower, "do ye nay ken? This tis the last space journey I make. I am nay a Warrior." He nodded at Jarvis and moved away.

Slender he may be, thought Jarvis, but even under the protection clothing Kahli's corded muscles rippled. For Kahli was never truly at rest, energy surging through him like volts in a storm laden cloud. If Kahli were motionless, it was as though the lightning was ready to strike. When they were young, Kahli was one of the few to stand against him by using rapid blocking moves and then move in closer to land a blow. Kahli was Ab born, but he had won the respect of the others at the Academy.

Jarvis grinned and hurried after him, his powerful legs pumping to match the long strides of Kahli. When he caught up, he threw his arm around Kahli's shoulder and cursed at the suits that kept them from touching. "Old friend, it tis nay the time to quarrel."

Kahli stopped. "Jarvis, it was nay a quarrel. I said what was in my heart."

"Aye, and ye have a temper as bad as your brither's. Now about that flight home, tis there anything else I need to ken?"

"Nay, not till something else goes wrong."

They walked back, arms thrown around each other's shoulder, at a comfortable matched stride.

Chapter 3

Journey To Brendon

Once they were on board, Jarvis delegated Tamar to set their course for Brendon. The prisoner he sent to Medical and ordered him restrained. He then informed the crew via the communicator as to their destination and the problems.

"There will be nay brew till we are sure there are nay other predators in this quadrant. All the Captains and Directors will join me in conference. While the supply system tis being repaired, everyone tis restricted to showers every third day. We'll rotate through the ranks and the schedule will be posted. Thalians, ye have done well."

Kahli's white teeth flashed as he entered. "And do ye think they'll thank ye when ye change the showers to every second day?"

"'It tis an edge in case something else goes wrong."

The seats were filling by the different Captains, and Directors. Lillie, as Recording Director sat beside Jarvis.

Malta, Captain of Medicine, from the House of Medicine entered. Her black hair was pulled back and in a clasp before cascading down to her backside. While she was shorter than most of the Houses, standing barely six-foot tall, she had the supple grace of Ishner. A purple sash representing the House of Medicine circled her waist. She had the darkest eyes in Thalia and was much sought after as a win in the Arena. She bowed formally and handed her crystal to Lillie and sat down next to Kahli.

"Malta, give your report."

"Aye, Captain. The prisoner has been sedated, but he tis also electrically bound for safety's sake, and a trooper has been assigned to stand guard. We request that the duty be changed every four or five hours."

"Agreed. Pillar, ye attend.

"Lillie, your report."

Lillie had consulted the various crystals. "We have sent space messages to the Justine League and to the De'Chins advising them of the outposts' destruction and suggest they set out patrols. They may nay receive it any sooner than our arrival in Brendon."

"Engineering reports that the Supply Sector tis under control, but some of the hydros are nay repairable without more water." She frowned as she scanned Kahli's crystal and looked at her brither with a frown. Kahli kept his face bland.

Jarvis broke in. "Ye have all heard my announcement about the showers. As soon as we determine that we are not pursued in any manner, I twill issue the last of the brew. There will nay be any more till we arrive at Brendon." He ignored the stunned faces.

"Lillie, I want ye to make extra crystals of all our reports and seal them in a space container. If anything happens to us, they must reach Thalia. The alien nay suited up when he burst out of the compound. I dinna think they expected us. Mayhap someone notified them of the false going home message we sent off six months ago."

"Kreppies!" Lillie spat out the word.

"Aye, mayhap, but we have nay proof. All are to remain battle ready and rations will be lean. Any problems will be routed to me immediately. All routine reports are expected every four hours. Any questions?"

Malta spoke first. "The alien's blood shedding was a large amount, but his blood type does nay match ours. It tis more like that of a Kreppie, but we dinna have any in supply. If Kahli (and her saying the name was like a caress) could devise a filtering system for ours, we could make him more comfortable."

Kahli scowled at the thought of wasting water on an enemy. "Can ye keep him alive without it?"

"I canna say. He tis an alien and nay cooperates. He may decide to expire and it will be necessary to use liquids to keep him alive."

The scowl spread across Kahli's face and Jarvis hurriedly asked, "What about the De'Chin? How tis she?"

"She was badly abused, but she should heal without any problems. She tis tranquil now and will remain so for six hours."

"Did ye get any information?"

"'It tis on the crystal, but it tis nay much. According to her, the beings came in to steal the minerals and ore already extracted. She was the only one kept alive for beddings, so whoever we killed in the outpost was nay De'Chins. She, like all De'Chins, tends to be hysterical about such things." Malta shrugged, dismissing the De'Chins as nay Warriors.

"The attack was to rob and destroy. They were nay interested in prisoners or what could be learned about the De'Chin planet. I think they already ken. Thalia must have this news."

Kahli spoke next. "Since we will need extra water for both the alien and the De'Chin, showers remain at every three days till we need to go to a full week."

Jarvis nodded. "Our course tis toward Brendon. We'll arrive a bit weary, but nay too famished or athirst. Mayhap we will offend from nay showers, but the Brendons are the politest of beings. By then we will have transmitted our news to the Justine League and Thalia. The first scheduling for showers will be out this evening, and all those who participated in today's foray will be listed. All may return to your duties."

* * *

Freshly showered, Jarvis was not weary enough for bed. Today had been what any Warrior craved, and he believed more campaigns would follow. His body surged with energy. Nay bed, but a bedding was his need. He donned the black loin thong and headed for Lillie's quarters. The temperature was nearing eighty-four instead of seventy-two, and clothes were too hot for comfort. It was one formality he had eased for all off duty.

Jarvis touched the DIP (door imprint) that admitted him. As Captain of Flight, he could open any door within the ship, but he and Lillie had reached an agreement and he was welcomed at all times. All kenned when he was on or off duty and where he would be.

Lillie's wide face beamed with pleasure. "Jarvis, tis welcome ye are." Her magnificent broad shoulders, wide torso, and heavy legs rippled as she strode toward him as unencumbered of clothing as he. Her dark eyes bubbled with anticipation. "Ye are a Director who kens the needs of your Captain."

Later, hours after Jarvis had gone, Lillie scanned her crystals with satisfaction. "Jarvis, darling, someday ye may find these fascinating. What a magnificent body ye have." Quiet descended over all but the piloting section of the ship.

Kahli had made his bed in the Supply sector nearest the hydro beds that had been repaired. To the crew it appeared he wished to be near if the repairs should fail, but they were homeward bound and it was his way of signaling the end of beddings. That Malta might fume did not bother him. And Malta had her own worries in Medicine.

* * *

Tabor carefully breathed the air around him. It was a thin mixture approximating his needs. He realized he was laying on cloth with arms and legs attached to glowing posts. He peered with half-lidded eyes to determine his location, ignoring the throbs in his head and left leg. He was drowsy, too drowsy. He had been drugged. Anger began to boil inside of him. Who had dared to do this? It could not be the insignificant creatures they had bested on that sand, blasted asteroid; nor could it be the sniveling creatures that called themselves Krepyons. He noted with interest the tubes running into his left arm, then realized another was threaded through his nose and into his throat. He was puzzled. For what purpose? And the thought that it was probably for drugs and nourishment. The fools! No Draygon would submit to capture.

He let the anger course through him, building his strength, pushing back the edges of darkness still clinging in the recesses of his brain. He forced his body to lie still while searching the room for any sign of movement. The clear, tent shroud over his body prevented his nostrils from identifying the source of the creature he knew must be somewhere in this room. Someone had to be here, waiting, watching for some movement from him.

Then across the room, someone moved into view. He sensed that this one was female, although the figure was wide and muscular, like most species there seemed to be a hint of mammary glands in the upper portion of the torso. He began the breathing exercises, gradually expanding his lung capacity. Where, he wondered, were his mates? Their scent wasn't mingled with the other alien, gagging odors. Had they all died while he lived? He would take his revenge through death. His mind told him she must be one the Thalians the Krepyons had warned them would be the dangerous ones. They might fight, but they would not win. He filled his lungs again and arched his back against the force, howling his rage.

Trooper Tene was atop him immediately, holding the lunging body with her weight. Median tried to inject a stronger drug directly, but she had to move the sheeting out of the way. She was too late with the drug. Trooper Tene's face was gashed and bleeding from the creature's fangs. Worse, the struggle had upended the water sitting on the built out tray and the sheeting torn. Any bacteria the alien breathed or carried could be harmful. The whole room would need cleansing. The mapping of all the tissues and bacteria found wouldn't be completed until morning. She cursed inwardly as she shouted for her assistant. "We need vacs."

Meler was prepared and at her elbow with the equipment.

"Do the suctioning now. There are red welts growing on Tene's face from the bites." Median gave her orders and set about re-sheathing the alien. She'd worry about Malta's and the Captain of Flight's wrath after things were cleansed.

It took an hour to cleanse Tene and the room. Then she put Mali in charge while she went and made her report directly to Jarvis.

Jarvis asked a few quick questions.

"Did the alien break the force?"

"Nay, he was nay strong enough."

"Thank ye, Median, make sure that Lillie tis forwarded all medical crystals."

Once she left his room, he summoned Kahli and Lillie to the Control Room and explained the extra water usage. "Malta tis running a program to determine if the bacteria are harmful. We'll know by tomorrow if more cleansing tis necessary. If it tis, we'll need to cleanse anyone near him when it becomes necessary to remove the sheathing. We have him so heavily sedated, nay questioning tis possible till we reach Brendon. Can we spare the extra water?"

Kahli's face had whitened. "I dinna. We had some leeway, mayhap more than enough. We could let the brute starve."

"Aye, and then what? Search empty space for their planet?"

"They canna be too far. Their ship was comparable to ours."

"Aye," he answered "and Thalia has been looking for them for almost sixty years. They ken where to attack us."

"That means they have the help of the Kreppies." Kahli spat out the hated word.

"But we have nay proof, Kahli. It tis ye who must decide the division of sustenance and the clime for the ship." Jarvis nodded at them both. "Thalia's Council will decide on the captive. When ye have your data, let me ken. The crew will abide by our orders and we'll endure till we reach Brendon."

Kahli's face was back to its normal reddish hue. "By Gar, Jarvis, have ye anything else to throw at me?"

Chapter 4

Brendon

Three months later they hovered over Brendon and waited for official landing coordinates. They had explained their situation and the alien being in the Medical section. The Brendons sent the coordinates, but asked that the alien remained sealed in the ship's Medical while repairs were completed in the Bio area and water transferred aboard.

Crew members that weren't chosen to be among the first to bathe in Brendon's cool, green waters were promised the Brendon brew that was on its way to the ship. They hadn't fared too badly, although all had lost weight and slept ill in the warm cabins. The grumblings against Kahli's parsimonious ways turned to cheers when the Brendon ship dock with a new supply of food and brew.

Jarvis detested the polite diplomatic maneuverings of landing on another planet, but the process went smoothly. There were times he regretted not having his Mither Jolene's or Elder JayEll's devious tongues and their ability to move among the different political groups. The Brendons remained the same staunch allies they had been during the Justine War. They had suffered much from the Kreppies during the Justine rule. The ambassadors from Thalia were from the House of Rurhran and had taken care of all the rituals. As Maca, he outranked them, but he was grateful for their skills and laid his head on both their shoulders, lingering a bit mayhap, on the soft expanse of Rollan's milky opulence.

"What ails ye, man?" laughed Rollan as she pushed him back.

"It tis thanks I owe ye for the ear blustering ye have saved me." He grinned at them. "I believe the Brendon's speeded up the ceremony to speed me on the way to a proper cleansing."

Rollan crinkled her nose. "It would be a relief for all," she agreed and gestured toward the back of their home that was built in the rounded Thalian manner.

"Your room tis the first to the right, complete with the shower and a robe. The crew has been given accommodations at Complex Two in the Visitors section. The Brendon's are quite picky about who may step foot on their soil."

"Aye, and as Captain of Flight, I thank ye again." He nodded and hurried down the hall. He liked Rollan and her counselor, Rhode, as he had kenned them nearly all of his life. Like most from the House of Rurhran, they were tall and heavy though without the heavy, corded muscular physique of Ayran, Don, Breton, or Troy. Few of the House of Rurhran went into Flight. The exception was Rollan's brither, Ribdan. Nay did Rurhran produce many Warriors, but perhaps that was the way of farmers everywhere.

The water, wonderful cool water, splashing over his body was savored and almost as refreshing as a bedding. Gar, how he had missed both. Lillie had become snappish with the heat and the stench from bodies and refused to let anyone near her. In truth, there was more pleasure when circumstances were normal. He pulled on his dress uniform. The officials of Brendon would expect it. He added a brilliant, red sash denoting the color of Ayran and headed for the front room.

"Are ye ready for a brew, Jarvis?" Rhode was handing him a mug twice the normal size. "We heard about your deprivation."

Jarvis tipped his head and swallowed long and well. "It was worse than being on Krepyon," he admitted.

"Rollan's changing for dinner. Lillie and Malta will be joining us. Kahli was asked, but he has excused himself claiming he has an old friend here to consider."

"Aye, I saw him slapping some poor, green and tipped with orange-haired Brendon on the back and dragging him into the ship when I left. I think they roomed together when they studied at the Justine Refuge."

Rhode considered. "Ye are probably right. There tis someone at their University who went to Justine and attended the school set up by the Laird of Don's Earth laddie. He would be entering the half-way point of a Brendon's life span."

"How long do we remain in the clutches of Brendon official-dom this evening?"

"Just for the evening banquet. We scheduled the official visit for tomorrow afternoon."

Jarvis finished his brew and waggled the mug for a refill as Rhode continued. "Nay only ye, but all the officers from the ship if they can be spared. The Brendons wish to honor ye."

"I'd meant to leave nay later than tomorrow afternoon. All we need are supplies and fresh water. The rest of the repairs can be done at Thalia." His jaw tightened. "Those beings are still out there and they may ken that we have caught one of them. Mayhap they are ready to attack the De'Chins' home planet."

Rhode nodded. "Jarvis, I ken, but we may need Brendon's support at the Justine League meeting. We canna go it alone. The Guardian of Flight has pushed through a new ship in your absence. If it becomes a true emergency, even the Justines will use their *Golden One*. Ye and the rest must attend. It would be offensive to these gentle, wee ones."

Jarvis's elation was rapidly changing to frustration. It seemed society demanded a certain level of political relations and keeping some powerful individual soothed.

Rollan appeared in the classic white tunic of the diplomatic corps over the gold, form-fitting leggings, her dark hair descending in loops over her chest and back, and the gold sash of Rurhran draped over the left breast, tied around the middle and floating halfway to the floor.

"If Pillar attends, ye will instruct him nay to give a graphic account of the battle while we dine. Ye might also try to restrict the brew he gulps into his gullet."

Jarvis raised his eyebrows. "Since when have ye kenned Pillar's ways so well?"

"Since his brawling days at the Flight Academy ere he was tossed out on his backside. That cooled his temper enough that they let him join the Army."

Chapter 5

The Interrogation

Jolene, Guardian of the Realm and Lass of Ayran, called for the prisoner to be brought out to stand before the Council and the Justine. Jarvis's message to the Justine Refuge had brought their representative, Adair.

He sat in the Honor Chair in front of the seating section for the visitors, lesser House members, Tris, and the few Abs that attended. The Krepyon envoys Fribay and Efrom had come with the Justine and sat on the right side of Adair. Trigrow, the Brendon Envoy assigned to Thalia was in the chair to the left of Adair.

Tabor was chained, but standing on a medhover when brought into the chamber. Two Thalian Army Warriors marched on either side of him and two of Medicine's House walked behind the medhover. Tabor had refused to walk and Jolene had issued orders. She looked down at the prisoner.

"Ye can step down or be dumped." She saw no reason for politeness.

Tabor looked at her and realized that she was as hard as anyone from Draygon. Her softer body did not fool him and he stepped down. With his fanged teeth, he looked like he was snarling at them all.

"Ye can either tell us the coordinates to your planet or the Justine will enter your mind and tell us." Jolene words were as forceful as her looks.

Tabor spat.

Adair stood, his long face composed, raised his right arm and pointed his index finger at the Draygon. Silence swept over the crowd.

After ten minutes, Adair turn to the seated Guardians of the Realm and announced, "This one is like many of the Earth beings. I cannot penetrate his mind."

Tabor snarled a smile and spat. "We will enslave all of you!"

Llewellyn stood. "Guardian of the Realm, I have a proposal. My laddie and I promised nay to ever use our minds on another being while on Thalia. We have kept that pledge, but Lorenz has a mind more powerful than a Justine. I suggest that ye lift that ban for tonight and let him enter this being's mind. Then we can discover who he tis, where he tis from, and what their plans are."

Jolene looked at her lassie and Counselor, JoAnne, Lass of Ayran. JoAnne nodded her head. She kenned how much JayEll and Jarvis trusted the Laird of Don.

Jolene swiveled and looked at the seated Guardians and their Counselors. "Do any of ye have a nay vote, discussion, or better idea? If nay discussion or idea, I consider this a valid solution. Remember, these are the ones that destroyed the Justine *Golden One*. The debris from the Draygon ship matched that collected so long ago. All in favor say, Aye."

The Guardians and Counselors looked at each other and said, "Aye."

"Any nays?"

There was silence. "Motion passed. Guardian of Don, do ye swear nay to use your mind on others after questioning this one?"

Lorenz stood, "I so swear."

"Do ye need time to prepare?" Jolene asked.

"I can question him now, but I just saw how difficult it was for a Justine. I ask that ye remove that stipulation from my Fither, Maca of Don. If necessary, he can enter my mind and feed me questions or relay my answers."

"Can nay the Justine do that?"

"I refuse to allow a Justine into my mind." Stubbornness was in his voice and his stance. Llewellyn tried to hide his amusement.

Jolene looked from the Guardian of Don to Llewellyn, Maca of Don and Guardian of Flight. She knew that arguing with Lorenz was futile and time consuming.

"The Guardian and Counselor of Don and the Guardian of Flight may nay vote on this, but if I hear nay "Nays," the oath tis also removed from Llewellyn for this eve."

The Guardians and Counselors were grim, but all voted "Aye." Jolene looked at Lorenz. "Do ye need to descend?"

"Nay, however, Fither, if it is difficult and I raise my arm, I'll need ye to come into my mind to relay the answers or feed me the questions I need to ask." Lorenz had modified his speech for the Council meetings. He didn't need to confuse the visitors with his Texas drawl.

He half-way closed his eyes and looked down at Tabor. His mind hit Tabor's and hammered away at the wall that had been erected. It took twenty seconds and he was into the alien's mind. The hate hit him like a red, hot branding iron. He balled his hands into fists and set his teeth. His response to hate like that was to retaliate and kill. His eyes were open and his lips were white with the effort to keep from killing that being. He was needed alive.

Llewellyn was looking at Lorenz with his eyebrows raised. He saw Lorenz's right arm lift up from the elbow. He glanced down. Tabor who was shaking his head as though to dislodge something.

'How many starpaths to Draygon from the DeChin's dwarf mining planet?' Lorenz used mindspeak to ask Tabor, but also said the words aloud.

"Aaaaaaaaaaa," came from Tabor's mouth as he sank to his knees, but could not cover his mouth or hold his head with his chained hands.

"His mind says twenty-six or twenty-five. He is not sure. They would have headed in what we consider up and veering right." Lorenz's voice was stilted and wooden without any emotion.

'Do you have a more precise number of starpaths from one of the inhabited planets in this section?' Lorenz probed at Tabor's mind.

"From the planet Krepyon it is thirty-four starpaths." Lorenz's strange voice carried the horrifying news.

'How did you contact the Krepyons?' Lorenz sent that question into Tabor's mind while intoning it aloud. Sweat was forming on Lorenz's brow and on his temples.

Once again the strange voice came from Lorenz. "We captured one of their expeditions to an asteroid. Then after we learned about this area, we captured another ship and sent it back with a dead and tortured crew. We promised them leniency and part of Thalia and Brendon if they would join with us. We convinced them we could demolish the Justines."

The Krepyons in the audience were yelling, "Lies, all lies."

Jolene motioned for the guards to surround them and keep them silent. To Lorenz she said, "Ask him if they have contacted anyone else."

Lorenz sent the question into Tabor's mind. Tabor was swaying back and forth on his knees and shaking his head.

"No others. They aren't as spineless as the Krepyons."

'How do you know that?' Again Lorenz used both mindspeak and his voice.

"This was the second De'Chin mining area we've visited. They fought us." Lorenz said aloud.

'What is your planet's position in relation to the other planets in this quadrant?' Both mindspeak and aloud.

Tabor's mind showed a huge star map with the locations and coordinates of the known inhabited planets. Lorenz transferred them to Llewellyn.

"I've got it." Lorenz shouted. "I can draw it out for everyone."

Tabor had lowered his body and was banging his head on the floor. Medicine ran to him to stop the mutilation.

Lorenz shook his head before speaking. "Do y'all need anything more?" This was almost a normal voice, but somehow the strangled anger was in the sound.

"No, not until I have conferred with Flight and Army," replied Jolene.

"Good." Lorenz looked at the seated Llewellyn. "Papa, I have to go throw rocks or I'll finish him. Y'all can explain it to them. You have the locations in your mind. I'll draw it out when I return." He left the Guardian's section, ran down the stairs, and slammed out of the door; the anger from the Draygon raging through his system and he wanted to kill, to destroy, to avenge all the wrong he had seen as a child.

Chapter 6

War

The Krepyon planet lay in ruins. Its factories, cities, and underground facilities blown apart for the second time within two of their generations. The hatred for the Justines, Thalians, and Brendons became imbedded in their collective memories.

Those in the *Golden One*s, Thalian, and Brendon warships did not care. They had a mission: Seek and Destroy.

As Guardian of Flight, Llewellyn had selected his crew and ships before going on to Brendon with the recordings of the Guardians of the Realm Council meeting. The Brendons added their space fighters to the fleet. The Krepyon envoys were detained on both Thalia and Brendon.

The Captain of Flight for the largest and newest Thalian warship was Daniel. His second in command was Captain Aretha. Neither mentioned that both had once been Abs. Daniel was computing the likelihood of a starpath appearing before the one laid out by his Elder Fither, Llewellyn, now serving as the Commander of the Fleet.

A slight smile came across Daniel's face and he tapped out the message on the circle to his Elder Fither. "If we move sixty degrees upward and to the left we will be there a day sooner. Any Kreppie craft that escaped would be left behind."

"Are ye certain?"

"Aye, Commander."

"Tis it as wide?"

"Nay, it would be one by one."

"And what if the Draygons have already discovered this starpath?"

"They already ken the other one."

There was silence and then Llewellyn's voice came again. "I will go first. Then three Thalian ships, three Brendon, and then Captain O'Neal behind them. They will nay be expecting two *Golden One*s. The rest of ye follow in the same order: Three Thalian, three Brendon until all are through. It will be lively. All data has been transmitted to the other ships."

Daniel frowned. He had wanted to be first, but he was in position to follow directly after Llewellyn and he took it. This was his chance. He knew Jarvis was sulking on Ayran, prevented from accompanying them by his long years in space. Daniel had been given the nickname of Pathfinder at the Warrior Academy, but most thought Jarvis would be the better Captain in a space fight. Until now there had been no real battles. Just simulated ones. Finding the starpaths in their training flights had been real, as real as this engagement, and he found himself leaning forward in the seat.

They rocketed through the rounded area on the tail of the Golden *One* and broke free in the middle of a battle. Five of the Draygon ships were closing in on the *Golden One* and Aretha began firing.

Daniel saw more Draygon vessels veer off and swing towards the open starpath, and he yelled, "Aretha, aim at the ones I am closing in on. Our Commander's *Golden One* will hold the others. The rest must get through."

Aretha leaned as the ship skewed and turned. One Draygon vessel was firing at the next Thalian ship bursting out into space and she recalculated her aim when a burst of flame from the ship reached out and slammed into the Draygon ship. She froze. Her shot would have downed the Thalian.

"Are ye piloting or firing?" she screamed at Daniel.

She could not see his face to see his eyes gleaming and a small smile on his face. "Both, but ye are correct. Ye guard the starpath, I'll fire at the others."

Another Thalian ship was through and both were engaging the Draygons surrounding the *Golden One* like a swarm of stingers after the nectar of the brambleberries.

Daniel went above the starpath to give Aretha and himself the chance to fire at others that might try to stop the rest of the ships. The second *Golden One* burst through and O'Neal's crew swept the area of the oncoming Draygons.

"Mac, are you all right?" O'Neal's voice came over the com as the last enemy ship spiraled into the blackness of space.

"Aye, thank ye, my friend," came the deep, rumbling voice. "Your arrival was most welcomed. I believe we should head for their planet and destroy their plants and bases. After that we can secure a treaty."

"One of the *Golden One*s stays above. I don't trust them. They will probably lie about keeping any treaty." Red's voice was flat, devoid of the Irish dialect he sometimes used. "Anyone that allies with the Krepyons can't be trusted."

Chapter 7

The Treaty

Llewellyn had issued his orders once the Draygons sent word of their surrender, He confiscated the fanciest building left standing in the Draygon capital of Leshidan for meeting with the Draygons.

"Any remaining ruling members of the Draygons will meet with me, Llewellyn, Thalia's Commander of Fleet and Guardian of Flight. The Captains of Flight from the ships of the Justine League will also be present. The treaty has been beamed down to a being identified as Quosalle Tabon, Grand Marshall of Draygon. The meeting will be in the morning at the building where our carrier has landed. Our ship will be overhead. Any hostilities and all Draygons will die."

They arrived at the still standing marble-like building early in the morning. Llewellyn deployed a contingent of troopers around the building and the carrier before sending another unit of troopers to search, scan, and destroy any trap inside. He then selected one of the rooms and saw to the placement of table and chairs. Anyone entering would be scanned.

He had given orders that all wear their dress uniforms. He was resplendent in the black suit with the sheer sleeves that permitted the display of Thalian muscles. The black shoulder band ran down to the black, fringed sash. O'Neal he could not force into a uniform, but Red surprised him by showing up in a tailored suit from Earth's twentieth century. The Western hat was set at a rakish angle when he entered. Red winked and placed the hat on his lap.

Lorenz was not in Flight, but as a Laird, he was given the honorary title of Captain and he was dressed as his father except the shoulder band and sash were in Don's blue. Daniel, was dressed as his elder fither, but there was no shoulder band. Captain Lili of Army was also dressed in black with a black sash.

The two Brendons wore their colorful autumn colors of red and yellow uniforms. L'lana Badder, the De'Chin Commander, wore his robe of scarlet satin and golden stars splayed across the material. His skull cap was a matching color and pattern.

Troopers escorted the Draygons into the room and stationed themselves outside the door should any disturbance arise. The Draygons glared at the assembly but proceeded to the empty chairs. They were spared the indignity of standing like prisoners. The list of their names and ranks had been transmitted the day before.

Their leader, Quosalle Tabon, sat in the middle facing Llewellyn. The rest were Vatta Fallown, Raffen Daveren, and Jaffa Jemina. They were what was left of the Diet of Treat. Their faces were hard and set. They hated their conquerors and the shame brought on them by losing. Their planet survived, but the cities, towns, and lands were destroyed. Their populace decimated by half.

Llewellyn's introduction was brief; their names and the planets they represented. He then began discussing the conditions.

"Ye were sent the treaty and the conditions by our Justine League. If ye dinna sign, we will finish destroying this world."

"We were told the Thalians would use a challenge to determine the winner," Quosalle Tabon hurled out. "Do you so fear us?"

"I am nay doing this for Thalia alone. We are the Justine League."

"I say you are afraid to match one of you against me." It was Vatta Fallown, the Draygon. His jaw jutted outward under the resplendent nose and bulging brow.

"Enough, such a fight would be as being against being. Nay for the treaty. Do ye intend to sign?" Llewellyn's roared out.

Quosalle swallowed and marked both sets of the thin sheets of metal.

"We will station a few troops and ships here to verify that all tis complied with according to the new laws. If at such time ye wish a one-on-one fight, I am sure one of our Thalians Warriors would agree."

"I would be happy to meet that challenge in an arena," Daniel said and smiled.

"Would now change those terms?"

"Nay, Supreme Draygon Quosalle. It would be a fight between my Captain of Flight, Daniel, Lad of Don, and your volunteer such as we do in our Arena," answered Llewellyn.

"Then let it be this afternoon at two of our hour. That is six hours from now. Vatta will need time to prepare. Do you have a better opponent with you?"

Daniel's eye's hardened, but his smile was innocent. Lorenz was frowning.

"He tis our best."

"Good, our stadium is beneath us. We need a victory." The Draygons rose and left.

"What the hell do you two think you all are doing?" Lorenz exploded. "That being has talons. He'll use them like knives."

"Fither, I am taller than he. First he will have to reach me."

* * *

"The fight will continue until one of you concedes or is unable to rise after thirty seconds." The Draygon official finished his instructions and stepped back to officiate.

Daniel and Vatta entered the ring for the fight. Llewellyn had had the room cleared and scanned for the second time that day. From somewhere there appeared about fifty Draygons to watch. They were the ruling elite who had hidden deep in specialized spaces beneath the ground.

Both Daniel and Vatta were clothed in their thongs and both bounded into the center of the ring. They were in magnificent condition with muscles rippling downward. Vatta had been oiled and his talons gleamed in the light. A hush fell over the watchers.

No gavel descended for Daniel, nor did the official of Draygon shout go. They advanced towards the middle with Vatta waving his hands faster and faster. Daniel had already considered the possibility that the Draygon would not use his fist and his eyes watched the man advance and Daniel began to sway.

As Vatta rushed forward the talons flashing through the air, Daniel spun, leapt upward, twirled, and came down on Vatta's left side and sent a smashing blow into the man's cheek with his right and bringing his left down on the back of the man's neck.

Vatta stumbled, but managed to scrape Daniel's right arm and buttock with the talons and blood began seeping out. He was unable to slash Daniel again as Daniel had spun away and was coming toward him with his fists clenched.

Vatta came straight at him flashing his talons and expecting Daniel to whirl away to the right. Instead Daniel lashed out with his foot and caught Vatta on the knee and then moved to Vatta's right side at the stumble and drove his fist into the right side and spun away. Vatta barely managed to scratch Daniel's left arm.

This time Vatta spun with Daniel and managed to slash at his cheek and then thigh. Blood began to run freely.

In the audience, Llewellyn had enfolded Lorenz in his arms. Lorenz's face was hard and he had risen as if to jump into the ring. The two swayed back and forth as Lorenz would not use his mind on his father.

Once again the opponents came straight at each other and bobbed and weaved, with no contact. Daniel set his teeth and dove for Vatta's midsection, his four hundred and fifty pounds bearing Vatta downwards.

Vatta's arms flailed outward and then he brought them together to rake down Daniel's back and sides. Daniel smashed his fists into Vatta's face breaking the nose, then the jaw and cheekbones.

Daniel bounded upward and came straight down with his knees into Vatta's ribcage and his ears heard the cracking of bones. Blood started from Vatta's mouth and Daniel stood up and away. He noted all were looking at their coms or devices whether on the back of the hand or the wrist and a slight smile started. At the end of thirty seconds, the Draygons raised their eyes and rose to leave.

Daniel turned, pumped his fists into the air, and roared, "Thalia!"

Gary MacDonald was running toward him, the medical spray of antiseptics, antidotes, and sealants aiming for his arms and sides. "Hold still, dammit," Gary yelled at him. "I need to scan you to for any bacteria or poisons."

"Are you all right?" His father was beside them and shouting at him. Llewellyn followed.

"I needed to restrain him," explained Llewellyn.

Daniel grinned and enfolded his father while Gary muttered more invectives at him.

"We will leave now." Llewellyn spoke into his com and Daniel grabbed two brew cans from his valise that Lorenz was holding.

"I must congratulate my opponent on a match well fought." Daniel bounded off while the others stared in disbelief.

He rushed into the room just off the hall that had been designated for whoever lost and shouted to the man on the cot and boy and man standing beside him. "It was a magnificent fight. I have come to share..." and his voice died away.

Daniel remembered protesting that medical should be there, that he had not meant for the other to die. He never remembered the words of comfort he tried to murmur as he backed out of the room.

The two shamed Draygons would remember his words and vowed vengeance on Thalia and on Daniel.

Chapter 8

The Maca of Ayran

Jarvis, the Maca of Ayran, was in a foul mood. The fighting fleet had left, and he, Jarvis, was still on Thalia. Worse, he was expected to be the one directing the affairs of Ayran.

Llewellyn, the Director of Flight, had ordered all who had been on the prolonged space flight grounded for two years. It mattered nay to Jarvis that Pillar was as upset as he was. Jarvis had protested the order.

"The Justines and the ones managing the *Golden One* are on longer flights with less off time. Why do ye impose this on us and deny us the opportunity to perform as Warriors?"

"Our technology tis nay the Justine technology." Llewellyn's voice and words were just as adamant. "These rules were set down before Thalia was conquered and there was a reason for them."

"We no longer need them. My flight proved that."

"It proved nay! Ye and the rest of those that went with ye are grounded."

His arguments had not swayed the Guardian and here he sat, shifting through the screens detailing the amount of metals withdrawn from underground, the scant number of jewels, the loads from the asteroid mining, the production of armor clothing and crystals, the food and credits distributed to the different Ayranians, and it was boring.

Jarvis stood and paced. He could see his sister, JoAnne, coming down the corridor with Jeken, the foreman in charge of mining production and the mine crew.

"Where tis JayEll?" Jarvis snapped at JoAnne.

She raised her eyebrows at his tone, shrugged her shoulders, and smiled sweetly. "He tis performing his duties as Counselor of the Realm for our Mither. Ye will have to take Jeken's report and issue the orders for the morrow. I am due at the Training Center for my stint at the weights." JoAnne nodded at both and continued down the hall.

"Come in," Jarvis tried to make his voice less than impatient. Jeken wasn't to blame for his grounding.

Jeken handed over the crystals. "That tis yesterday's total. According to JoAnne we have more orders for the rare earth that will be mined at the Six A asteroid. A flight is scheduled in two days' time."

Jarvis looked up. "And who pilots this flight?"

"The Flight Academy schedules one of the best cadets. It tis only a five path star trip. Six back I'm told to prevent any accident."

A broad smile went across Jarvis's face. He would be back in space and still be tending to the business of Ayran. JoAnne and JayEll could tend to the business of Ayran just as they had while he was hunting down those that were the unknown enemy.

He ran the reasons through his mind. The Maca was needed to encourage the Ayranians that were living and working there. He could have the cadet as a co-pilot and the trip would be smoother and faster, and, he, Jarvis, would be back in space. Damn any reason the Director had for grounding him. Some rule devised before the Justine War could not be valid almost two hundred years later. He would prove this to the Director of Flight. Nay could go wrong with his plan.

Chapter 9

Lilith's Vision

Lilith had loved coming into Donnick with her parents when she was a wee one. She was there every day for school, but that did not count. The children from the town of LouElla would board the carrier in the morning and return by carrier in the afternoon.

When her parents went to Donnick it was usually to trade and the buy goods at the First Center. There was always a treat of some sort and maybe a blue ribbon for her sun-streaked braids. Then she would roam over the grass and around the Center's other businesses and public places. She tried to avoid the waterfront. It smelled of brine, Ab boats, and odors from the brew halls that lined the way. One place in the First Center always intrigued her and she would stand in front of it and stare while dreaming daydreams.

It was the Shrine of the Kenning Woman. No Kenning Woman lived there when Lilith was young. It had been destroyed by the Sisterhood, but the Maca of Don had restored it. The stand at the front had the slot where one could drop a request or sit silently on a bench. If the old Kenning Woman, who was not really old, was there, visitors would tell her their troubles. It was rare that any vision was given, although some declared that she did just for them.

Lilith had doubted it. She was the new Kenning Woman. The old one had proclaimed it, but cautioned those that heard it to secrecy until Lilith was of age. She had been given her mission by the old Kenning Woman. Lilith had been perplexed and still puzzled over it. How could one find what had been destroyed by the Kreppies and the Justines? She would shake her head and continue to wander the grounds and look at the fountain gurgling blue water. Sometimes the water would still and reflect her solemn face, her dark eyes, and her dark hair pulled back from her oval face. She would hug herself and think someday I shall live here.

Then she would close her eyes and try to concentrate. She had known she could not live at the Shrine until her visions began. They would revealed where she was to search. Always, it had been a disappointment when no vision came.

Today, so many years later, her body grew rigid and her breath became short gasps. She began to fear she would never live here. She could visit, but the vision showed a cold, barren land overlooking a cold sea with the wind whipping her hair and cape, and her heart ached.

Chapter 10

A Vision Proclaimed

Lilith stood on the shores of Ayran's misnamed Lake Bliss. Its waters glistened with a greenish, metallic tint from long ago mines, minerals, and acids. She studied the water and tried to raise a new vision. Why had her last vision said to come here? It was cool and the wind whipped at her hair and the long, over garment that the traditional Kenning Woman wore. Her gaze was so intent she did not hear or see the red fliv land beside her blue lift that seated but two. She did heard the crunch of a step behind her and whirled to face whoever appeared.

The man coming towards her was JayEll, Lad of Ayran, and suddenly the mist enveloped her. Instead of Ayran's red cape, the man wore a dark brown cape over the red clothing of Ayran. His hair was longer, almost to his shoulders. His right hand held the Staff of Martin and his left held a metal, oblong plate lifted into the air. His hair seemed to turn grey, then white. She saw herself standing next to him with her staff dressed in her Kenning Woman cape and like him her hair slowly grayed and then turned to white. Her vision cleared, her breath was coming in gasps, and she was looking at a puzzled man.

"Why are ye here, Kenning Woman?" he asked.

Lilith raised her right hand and pointed at him. "Ye are to be the long-lived Martin and I, as the Kenning Woman, will serve with ye."

"I'm sure the current Martin would object and so will his Handmaiden."

"The current Martin tis a fraud and a tool of the Handmaiden. It tis she that controls what few seasonal worker Abs remain. Ye will be the Martin for all of Thalia, nay just Abs."

JayEll shook his head. "That tis folly," he snapped in annoyance. "Did ye come here just to tell me that?"

She looked at him. His features were comely, but his upper body was more slender than the heavy, muscled legs of someone from Ayran. She smiled at him. "I dinna ken why I came here till I had that vision. The previous vision said I was to come here and look at Lake Bliss. I thought it was for the Book and I was puzzled for if the Book of Gar had been thrown into that tarnished water, it would have dissolved. Then I saw ye and the new vision started."

"I am not qualified to be the Martin. Nay are qualified as our Book tis gone. If it were found, nay would ken its words."

"That will change when the Book tis found." The wind picked up momentum and her cape billowed around her. The fumes from the lake were beginning to make her ill.

"It tis time to leave now." She inclined her head and walked to her lift.

JayEll watched her take off in the two seated carrier and went to his own vehicle in a sour mood. He would ignore her vision. His days with the Abs were long over and so was his desire to be the Martin.

His mood was not any better when he walked into the dining area of the Guardian of the Realm's home on Ayran. It was the evening dining hour and he bent to kiss his Elder Mither's cheek and give the Thalian greeting of putting his head on the right shoulder and then in the left while making the "tsk' sound in each ear.

"And who was the interloper?" Jolene asked as she returned the greeting. She was starting to age, but her mind and plots still worked with superb precision.

"It was the new Kenning Woman." JayEll saw no need to elaborate as he seated himself.

Jolene looked at him with her bright eyes and motioned the Keeper to set the dish down and leave.

"And why would the new Kenning Woman visit the shores of Lake Bliss?"

"To have a vision."

"Ye are withholding something. What was her vision?"

JayEll looked at his Elder Mither. Of course, she could tell. They were so much alike. "She said I would be the long, lived Martin."

It was Jolene's turn to snort. "Were ye and Rolla nay planning to ask permission to Walk the Circle? A Martin canna wed."

JayEll watched her spoon the hearty stew into her bowl before reaching for the tureen and filling his own bowl.

"We have nay plans to ask permission to Walk The Circle. Rocella tis upset that Rolla was considering me. She really wanted Rolla to be with JoAnne. Neither of the two are even interested in each other."

Jolene slapped the butter of Don on her fresh, just baked roll and nodded. "Rocella would like to return to the days of the Sisterhood. Tis a shame Ravin appointed her as Guardian of Rurhran till the new Maca tis of age." She smiled at JayEll.

"Ye two should patch up whatever went wrong and Walk the Circle. Then your babe would be the new Lad of Rurhran and Ayran would finally have some control or at least an edge over the agra-business of Thalia, and it would give Thalians something to talk about instead of wondering how our Warriors fare."

JayEll smiled, halfway for her and halfway for his own amusement. Jolene could not stop her plotting, and he would not be Martin. The vision of the Kenning Woman was wrong.

Chapter 11

The Warriors Return

All of the Thalians that could be spared from their posts were at the Warriors Field on Don. The Guardian and Counselor of The Realm with the Guardians and their Counselors from all the Houses, Ayran, Betron, Don, Ishner, Medicine, Rurhran, Troy, Flight, and Army, plus the less than one hundred-years-old created Houses of Manufacture, and Trade were in the viewing stands.

The Maca of Ayran, who also acted as Guardian of Ayran, was absent. Jarvis had ignored the Director of Flight's command that he, Jarvis, was grounded for two years after being in space for almost nine years. He had twice boarded the Ayran freighters to oversee the asteroids and the mining operations in space and had not returned from the last flight.

Llewellyn, Maca of Don and Guardian of Flight, had forwarded the news from space about the battles and successful treaty negotiations with the Draygons and Krepyons. Jolene, Guardian of the Realm, had ordered a huge celebrative banquet for the evening and directed that all would be honored. She regretted her laddie was not among them, but perhaps it was better that Jarvis was not here. He was resentful enough that he had been left behind and Daniel, Lad of Don, taken. He did nay care that Kahli, Lad of Don, had been left behind. Kahli was not a true Warrior.

Wild cheers erupted as Llewellyn, Maca of Don, and Lorenz, Laird of Don, appeared in the doorway of the ramp leading down from the *Golden One*. The other spaceships had their ramps down and their Captains and Directors were on the ramps. Even the *Golden One* belonging to the MacDonald Corporation had landed to permit the Thalian portion of their crew to take part in the festivities. Jolene was delighted. Captain O'Neal of the *Golden One* was a wonderful bedding partner. It seemed strange for he was a Justine-Earth being, and no Thalian blood ran in his veins.

The crews must have had their instructions. They all lined up and bowed to the Guardians and Counselors of the Realm and then to the beings of Thalia. Llewellyn, and the lead officers of each ship continued toward the Guardian and Counselors. The lesser members stood at attention waiting for the welcoming speech so they could break ranks and run to their waiting loved ones.

"Welcome home, Warriors of Thalia. We offer our thanks for your stupendous victory and the peace you have brought to this quadrant. The banquet tis this eve at the Guardians of the Realm Complex in Don. We ken ye are anxious to return to your own homes. Llewellyn, Maca of Don, ye and your counselor, Brenda, Maca of Betron, may greet, but then, please join me in my office for a full report since ye are also Guardian of Flight. The rest of your crew may all greet their House and their loved ones." Jolene's voice was amplified by the speakers set around the Warrior's Landing Field.

Llewellyn bowed and turned to those behind him and yelled, "Dismissed," the deep, huge bass rumbling out towards them all. The crews of women and men began running to the ones who had remained on Thalia.

* * *

Jolene and Llewellyn sat drinking their brews in her Guardian of the Realm office. He had finished his debriefing and handed over the crystals containing the reports of their flight and their battles on Krepyon and the planet Dragon. He also gave her the crystal and the metal sheets with the Draygon and Krepyon Treaty inscriptions. Before joining her, he had taken time to hold his counselor, Brenda, Maca of Betron, their lassie, Lillie, and his claimed laddie, Kahli.

"Did anything exciting occur while we were gone?"

"Nay, Llewellyn. It was as though all were going through the motions of living till they heard of ye and your ships return."

"And how does your House? Tis Jarvis settled into being the Maca for a few years instead of space Warrior?"

"Aye, that he has. He tis inspecting the operations on the Class D1 mining outpost."

"What? That means he used a spaceship. He tis grounded for two years. The manual clearly states that after prolonged flight, the crew must remain grounded for that time period. Then Medicine must determine if it tis safe for them to return to space."

"Really, Llewellyn, the Justines have stayed out much longer and so has our friend Red O'Neal and his crew."

"Agreed, but the rules for our spaceships are different. We have rounded vehicles as do the Ayanas and De'Chins. The Brendons, Kreppies, and Draygons use a cylinder. The Justine's *Golden One* tis larger and ovoid in shape. We canna duplicate that, although we are creeping closer. I believe it may be sheathed in gold inside and outside and there tis nay enough of that metal here. There tis something different in their metal and their shielding. We canna determine what it tis without destroying our ship or that belonging to the Earth corporation. We canna afford to lose either of our *Golden Ones*."

"Mayhap it was rare minerals from the ground of their planet."

Llewellyn nodded. "Mayhap, but their planet tis nay more."

"There could be debris from it on the other planets of their sun. It tis too bad ye did nay bring some of the debris from the Golden One the Draygons destroyed years ago. Could ye retrieve it now?"

Llewellyn smiled at her. "Ye are thinking like someone who has worked with ores and metals all your life. We tried, but there were nay pieces of metal on the asteroid, and we could nay pry or cut any loose. I am, however, still worried about Jarvis."

"He was fine when he returned from his last trip to the other two asteroids."

"Last trip? Ye mean, this tis his second time? How long will he be gone?"

'He should return within two to three months. He tis delivering supplies, a new crew, checking the operations, and bringing back a load of ore. Tis but a short run."

"I shall leave him a message to report to Medicine and then to me." Llewellyn stood as did Jolene. They bowed to each other and moved around the desk for the Thalian goodbye.

Chapter 12

Lilith's Mission

The Kenning Woman checked the reception room on the bottom floor. It was empty. Nay had appeared for a vision or for comfort since the return of the Warrior Fleet. She decided that now was the time for her to resume her search, but where?

The old Kenning Woman had whispered it to her when she was but ten-years-old, and assured her that her visions would lead her to it. Almost one hundred years had passed, but there had been no visions at all until her vision of Bliss Lake. There had been nay about Gar's Book she was to find. All of Thalia said that Gar's Book was gone forever.

Lilith ran a comb through her hair and slipped her light blue cloak over her shoulders. Mayhap a trip to the mountains? Nay, that did nay feel right. She decided to take the lift and head to the land around Devon and walk on the coast there. People avoided it as it was craggy, cold, and windy in the fall.

She entered her lift and started to enter the coordinates for the cold beach area into the panel when the vision was there. She sat like a statute with her mouth open and her eyes unseeing while the vision played out before her.

She watched the dark-haired woman with a white streak of hair in the middle of her head approach the cave. To the south-east was Lake Bliss. The woman flew the fliv into the cave, went across an open space and landed on wide ledge. Then she stepped out of the fliv with a small metal case and approached the soaring mass that rose upward. She knelt beside it, used a rockpick to scoop out a space, and placed the metal object into the rocky soil. Then she piled rocks in front of the small hole and to the sides of it. A loud noise made her turn and the side of the ledge holding the fliv plummeted downward. A huge jagged gap against the black emptiness and wall appeared where once rested a fliv. The woman stood, terror filling her face as she looked at the opening across the crevice separating the ledge from the opening to the outside. She seemed to stumble as she went to the side where her fliv had disappeared. The rock crumbled again and she followed the fliv downward. The words she screamed burned into Lilith's mind.

Lilith was left gasping, but she knew where she needed to go and what she needed to do to succeed in fulfilling her mission. She climbed out of the lift and went into her storage pod and removed the cable slingshot for climbing the steep terrain of the Skye Maist Mountains.

Within minutes she was at the cave in Ayran. She had ignored the demand from the Ayranian Director asking for her identification and reason for penetrating Ayran's airspace. Once inside the cave she looked across the opening and decided where she would shoot to anchor the cable. She shot the cable across, pulled on the line to make sure it was secure, went outside to attach the cable slingshot to her lift, returned to the cave, and began going hand-over hand to reach the ledge.

She had ignored the stench when she entered the cave, but it was worse over the deep clef and overpowering on the ledge. She wished she had brought oxygen and a globe. Instead of returning to the lift, she knelt and pulled away the rocks at the place she had seen in her vision.

For a moment, she sat wide-eyed as the metal box appeared. Then she pried it open. There it was: an ancient crystal and metal sheets from another time. She closed the lid and clasped the box to her chest, and crumpled over.

Chapter 13

Bliss Cave

JoAnne. Lass of Ayran, was overseeing the transfer of ore from the far south mine. She had on a light jacket against Ayran's cold winds, and thankful she wasn't in Northern Ayran. Cold had come early this fall. Jarvis was still absent and JayEll was still serving as Counselor of the Realm for this term. The burden of running Ayran was hers till Jarvis returned. Her thoughts were interrupted by her com beeping and she lifted it from her pocket and hit the circle.

"Aye?"

"Someone from Don just flew a lift into the Lake Bliss area without permission. They refused to respond to my demand for their reason and identification. That area is posted. Do ye wish a contingent sent?

"There canna be more than two people in a lift. Why would we need a contingent? I'll go check it out."

JoAnne entered her own lift and flew to the Lake Bliss area. As she circled she saw the blue Don lift near the old mine entrance. Someone had removed the wire covering the opening. What fool would wander in there, she wondered. The waters that formed Lake Bliss ran through there. Then she realized it looked like the Kenning Woman's lift with that little white cloud insignia on the side.

"Who tis down there? Respond." JoAnne used the code for the Kenning Woman, but there was no response. She landed her lift.

"I'm going to check the inside of the cave," she used the com to contact Director Jada.

"Dinna go in there," came Jada's voice.

"It should be safe enough at the opening as the wind tis blowing and I have the mine mask with me." She didn't mention that she had left it in the lift.

Inside the cave she looked across at the fallen Kenning Woman. Silly creature, thought JoAnne and backed out. She felt the sick feeling in her stomach from the fumes and retrieved her mask and cable slingshot before entering the cave. Then she remembered to call JayEll. He was her backup for the mines as the Guardian of the Realm had other helpers; plus there wasn't another meeting of the Council of the Realm until next month.

JayEll was at the Warriors Academy with Daniel, Lad of Don, exercising. Jolene insisted he must retain a Warrior's body while representing the Council. Neither JayEll nor JoAnne understood her reasoning, but arguing with Jolene about appearances to the rest of Thalia was futile.

"JayEll, the Kenning Woman has collapsed in the Bliss Cave. I am prepared and going after her. Enter the charges for trespassing in Ayran and entering posted areas."

She didn't bother to wait for an answer and turned off the com. She studied the wall above the ledge and saw the line that Lilith had used hanging over the ledge. The woman had used it to pull herself over, but somehow it had become loose on that side or the rock was crumbling.

Her com was giving off annoying beeps, but she ignored it and used the slingshot to put her own line across. She did nay trust someone else's equipment. JoAnne pulled on the line and it seemed secure. She kept the line taunt while she went back outside to wrap the line around a large boulder and clamped it into the cable lock in her lift. JoAnne donned the mine mask and returned to the inside of the cave.

The line held steady as JoAnne went hand-over-hand across the opening. She realized too late the mask was nay adequate for these fumes.

She landed on the ledge, and held onto the cable to walk over to Lilith, and bent down. The fumes had entered her mask and she was too dizzy to pick up the woman and carry her back. She rose to return to the outside and went down on her knees. She pulled out the com, hit the emergency circle for JayEll and yelled, "I'm down, Bliss Cave, dangerous."

Chapter 14

Rescue

Both JayEll and Daniel, Lad of Don, heard the frantic call and stopped their weight lifting. They looked at each other's wide eyed, opened mouth face before running towards the door. JayEll stopped long enough to grab his clothes and the com before following Daniel's wide shoulders into the hall.

"Where are ye going," he yelled at Daniel as Daniel headed into another room. "We need proper globes and air," Daniel yelled back. "Wait here as they are awkward to carry. He disappeared.

Within one minute he returned with two globes and two canisters and handed one unit to JayEll. "We'll take my fliv. Tis better outfitted for an emergency than your fliv." They raced to the padport.

Once at the fliv, the equipment was stored in the back and they took their seats. Daniel set the coordinates. "JayEll, alert Ayran that we are headed to Lake Bliss and call Medicine."

JayEll nodded at him as he spoke to Jada. "Mishap at Lake Bliss mine cave. I'm in a Don fliv. Permission to land."

"Aye," came the voice do ye want me or anyone else there?"

"Alert others that Medicine will be coming." He punched the circle for Medicine.

"Two people down inside the cave at Ayran's Lake Bliss. We need ye, a Medvac, and probably hover gurneys."

By this time Daniel was over Ayran and streaking towards the Lake. He could see other dots headed there. Probably a crew from the mines, he thought and guided the fliv down. Once on the ground he turned, grabbed a rope that his fither insisted he carry, his globe helmet and air, a cable slingshot, and bounded out the left door, pausing long enough to anchor his slingshot. JayEll watched his broad back and heavy legs carry him towards the cave. Within moments, Daniel had entered the dark confines of the cave.

JayEll emerged from the fliv as two of Ayran's flivs landed and two of Medicine's. He slipped the globe helmet on, adjusted the air, and the built-in com, and followed Daniel into the cave.

Daniel had his globe on and was aiming his slingshot at the looming rock above the ledge. "Ye might wish to wait for Medicine and guide the hover gurney over."

"How?"

"They should be able to connect to the cable." Daniel replied. His shot was perfect and he began the hand-over-hand crossing.

Once on the ledge, he knelt beside JoAnne and realized that green fog was accumulating inside her mask. He ripped it off and held her close before wrapping the rope around her body and himself. He finished tying off the knot when JayEll's voice came over the com.

"Tis JoAnne's line secure? If it tis, Medicine wants me to use it."

Daniel stood, JoAnne's two hundred and ninety pounds a dead weight, but he lifted his arm and tested the other line. Rocks began falling and the line came loose. He then tested his line. It was more in the middle of the rearing rock and held firm.

"Secure the gurney and use my line. Dinna try another shot. This rock tis nay stable."

JayEll tuned to the two Medicine responders. Both had on the globes. "Did ye hear?"

"Aye, we are securing both gurneys to ye and the cable. Both will have lines to pull them back. Put the lassies on them. If necessary put yourself on it too. This air tis poison. All should be out now."

JayEll ignored the slur on his abilities. He kenned it was in reference to his less developed arms. He was a scholar and a diplomat, nay a Warrior like Daniel.

Medicine used belted clips to secure the hover gurneys on either side and JayEll began his crossing. It was more wearying on his arms than he had thought. He was thankful the gurneys were there.

Once he was across Daniel was also holding Lilith. How could he do that with JoAnne's weight on him too? Daniel placed Lilith on one of the gurneys and turned to JayEll. He realized JayEll was kneeling where the Kenning Woman had fallen. In JayEll's hands was a metal box and he was struggling to open it.

"Leave it," Daniel shouted.

"Nay, tis why she came here." JayEll stood with the most defiant look Daniel had ever seen on his friend's face.

"Get on the gurneys, both of you." They recognized Lass of Medicine, Melanie's voice. "Jada tells me the rock inside that cave was undermined centuries ago. Weight will make that ledge shift."

"Will the gurney hold both JoAnne and me?" Daniel yelled back.

"Aye, it tis a hover gurney and was built for the battlefield. Go, go, go."

JayEll sat beside the Kenning Woman and Daniel settled on the other as the Medical people guided the gurneys to the front.

JayEll and Lilith arrived first and JayEll started to step down. "Stay right there. Ye are all going to Medicine.

"We did nay breathe that air."

"Ye were in that cave. That gas works its way into the clothes, the skin, and then into the blood. Ye all must be cleansed. Medicine will alert your Houses."

Chapter 15

Medicine

They landed on the padport by Medicine's facility just to the left of Medicine's Maca's Tower. The purple doors swung open to admit them, but Melanie stopped the gurneys.

"Strip," she commanded, her brown eyes hard and demanding.

"Uh, if ye will note, there tis very little to strip." Daniel looked at her. "I did nay stop for clothes when we left the Warrior's Training Room."

"I dinna care. Anything ye have on will be burned. Stay on that gurney and strip or I'll cut it off."

She must have given orders while in flight as several purple and lilac clad Medicine Directors and Keepers were there stripping the clothes off Lilith and JoAnne. JayEll had slipped off the shirt he had grabbed and his thong. Keepers had cut the rope that bound Daniel and JoAnne together and tossed that into the container for burning. Daniel knew he would have to explain to his fither as it was an Earth rope, not the gray, slender rope produced by Ayran. He grimaced at that thought and removed his thong.

They advanced through the double doors and a mist came down over them and a tent-like, clear plas settled over each individual. Melanie, Director of Medicine, guided his gurney into a room. He saw Marta, Guardian of Medicine, tending JoAnne before the door closed on them. Then his gurney was beside a bed.

"Off," came Melanie's command.

Daniel rolled off the gurney onto the bed. The gurney was whisked out through an opening that appeared in the wall. All was fascinating as Daniel had never been ill, nor had he been in an accident. This was his first experience here. The tent remained around him, but the folds were drawn up into a descending tube and seemed to close around it. Daniel looked up to watch.

"On your back and close your eyes," was Melanie's next command. "The quicker we do this the quicker ye will be out of here."

Daniel complied and another mist came from above. Melanie's hands were enveloped by the plas tents, but it didn't stop her from lifting his penis from one side to the other. Instinct made him grab her wrist.

"Keep those eyes closed. This is to wash off the residue from the cave."

After five seconds her voice came again. "Turn over and blink your eyes and then close them again."

Daniel complied and the mist settled on him again and he felt his butt cheeks being separated.

"Now turn over."

Since the mist had stopped, Daniel turned, looked up at her and gave her one of his innocent smiles. Before he could say anything a tube snaked down from above.

"Put that in your mouth and breathe in and out a couple of times."

Since the laws of Thalia clearly stated that Medicine ruled in their area, Daniel again complied. Then he looked over at Melanie checking the visual.

"Hah, you are fortunate. You weren't in there long and you were efficient." She threw off her plastent and pushed a button on the wall. The pipe inside the tent retreated into the ceiling and the tent collapsed around him.

"JayEll has already been released, but insisted on remaining with that retrieved item from the cave. Your parents are waiting for ye. I believe someone from Don has clothes for ye as both Houses were alerted.

Daniel swung his feet to the floor. "And JoAnne and Lilith?"

Melanie smiled at him. "They will take longer. Their exposure was greater."

Daniel stood, smiled, threw his arms around her, and laid his head on her right shoulder then her left, and made the "tsk" sound in each ear.

"Thank ye, Melanie, Director of Medicine. I am most grateful."

Melanie smiled at him, the dimple showing in her right cheek. "Daniel, there was nay way I could have let anything happen to ye. Your fither and mither would nay have forgiven me."

Chapter 16

A Thalian Proposal

As Daniel stepped out of the door, his mother's arms enfolded him. "My darling laddie, why do ye take such risks?" Diana was six inches shorter than her laddie, but she had a magnificent Thalian muscular structure. Her eyes and hair were the same light brown as his, and unlike most Thalians her hair fell in waves.

Daniel returned the hug. "I could nay leave JoAnne in there, nay Lilith, and JayEll could nay have rescued them both."

Jolene, Guardian of the Realm was pacing back and forth. She looked at Daniel with approval, but kept frowning at the doors that held her lassie and younger.

"Ye might wish to put these on ere ye greet the rest of us." Llewellyn's dark eyes were brimming with amusement as he handed Daniel a thong, but retained the one piece Warrior's black outfit.

"Aye, thank ye, Elder Fither."

Since there was no place to change and the crowded entry way was now the waiting area, Daniel pulled on the thong on and adjusted it. Then he accepted the outfit of black and pulled it on, the fabric stretching over and around his muscles.

Another door opened and JayEll entered holding a metal object that was twelve by twelve inches and four inches thick. In his other hand, he held a crystal. His black eyes were glowing and a look of reverence filled his face.

Jolene wrapped her arms around him. "Ye would pick a most dangerous place to prove ye are a Thalian Warrior." Her voice was husky and the half-reprimand half-compliment made JayEll smile and bend enough to give her the Thalian greeting.

"Thank ye, Elder Mither, but look what the Kenning Woman has returned to Thalia."

Jolene barely glanced at the objects in his hands. She was more concerned about the door keeping her from her lassie. "Her foolishness put ye all at risk."

"It was necessary. Look! It tis the Book."

Jolene whirled. "What book," she snapped. "I dinna care about such ancient things when my lassie tis near death."

"She tis nay near death."

The door opened and a nude JoAnne appeared to be enfolded by Jolene. Someone handed JayEll a robe of red and he managed to sling it around himself without letting loose of the objects in either hand.

Jolene released JoAnne expecting her to take her clothes. Instead, JoAnne saw Daniel standing there and threw her arms around his neck. As he lifted her, she wrapped her legs around his midsection and began kissing his lips.

Daniel kissed her back while Jolene was yelling. "JoAnne, here tis your robe."

"Daniel, keep your bedding rituals in a private place." Lorenz growled at his son.

JoAnne lifted her head and looked at Daniel. "Since I am acting Guardian and Counselor of Ayran, I welcome ye into my heart and my House, and give my approval for us to Walk the Circle. I do think as a courtesy, we should ask my mither next, and then your parents."

Daniel smiled and let her slide down and took her hand while Jolene was busy stuffing JoAnne's right arm into the robe.

JoAnne obliged and let Daniel's hand drop. She slid her left arm in and took hold of Daniel's hand as they both turned to Jolene.

"Mither, ye have kenned Daniel since he was a laddie. We wish your blessing to Walk the Circle."

Llewellyn had the distinct pleasure of seeing Jolene stand there with open mouth and no words issuing forth. How many times had she done that to him?

"When did you two discuss this?" Jolene finally found her voice.

"We just did with the kiss. He choose me in that cave."

"How did ye ken? Ye were nay conscious." Daniel was puzzled.

"I was more conscious than ye think, Daniel.

"Well, Mither?" She was staring at Jolene.

"Of course, of course. Daniel, ye are welcomed into my heart and my House. Now while ye ask his parents I will alert the staff for the celebration."

As Daniel and JoAnne turned toward Lorenz and Diana, the first Medical door opened and Melanie appeared. She ignored Lilith's Tri parents waiting patiently in the background.

"Guardian of the Realm, I hate to intrude, but the Kenning Woman is making herself ill again. She insists she must deliver a message. The poison tis cleansed, but it has left her weak. Would ye consider calming her? She tis crying for that book too."

JayEll stepped forward. "I was but keeping it safe for her." He did not relinquish it.

"What tis this fuss about a book?" Jolene snapped.

"Elder Mither, it tis the Book of Gar that ye had someone hide."

For a moment Jolene looked at him, her black eyes bewildered. Then she turned and rushed into the room that held the Kenning Woman. "What tis your message?"

Lilith stood and looked at Jolene as tears slipped down her face. "I saw an Ayranian clad woman land a fliv in the Bliss Cave. A white streak of hair ran from the forehead to the back.

She knelt in the middle of the ledge by the rock that raises to the ceiling and removed stones and dug at the rock with a rock-pick. There was a rumbling and the part of the ledge where the fliv rested fell away. She pushed the book into the space, put the rocks around and over it, and walked towards the edge as though she would climb down after the fliv. She stumbled. The gas must have been weaker then, but as she stumbled and fell more of the ledge gave way. She screamed these words: Jolene, my lassie, my wee lassie!" Lilith buried her face in her hands, then raised her head and continued speaking.

"I am so sorry, Guardian of the Realm, but it was something I had to tell ye. Forgive me."

"Dear Gar, that was my beloved Janet." For a moment Jolene closed her eyes and swayed back and forth. JayEll put his arm around her, but she opened her eyes and looked at Lilith.

"All charges against ye for trespassing are dropped." She swept out of the room, then stepped in far enough to speak to JayEll.

"Are ye coming?"

"I thought I would take Lilith home if her parents will let me. They have brought her clothes, but the Book must go in her Kenning Woman's stand and the crystal properly aligned."

Jolene looked stern. "The celebration for your younger and Daniel will be early this eve. Will ye be there?" Her voice implied he would be.

"Of course, Elder Mither. That way I can slap Daniel on the back and he can nay retaliate."

Chapter 17

A New Martin

The members of the House of Don arrived at the House of Ayran with platters of meats, sausages, cheeses, and baked brool breads and pastries. To Lorenz, the latter were the apple and yeast bread concoctions called apfel kucken, apfel strudel, and apple pies of his German forbearers and deserts of his country. He was adamant that it was not a festive occasion unless they were there.

Ayran had piled platters of smoked fish from Ishner, fresh crackers piled with vegetables (both raw and cooked), and pitchers and pitchers of Rurhran's finest brews. Ayran did not have the House members that had repopulated Don after the Maca's return, but Jolene compensated by having the Directors from the mines with their families and the head Keepers and their families attend.

JoAnne was resplendent in a clinging, one piece red suit and Daniel in his dark blue House of Don's formal shirt with the ballooning sleeves towered over everyone but his Elder Fither Llewellyn.

Lorenz gave up trying to avoid the many Thalian hugs. It was not possible. Why, he wondered, did they never tire of it?

Jolene banged an empty mug on one of the tables. "Thank ye all for coming. As ye ken, my lassie JoAnne and Daniel will request the Council of the Realm for permission to Walk the Circle as soon as Jarvis returns and gives his permission." That Jarvis would not give it did not occur to anyone. All knew that Daniel had severely injured Jarvis in the dining arena when Jarvis had angered Daniel. They also knew that Daniel had hidden his Maca's hands for years, but had not challenged any reigning Maca. Jarvis would give his blessings and breathe easier. Jolene continued with her announcement.

"All here have always kenned that JoAnne was nay my lassie by birth, but none dared or cared to dispute my right to raise her as my own. She was a delightful wee one and she tis a delightful adult capable of running Ayran when necessary. I nay claimed her for I dinna kenned where her Mither had gone. I thought she might reappear someday. Instead, we have discovered that she gave her life for Thalia during the time of the Justine and Kreppie occupation. She was successful in killing one of the Justines and hiding the Book of Gar and its crystal for me." The hate that Jolene bore for those alien beings was in her voice. She swallowed and continued the tale of what had happened to Janet. Some of the Ayranians were sniffing or dabbing at their eyes when she finished.

"Now ye all ken my reason for nay claiming her. I felt if Janet was alive, she would come back and acknowledge her. JoAnne has always been Lass of Ayran as that tis her right. Janet was the lassie of my Elder Jessup. She doted on me when I was a wee one. I canna say who JoAnne's fither was as I dinna ken." She turned to JoAnne.

"All these years, ye have been as dear to me as my own. The home I gave ye at your Confirmation Rite, tis your Mither's. Ye have every right to keep it. If now, since ye ken the truth and wish me to Claim ye, I shall do so. Ye have been, ye are, and will always be my lassie, and the title of Lass of Ayran tis your birthright."

JoAnne was staring at Jolene and then went to her and put her arms around her and her head on each shoulder. "Ye have been, ye are, and ye always will be my Mither." She looked down at Jolene. "But, Mither, I would like to honor that brave woman that birthed me and be known as the descendant of Jessup, Lad of Ayran, if this meets with your approval."

Jolene nodded and hugged JoAnne.

"I will construct a monument to Janet at the front of the cave once it tis sealed." Jolene announced to the group. "More brew everyone?" She smiled at all and began circling the room as a good hostess, but trying to find Lincoln and Kahli.

After seeing that the platters of food would be renewed, Jolene managed to corner Kahli, the claimed laddie of Llewellyn while he and Lania, his counselor, were talking with Daniel and JoAnne. "Do ye still do your artwork?"

"Aye, now that I have more time for it," Kahli answered.

"When I seal Cave Bliss, I will install a monument to Janet, Lass of Ayran. Can ye make a suitable, embellished plaque? I would pay ye, of course."

Kahli nodded his head. "It would be my pleasure, but I am nay sure I should charge."

"And why nay? Your younger Lincoln has nay qualms charging for the vacation homes he builds along the coasts or high in the forests. He will charge for the small structure for the plaque ye will be making. That tis where it will be embedded."

"Guardian of the Realm, I do my art for pleasure. My work tis at the Warriors Academy where I am in charge of bios for spaceships. Lincoln does his drawing of buildings and their construction for a living. More important, this artwork will be for a forgotten Warrior of the Justine Wars."

"That tis beautiful." Jolene laid her head on Kahli's shoulders. "Keep the part about The Forgotten Warrior in the wording." She hugged him again and whirled away.

JayEll was an hour late in arriving and headed straight for Daniel and JoAnne who were again talking with Kahli and Lania. He was able to give Daniel a hearty slap on the back before being detected. Daniel turned to great him and the old friends hugged and exchanged the Thalian greeting.

Daniel's head lifted and his brown eyes surveyed his friend.

"Ye are nay longer hiding your Maca hands."

"I nay longer need to as I am the new Martin."

"What?" JoAnne was pulling at his arm. "And have ye nay greeting for me?"

JayEll greeted her and smiled. "May your days together be blessed, and now I had best greet Kahli and Lania. Then I need to find Elder Mither ere she sends out a search party for me."

He and Kahli embraced while JoAnne watched with a frown on her face. It deepened as Kahli too looked at his boyhood friend.

"JayEll, do ye ken what ye may start?"

"Aye, but that like Gar's Book canna remain hidden anymore." JayEll smiled and greeted Lania. Before JoAnne could speak Jolene appeared.

"So there ye are." She too greeted JayEll and snapped her head upward.

"What tis this?"

JayEll smiled. "I am the new Martin, Elder Mither. Tis something I have hidden for a long time."

"Now we talk," Jolene commanded her younger.

JayEll smiled and nodded at the others and took her arm as they walked through the crowd into a small office near the great room. Once the door was closed Jolene spun on him.

"How can ye be a Maca?" Rage was in her voice. "And how could ye have hid it all these years?"

"The same way Daniel hid his all those years from everyone with the exception of the Maca of Don. Evidently, he kenned."

"And he kenned about ye too?" Anger began to redden her face.

"It seems Daniel confessed all who were gifted as Macas when his Elder Fither congratulated him for being a Maca."

The red left Jolene's face and she stared at her younger, her mind sorting through all the possible scenarios for disrupting Thalia. "All? Ye mean there are more?"

"At least one that we ken, but he does nay care to have it aired. He fears ripping Thalia apart just as Daniel does."

"Are ye saying ye have nay such fears and ye will challenge Jarvis?"

"Nay, Elder Mither, Jarvis tis Maca of Ayran and he would beat me to a pulp before he killed me. I am Martin, nay Maca of Ayran."

"Martin tis an Ab, nay a Maca." Scorn was in Jolene's voice.

"Is he truly an Ab? I dinna believe that anymore. I have read but a small portion of the translation of Gar's Book. The little I have read makes me doubt that a Martin must be an Ab. It refers to the first Martin as an Abanian Laird."

"Bah," Jolene disputed his words. "The old prophesy said that Abania would once again rule Thalia. The old Martin also preached that the Abanians would once again rule Thalia through the Ab Martin. There tis nay Abania."

A small smile tugged at the corners of JayEll's mouth. "Elder Mither, we are descendants of the Abanians and ye do rule Thalia."

"And now ye want that rule?" Jolene kenned that he was clever enough to outwit most of the Guardians.

"Nay, Elder Mither. I am the new Martin. I need this authority to be authentic. The old Martin should nay have taken that title from me and given it to Jarvis. Jarvis was a Warrior then and he tis a Warrior now."

"Ye were but a laddie. Ye could nay have disputed Martin."

"Oh, but I did. I continued to preach the known words of Gar. Martin trumped up a charge of thievery against me and sent me to Ayran. I was too young, but that bothered nay and when ye rejected me I decided that somehow I would be Ayran."

"When did I reject ye?"

"I had fallen and broken an arm while in the mines. They told ye I was your younger, but ye screamed at them and at me that I was an imposter."

Jolene stepped close and hugged him. "I sorrow, my younger, but at that time I was so angry with your mither that I was sure she did nay even bed lassies. I did nay wish to hear anything about her. Right now ye are needed to run Ayran. I intend to announce that JoAnne tis my Counselor of the Realm. She needs this time to Walk the Circle with Daniel."

"Elder Mither, Jarvis will be back any day now. The Ayranians working as Directors and Keepers are excellent at running the mines and the manufacturing units. The Accounting tis automated except for finalizing that all the Directors do. The most important job tis to continue analyzing the minerals and metals that are returned from outposts and any new asteroid that tis discovered. I can do both till Jarvis returns and he can take over"

A knock was at the door. "Guardian, should we bring up more brew? It seems some of Daniel's Warrior friends have arrived."

"Dear Gar, they will destroy the place. JayEll, we will talk more later." Jolene rushed out to keep order.

Chapter 18

A Warrior Returns

Jarvis landed the Ayranian freighter in the docking zone and switched off the power source for landing. He was irritated about returning to land, but it was necessary to download, submit his prelim reports on the rest of the asteroids in that field, and visit Lillie. The latter was his only pleasant thought. Then he remembered that the last incoming message told of the space fighters return and his mood blackened with bile.

Daniel, he thought, tis probably covered with glory and he will smirk at me in the Arena. He kens I dare nay challenge him again.

"Maca, we are ready to accept the load." Jadda's voice came over the com.

Jarvis hit the com buttons. "Jalin, open the doors."

He stood. The rest of the Ayranians could remove and store the ore wherever it went. He needed his personal rooms and a proper cleansing. He walked to the back, ignoring the buzzing mechanical loaders and their operators that waved at him. Why, he wondered, am I even here?

He ignored Jadda's wave. Who would be at the mine office today? JayEll? The message had said JayEll and JoAnne had traded chores, but had nay given a reason. Why hadn't JayEll greeted him? He walked into the red stone building and nodded at the novice commanding the console.

"Where tis JayEll?" he asked.

The novice stood and bowed. He was studying to become an ore analyst and a stint at the console was expected as part of the training for kenning the workings of Ayran's mines, metals, and processing works. Those studying joked that it was Ayran's way to keep from paying credits to Tris or Abs.

"He tis at the Kenning Woman's home on Don."

"Don't tell me JayEll has finally found someone to spend his nights with instead of here and alone."

The novice grinned. "Tis probably an inducement."

Jarvis walked out to his fliv. He never bothered with the two passenger lift. Too confining. Far more suitable for the young learning to navigate. Within minutes he was at the Ayranian Maca's home and heading for the cleansing room. Jackon, the Director of the Maca's Home was miffed that he had not been greeted, nor had he been complimented on his care of the home during the Maca's absence.

Jarvis emerged from the shower and was about to call Lillie when his screen lit up. It was Llewellyn, Maca of Don and Guardian of Flight.

"Jarvis, welcome back to Thalia. Ye are to report to Medicine immediately."

"Guardian of Flight, I must first secure all the ore that I have brought and make sure all entries are in Ayran's accounts. Then I need to attend to certain personal matters as there tis nay need for Medicine. I am fine." Inside he was raging. Why this constant surveillance? He was not a child.

"I will accept that last statement as soon as I see Medicine's report. I do realize ye will have one personal matter to resolve." At least the Guardian smiled widely on that remark. What matter? Did he ken about his feelings for Lillie? His head was beginning to throb when the front announcement chimed and Jackon's voice came over the com.

"JoAnne, the Lass of Ayran, and Daniel, Lad of Don, are here to see ye, Maca."

"As soon as I'm dressed," he snapped. Now what, he wondered as he donned a red suit and pulled on shoes. Why would they arrive at this hour?

JoAnne threw her arms around him as he appeared in the great room and gave a hearty Thalian welcome. Before he could greet Daniel, JoAnne was beaming at him.

"Ye dare nay say nay. Daniel and I wish your blessings for Walking the Circle. Ye have kenned him since ye were laddies."

For a moment he was stunned. Daniel wedded to his sib? But then he realized this would keep Daniel from challenging him to the death to be Maca of Ayran. He looked back and forth between the two. Daniel had that innocent smile on his face, but his eyes were hard as though he knew how much he longed kick Daniel out of his home. Jarvis wet his lips and bent to hug JoAnne again. "Are ye sure, my darling sister?"

"Of course, I'm sure. He picked me when he rescued me and the Kenning Woman from Bliss Cave."

"He what?" What was she blathering? How could Daniel become a hero here on Thalia if he were off in the universe fighting Draygons? His head was throbbing, throbbing, but he could not show weakness.

The hate inside must have shown through when he looked at Daniel for Daniel stepped closer and laid his head on one shoulder and the other, but his hands reached out and clasped Jarvis's biceps with his powerful Maca hands.

Jarvis looked up at Daniel and saw that same innocent smile and hard eyes. Inside, Jarvis knew he had lost. This Maca without a claimed land was more powerful than any others and Jarvis felt his manhood shrivel. He knew if Daniel bent to kiss him or kick him he could offer no defense, and he nodded his head yes.

"Welcome into our hearts and our House, Daniel, Lad of Don."

He heard Daniel chuckle and it became a group hug.

"I'll have Jackon bring us all a brew, but then I must return to the mines. Would ye like to come with me, JoAnne?"

"Jolene, Guardian of the Realm," announced Jackon.

They all turned towards the door and Jolene rushed in to enfold first Jarvis and then the other two.

"Welcome home, my laddie! Tis this nay wonderful? Our darling JoAnne and Daniel will Walk the Circle, and I, as Guardian of the Realm, shall wed them."

She did not wait for an answer. "I've ordered Jackon to serve us all lunch and we will catch up on all gossip; including the fact the current Kenning Woman tis truly amazing. She has found the Book of Gar."

Inside Jarvis could only seethe. If he was going to win the fight with Llewellyn about going back to the stars without all the Medical exams and eliminating the waiting periods between flights, antagonizing his Mither, the Guardian of the Realm, was not the way to do it. He'd worry about getting JayEll back this afternoon.

* * *

"Maca, the lab reports the earth ores ye returned from the asteroid marked as Ayran 47 tis showing promise." Jada's voice was a compromise between awe and excitement. "I've told them to continue the experiments with the rest of the shipment, but thought ye would wish to ken."

"Thank ye, Jadda. Tell them to report to me directly if they discover an ore that fits the description of the earths from the ancient Justine crystals." Jarvis sat back and nodded his head. Finally things were going in his direction. It had taken all afternoon to go over the details of cleaning the freighter and getting it ready for the next trip. Then all the information gathered on the crystals had to be transferred into Ayran's Operations Center. It seemed like anything that could possibly delay the process happened and his mood was foul. Where was JayEll?

He hit the circle on the personal com for JayEll and heard the familiar, "Aye?"

"Where are ye?"

"I am at the Shrine of the Kenning Woman in Don. I thought ye kenned."

"That was this morning. Why are ye still there?"

JayEll's smiling face appeared. "I am reading the translation of the Book of Gar. By placing it in her Sanctuary Stand it connected with the display on the table top. It took a few hours of searching to find where the original table display had been stored. It tis amazing! I have nay had a chance to read much, but the old Martin lied about everything."

"Why tis that a surprise? He was an evil agent of Darkness when he lived, but I still need ye here. JoAnne tis gallivanting with Daniel whenever she tis nay acting as Counselor of the Realm."

'They are nay gallivanting. They are discussing with Lincoln the building of their home."

"She has a home here and Daniel has a home on Don." Jarvis roared back.

"Aye, but if ye wed and have a lassie the Lass of Ayran's home would belong to her. Both Daniel and Lincoln are living in the Lad of Don's home and JoAnne would nay want to move in there."

Jarvis shook his head "JayEll, I am nay wed. I need ye here."

"Jarvis, it tis near the darkening time. The dinner hour tis almost here. I will be there tomorrow." JayEll's face disappeared.

Jarvis frowned at the com. He should have ordered him back. He stood and paced, then sat again and pulled up the screen for communicating with the other Houses. First he checked the outside. Ayran was growing darker. How could he have spent so much time on crystals and records? He should have been in the gym.

He punched the key for Lillie's home. It took a minute and then her darling face was there. "Lillie, my darling lassie, what are ye doing this eve?"

"I am attending the party for my brither, Lorenz, the Laird of Don. It seems on Earth it would be his birthing date. All of the Laird's and Lady's Station personal and families are to be there, plus his immediate House. He tis having his version on an outdoor cookout. I'm sure he wouldn't mind if ye were to go with me."

The idea of confronting Llewellyn, Maca of Don, when he was this keyed up was not going to happen. "Nay, I was looking forward to an eve with ye."

"Tomorrow, Jarvis, tomorrow. I must be there or Fither and Mither will again yammer on and on about nay tending to House affairs."

"All right, tomorrow then." His voice was angry and he slammed his finger into the circle closing the screen. When did Lillie become so involved in House? What had he missed? She loved beddings as much as he did.

Chapter 19

Jarvis Takes Charge

For some reason he had slept late. Jarvis wondered if this were some kind of weird space syndrome after returning to Thalia, or if it was because he had neglected his training. That morning he went straight to his Maca Tower's gym and spent two hours with Jammie, the trainer for Ayran. Jammie also substituted as a fight opponent. This morning Jarvis enjoyed throwing Jammie and striking him.

Two hours later he headed for the showers again and his breakfast. He ignored the angry Jammie. What did a few bruises matter to an Ayranian Director of Training? The man best learn to take his lumps.

By the time he was at the mine, bells were clanging below. Something was hung up and he rode the lift downward with Jeken to straighten out whatever had set off the crew and the transferring of ore. At the bottom, they found a tram overturned and one of the rails split.

Jarvis whirled on Jedda. "What kind of Head Keeper are ye to miss a rail failure. Get out."

Stunned silence filled the area. Jedda's face turned white then red, He bowed and left.

"The rest of ye, clear that debris while I call in someone to do the repair." He followed Jedda to the top.

Back in his office, he called Jennie, the Ayranian that headed the Manufacturing Division. "We need a new rail at the bottom on Mine 45. Have someone install it." He signed off before he could see a sputtering Jemmie.

"Why would the Maca call me for that?" she asked the wall and called the proper Ayranian division.

Jarvis continued trying to make sense of the metal analyses and encode the crystals with the proper classifications. He had lunch served in his office and then debated in his mind whether to return to the gym. If JayEll were here, that would be doable. He punched the com for the information.

"Has JayEll arrived?"

"Nay, Maca."

He stared at the screen and punched the circle for JayEll. "Where are ye?"

"I'm at Lilith's home, the Kenning Woman's Shrine in Don. We are into the twentieth chapter of Gar's book."

"What do ye mean, Gar's book? Ye are supposed to be here."

JayEll's face smiled at him. "It tis the Book of Gar that Elder Mither had hidden so that the Justines could nay destroy everything about Thalia's past. Lilith located it while ye were gone."

Jarvis tried to keep his temper and his voice under control. "JayEll, ye explained that yesterday! I need ye here. Now!"

"I will be there as soon as we finish this chapter. It tis fascinating. I canna believe how much the old Martin lied."

"JayEll, the old Martin was evil. Why tis that hard to believe?" He was speaking through clenched teeth. "Of course, he lied. That tis nay reason to be there instead of here."

JayEll smiled at him. "Oh, but it tis. I am the new Martin."

"Ye are nay an Ab. Ye are House and I am your Maca. Ye are to come here immediately." Jarvis was yelling at the screen.

"Calm down, Jarvis. I shall be there in an hour or two." The screen went blank.

Jarvis was on his feet. He punched the circle for Security. "Have two enforcers meet me at the padport." He grabbed his Warrior's hat as he went out the door at a run. Disobeying a Maca was nay sufferable.

He nodded at the two enforcers, Jillin and John waiting for him. "We are taking the fliv."

The two enforcers climbed into the back seats. "We need to pick up someone in Donnick," was all they were told. They did look at each other, but presumed someone in Donnick had called Jarvis.

They were at the Kenning Woman's Shrine within minutes. Jarvis ignored the Don enforcer's voice coming over the com. She was saying, "Please state your reason for entry."

Jillin and John looked at him when he exited the fliv for he had landed on the street, nay the padport in the back. "Should ye nay answer her?" asked Jillin.

"Nay need, we are just going in here to pick up someone. Follow me." He ran up to the door and burst into the front area.

JayEll turned and looked at him. "I did nay expect ye."

In the once empty stand, the lume glowed its blue light on a copper-colored metal book. The book was opened and a portion of the metal sheets were on the left side. The counter faced the display. JayEll was closest to the door and Lilith was at his side.

"Ye are coming with me now."

"Jarvis, your demands are becoming wearisome. We have important work to do. I need to ken enough to set up a school or at least a class to start the proper readings and discussions."

"A school for what? Teaching an old myth?"

JayEll straightened and looked at him. "Tis nay a myth and I am Martin. I will need to train other Martins and teach them Gar's Book and how to use it."

For a moment the words stopped Jarvis and then anger took over. "Ye canna be Martin. Ye are nay an Ab."

"Neither was the first Martin. He was Laird of Abania. He trained other Abanians and Thalians to be Martins. It must have been the long ago war over technology that made the Martins Abs or confined the position to them. I must read it all to be certain."

"I am your Maca. Ye are to come with me now."

JayEll shook his head. "Jarvis, ye are nay being reasonable."

Jarvis doubled his fist and sent it at JayEll's chin. JayEll threw up his arm in time to block it and stepped around the edge of the counter to grab Jarvis's arms.

"What tis the matter with ye, man?"

Jarvis felt the jolt of a Maca's hands. What was this? Did JayEll dare challenge him? He drove his knee into JayEll's crotch, and JayEll doubled over.

"Get him into the fliv," he commanded as he pushed JayEll towards the two enforcers. "Use wires."

"Enforcers needed. We have been attacked." It was Lilith yelling into the com. Jarvis shoved her down and away. "Go, go, go." He was shouting at his enforcers. Lilith scrambled back on her feet and swung at him.

Jarvis grabbed her arm, spun her, and slammed his fist into her shoulder. That sent her to the floor again, and he ran out of the door. He could hear the voice coming from the com.

"Who attacked?"

He charged into the fliv. One enforcer was in the back with JayEll, his wrists and ankles confined by wires. Jarvis took off as soon as the belt had snapped around him. It took seconds to leave Donnick's airspace when a voice came over the alert com.

"Ye are to land. We are in pursuit." It was a Don enforcer's voice. The fliv was now out over the Abanian Ocean heading southeast towards Ayran. Llewellyn's voice boomed into his ears.

"I have just spoke with the Kenning Woman. Return with JayEll immediately or ye are banned from Don."

"Ye canna ban me. I am a Warrior and have every right to be at the Academies"

"Ye will be detained if ye attempt that without returning JayEll. I will be filing charges with the Guardians Council of the Realm."

"I am Maca of Ayran, and I have retrieved a subject who dared ignore my orders. Tell me ye would have done it differently."

"I would nay have brought Don's Enforcers into another's territory without permission. Nay would I have landed without verifying who I was. Tis a simple procedure. Return now or ye and your crew are banned."

Jarvis ignored the voice, the strained look on the face of the enforcer sitting beside him. He guided the fliv down on the pad-port by the Maca of Ayran's Tower, and turned to look back at JayEll.

"Are ye ready to go to work?"

"Jarvis, what tis the matter with ye. Ye are acting like a mad-man. Ye must make amends with the Maca of Don."

"Ye have nay answered my question." Jarvis was roaring.

"Ye canna force people to work for ye. I told ye. I am the new Martin."

"Lock him in the smallest cell," Jarvis commanded.

"Until ye change your mind and your naysense, ye are an Ab again and your name tis Pi as it was before. The Martin tis an Ab and since ye wish to be Martin, an Ab ye shall be."

He stepped out of the fliv and stomped into his office ignoring the greeting of Joven at the console in the lobby.

"There tis a call for ye," Joven said to his back.

Jarvis went into his office and pulled up the screen before touching the com circle.

"Aye."

"Jarvis, just what the hell do y'all think y'all are doing?" It was Lorenz, the Laird of Don, his grey eyes flat and hard like his voice.

"I have brought one of my workers back. He disobeyed me and tis now an Ab."

"Jarvis, hear this. Ye are to bring JayEll back or the next time I see you, I will pound you down into the ground." The screen went blank.

Jarvis wet his lips. The Laird had dropped the drawl, but why would that skinny-bodied alien think that he could whip him?

"Tis Daniel, Lad of Don," came Joven's voice.

Jarvis touched the circle again. He could see Daniel and JoAnne. What was she doing? Bedding him day and night?

"Jarvis, we were and are all friends. Why are ye doing this?"

"I am Maca, something ye dinna ken."

"Jarvis, pray that I find ye ere my fither does." The screen went blank.

Jarvis hit the circle for JoAnne's private com. Not that anything was private in Thalia, but they all pretended like it was.

"Aye," came her voice.

"When will ye be here?"

"I won't as long as ye are acting like that." The line went silent.

Jarvis clenched his teeth and his fists. If he tried to take JoAnne by force, Daniel might be there and he could not stop Daniel.

"Tis the Guardian of the Realm," came Joven's voice, and there was his Mither, Jolene, on the main viewing screen. Her face and eyes were puzzled.

"Jarvis, my laddie, why did ye violate Don's air space and take Ayran's enforcers into another Maca's continent? Llewellyn has submitted charges to the Council. It will need to be on the Agenda."

"Mither, I am being the Maca of Ayran. Ye are the one that kept pushing me to act like the Maca and now I am." He blanked out the screen and headed for the gym. He had to lift weights to relieve the anger and tension.

Two hours later he was at his dinner table in the Maca of Ayran's home. The work on his desk forgotten. He gulped down the last brew and hit his private com circle for Lillie.

"Lillie, my darling lassie," he said as soon as her face appeared.

Her dark eyes looked surprised to see him. "I ken ye canna be here this eve."

"What do ye mean? I just wanted ye to ken that I am on my way."

"Jarvis, my Fither has banned ye."

He smiled at her full face, straight nose, and adorable full bottom lip.

"Dinna worry, my love." He broke the connection and ran outside and past his fliv. It wasn't his only mode of transportation. He headed for the waterfront and his boat. Once inside the boat, he reached out to touch the circle to power on, but he swayed, stumbled as he tried to regain his balance, and dropped on his knees. He fought the blackness encircling his body and mind, curling his hands into fists as he swayed back and forth before folding over. His huge, brutal body folded into a fetal position and night crept across the bay. He did nay see his mother's fliv land at the walled padport beside the Maca's Tower and main mine.

Jolene stepped out of the fliv. When Jarvis did nay answer her, she had decided to remedy the foolishness he had brought on Ayran and contacted Jada. He met her at the office and they greeted each other as old friends.

"How tis my JayEll?" Was her first question.

"We have ignored some of the Maca's orders and have made him comfortable. He was locked in a cell below as he refused to work in the mines. I brought him sustenance despite the orders." Jada's dark eyes were stern as though daring her to rebuke him.

"I thank ye, my friend. Has Jarvis changed any of the locking systems?"

They had walked over to the lifts.

"Nay, Guardian of the Realm. They are the same as when ye ran everything."

Jolene nodded, and the entered the lift and went to the midlevel where the cells were located.

JayEll was the only occupant and he was sprawled out on the bunk contemplating the ceiling. He looked over as he heard movement and stood.

"Elder Mither, I am surprised to see ye."

"I canna think why ye would be," Jolene replied and touched the symbols at the side of the door, and pushed it open.

"We are leaving here now, JayEll. This is an abomination that must be righted now."

JayEll stood, walked over to her, and the two embraced in a greeting.

"Elder Mither, he tis still the Maca."

"And he tis behaving like a Kreppie!" Jolene used the vilest word comparison that came to mind. "He may be a Maca, but I am Guardian of the Realm. Ye will come with me now." She turned and walked back to the lift.

Jada winked at JayEll and the two followed her.

Chapter 20

Murder in Thalia

Lillie heard the alert from the com and recognized the form on the screen. Strange she was nay expecting that visitor. She would need to explain another was expected. It might end their friendship, but that had dwindled anyway. Lillie had a new love and it was Jarvis, not her. She slipped on her blue robe and glanced at the screen.

The visitor was dressed as always; totally clothed in black with the distortion mask over the face. How silly thought Lillie. Nay see the recording crystals but me, and she opened the door and started to refuse entry.

Two hands reached out and grasped Lillie around the neck and pushed Lillie's body against the doorjamb to prevent her from grasping a finger as the assailant's hands squeezed and squeezed.

As Lillie started to slump, the hands suddenly twisted her neck. It made a resounding crack and the body was cast backward into the room. The dark figure turned and walked back into the night. Blackness covered all and the hours fled into the morning sunrise.

Brilliant pinks and violets coated the eastern sky as the morning enforcer, Lorena, made her rounds in a lift. She swung back when the screen flashed an alert. Someone was stuck in the doorway of the Lass of Don's Home. How had she missed that?

She landed the lift at the padport and came running to the front. One look and she was on her com.

"Medicine, ye are needed in Don at the Lass of Don's Home. Emergency!" Before she could hit the circle for the Enforcer headquarters, Commander Lettuce was overriding anything that Medicine might have said.

"What tis wrong?"

In answer, Lorena lowered the com and pushed another button to show the doorway and body sprawled out on the floor to Lettuce.

"Have ye alerted the Maca?"

"I have nay had time. I just discovered her."

"I shall attend and be there."

Lettuce took a deep breath and pushed the emergency circle that would awaken the Maca at his home.

"Aye," came his rumbling voice.

"There tis a huge problem at the home of your lassie. I am on my way and will meet ye there."

"What problem?" The man was close to shouting.

"Maca, we fear she tis badly hurt. Medicine has been alerted." Her com went dead, and she fled the office

* * *

In his bedroom, the Maca grabbed his clothes, did nay bother with a shower, pulled on his shoes, and shook the shoulder of his counselor, Brenda, Maca of Betron. This was their week at his home.

"My love, something tis amiss at our lassie's home. I will let ye ken." He charged out of the door. He stopped long enough to touch the com circle for his eldest laddie's home.

"Lorenz, I need ye at Lillie's home. Fire!" He ran out of the door not bothering to wait for an answer. He kenned Lorenz would be there.

* * *

"That's Papa's emergency signal." Lorenz pulled away from Diana. "I have to go now."

"What? We had just started." Dianna was shocked. Nay had this man pulled away from a bedding before.

A quick kiss hit her cheek. "Sorry, darling. It's our code." He pulled on his clothes and boots before running out the door.

"Ye have nay cleansed." She was shouting at a closed door. Had he finally gone mad? Diana could think of no other reason for his behavior.

Lorenz flew his fliv to Donnick and landed by the crowd around Lillie's home. He could see several Don's enforcers' lifts and one Medicine medvac. His father was standing like a statue at the back of the crowd, his back rigid and his hands clenched. It looked like Medicine was ready to transfer someone to a hover gurney. He slid the fliv door shut and ran to stand beside his father.

Llewellyn turned, tears rolling down his cheeks, and he pulled Lorenz into his arms. The sorrow that was in him transferring to Lorenz.

Loren almost went to his knees and he grasped his father's arms. This was worse than when he was but fifteen and his father's sorrow of being alone without another Thalian on Earth had flowed from him into Lorenz's mind and soul.

"What is it, Papa? What is wrong with Lillie?"

"She tis dead." Llewellyn raised his head enough that Lorenz could see the anguished face and the bewilderment in his eyes. "Jarvis has killed her."

"What? Lillie? Jarvis?" Lorenz realized he was babbling, but this was wrong. She should be alive and Jarvis couldn't be that stupid.

"Then why is Medicine still here?"

"Like Earth, the Enforcers will complete a study of the surroundings before releasing to Medicine. Medicine will determine the cause of death before they take her to the Byre Berm of Don." His head went down on Lorenz's shoulder again, and the huge body shook with sobs.

Lorenz tightened his arms around Llewellyn. "I ken, Fither. I ken. It hurts and hurts to lose a child." It did not matter that Lillie was almost one hundred years of age and stood six foot five. She was Llewellyn's Thalian lassie. Lorenz's son, Kendall, had been fifty-three when he died on Earth and the ache was unspeakable. For a moment the two rocked together before Llewellyn took a huge intake of air and stood away.

"I thank ye, my laddie. I must now go to my counselor. Will ye bring the rest of our House to my home and find out when the charge against Jarvis tis official? Bring any news to me. I wish to announce everything and contact the Guardian of the Realm. I dinna wish anything on a com before then." His voice was harsh and his black eyes hard.

"I can't believe Jarvis would do this."

"He was the one coming to see her."

"He was banned. He would have been detected if he flew in."

"There tis always the ocean. They will need to check the harbor." He turned toward his fliv.

"Papa, don't y'all want me to pilot the fliv."

"Nay. If ye canna get any of the information before coming to my home tell Lettuce where I have gone." His steps to his fliv were steady and deliberate.

Lorenz took a deep breath and moved towards Lettuce. On Earth one wouldn't interrupt an investigation, but this was

Thalia, and he was Laird of Don. Those around Lettuce moved back for him.

Lettuce looked up from the screen. "Aye?" She tried to hide the annoyance in her voice.

"My fither wishes to ken when he can call the Guardian of the Realm and request the murderer be arrested."

"How can I do that when I canna tell who that person tis?" She paused the screen at the black clad figure standing at the door as Lillie was swinging it open. "Whoever it was stood between six foot three or five. We canna determine if the shoe soles had added height. The shoulders are broad, but what if they are padded? Tell me, Laird of Don, how many Thalians would fit that description?" The use of his title told him how upset she was.

"Most of them. Lettuce, but my fither believes it has to be the person who said he would be here. Fither said he would be at his Maca's home."

"He may request that the Guardians' Enforcers detain that person for questioning, but that tis all till we ken more. I now have work to do." She turned back to the screen.

Chapter 21

House Conference

Lorenz made his last stop at the Laird's and Lady's Station where he and Diana lived. He found her in the gym tossing weights around. She glared at him when he entered and then she realized something was wrong.

Lorenz walked over to her and put his arms around her. "Someone has murdered Lillie. Papa wants us all at his home. I've already notified the other members of House. We both need to hit the showers or we might not be welcomed."

Diana was looking at him her mouth open. "That kenna be right. Thalians dinna kill Thalians."

"Y'all forget. They did when there was a war on."

"We are nay at war now."

"Someone killed Lillie. The Enforcers and Medicine were still at her home when I left, and Papa is sure that Jarvis is the killer. It seems no one else has come to that conclusion." He stepped away.

"I'm going to take that shower. I'll meet y'all at the padport.

* * *

When they arrived at the Maca's home, their laddies, Daniel and Lincoln, were there. Kahli and his counselor, Lania, Logan,

Lad of Don, laddie of Andrew and Kitten, Tamar, honorary Lad of Don, Benji, Laird of Betron, and his counselor, Ilyan, Maca of Ishner, were also there consoling the two bereaved parents. Diana went to Llewellyn and Brenda to lay her head on their shoulders and take some of their grief. Lorenz followed behind to do the same.

Once the Thalian greetings were over, Llewellyn stood. "I am waiting for word from Lettuce that Jarvis will be charged with this murder. At least we ken that nay have attempted to leave the orbit of Thalia."

"Nay Jarvis," burst from both Daniel and Kahli.

"Aye, he was the one going to see her."

"I dinna believe it." It was Daniel. "Jarvis does stupid things to see what will happen, but he does nay murder Thalians."

"He would nay have murdered Lillie, Fither." Kahli was shaking his head. "They enjoyed each other too much. I was expecting them to announce their intent to Walk the Circle. Why would he kill her?"

"Only Jarvis can answer that question. All we need is for Lettuce to finish analyzing the crystals." Llewellyn disputed their outbursts.

"Ye two nay liked our Lillie." Brenda added her accusations. "Why else would ye defend that murderer?"

Daniel turned to her. "It tis nay a matter of like or dislike. Kahli and I were already in the Warrior Academy when Lillie was born. We had transferred into Flight when she went to the Justine Educational Unit. We were nay the same age."

"There wasn't that much difference," snapped Brenda with a sniff. Her dark brown hair was in a disarray, her eyes were red and puffy from crying. Her voice husky from the screams that erupted when she heard of Lillie's death. Her huge, muscular body still shook at times from the muffled sobs. Benji would pat her on her shoulders or bend to hug her.

"In truth, there were times she was embarrassed that Daniel and I had been Abs." Kahli felt he had to dispute what was said. "She did nay want us around when she was younger and had her parties."

Ilyan smiled. "She always invited the main House people." The implication was that neither Kahli nor Daniel qualified. "Of course, that was before I wed." She tossed her head, knowing that her longer locks would swing back and forth. She was a slender lass of Ishner and as the climate of the more northern continent was cooler, the inhabitants tended to have a longer hair style.

The com beeped and Lettuce appeared on the screen. "There tis nay proof of who murdered Lillie. I have alerted the Guardian of the Realm that Jarvis was expected and we would like to ken if he saw or heard anything. The Guardian tis in a rage at the suspected affront to her laddie, but did send her Enforcers to look for him when he did nay answer on his com. We are awaiting their report."

Jolene's face appeared, her lips pulled in a straight line. "Why do ye think my laddie has ought to do with such a heinous assault?"

"Guardian of the Realm, as I told ye, his was the only com conversation saying he would be there. Tis the only lead we have. Can ye suggest a better way to start?" Lettuce hurried to respond before her Maca caused a rift between Don and Ayran.

"Hmmph." And Jolene signed off.

The wait wasn't long before the screens were blaring again. "He tis gone. He canna be found."

"Check the mines."

"We have. He did nay go down there last night. His fliv and lift are still at his home. He could be anywhere in the hinterlands of Ayran if he took someone else's lift."

"Check the boats in the harbor." Llewellyn was roaring. "We ken he did nay try to fly into Don, but a small boat would nay cause alarm."

"He has his Maca's boat." Jolene's voice was pure ice.

"A red boat that size would have been recorded." Once again Lettuce responded. Frustration and anger were in both Llewellyn's and Jolene's voices. Why didn't the Laird of Don step in? She gritted her teeth and waited at her screen.

Ten minutes later the shout came from one of the Guardians' Enforcers. "Medicine and a Medvac are needed. We have found Jarvis and he does nay respond."

Chapter 22

Mystery

Llewellyn paced the great room of his Maca's home, his hands clenching and unclenching. Medicine had refused to relinquish Jarvis or allow questioning.

"He tis comatose. We need to ken if he brought this back from his last space trip and if the rest of Thalia tis in danger."

Brenda had retreated to their bedroom and the others had dispersed for various chores. Lorenz and Diana were arranging the burning at the Byre Berm and would return directly.

JayEll had met Lorenz and Diana as they left the Byre Berm. He greeted them and offered his condolences as he bowed.

"In the old days a Martin would conduct a service. If the Maca and his Counselor agree, I would like to say a few appropriate words for an honored Warrior."

Lorenz and Diana stood puzzled. There had been no Martin since the last one died. The Handmaiden supervised what few Abs wintered over the two months when no employment was listed. She insisted that one elderly Ab be called Martin, but he was either too befuddled to help or he slept.

JayEll smiled at them and broke the silence. "The fact that I am Martin tis what upset Jarvis. When I told him that I am the new Martin and will train others, he took great umbrage at that."

Lorenz's grin slashed across his face. "Others? Y'all mean you aren't going to claim a Pope-like position?" It may have been over one hundred years since he landed on Thalia, but his words could still leave others wondering what in Darkness he had said.

JayEll knit his eyebrows. "I think ye just asked if I was going to claim there could be no other Martin while I live. That tis nay the way it was in the old days. The first Martin trained many. It would be a blessing if I could recite a few of Gar's Words from the Book."

"Since everyone that attends is eligible to say something, why do ye even ask?" Diana looked at him. "Ye have kenned Lillie since she was born."

"Aye, but this would be about Gar, nay Lillie."

"Which means some might not want to hear His judgement about Thalians and how they behave and how they permit both sexes to do all things." Lorenz's smile had disappeared.

"The Book does nay state anything about genders except for the Martins, the Kenning Woman, and the Handmaiden. I have nay read the entire Book, but just the first part makes clear it tis for Thalians and our salvation."

"That tis ridiculous. Salvation from what?" Diana was upset. JayEll was sounding like her Counselor when he talked about his Book. Thalians would nay accept that.

"Salvation from the Darkness," JayEll answered before addressing Lorenz.

"What tis your decision, my Laird of Don."

"Ye Gods, JayEll, lay off the formality. It's fine with me, but I really think you should ask my fither and his counselor. I don't think Papa would object, but I can't say about Brenda."

"Very well, I shall go see them later. I need to comfort my Elder Mither till we hear from Medicine." He turned and walked back to the Shrine of the Kenning Woman.

Lorenz and Diana were no sooner in the fliv when the screen came alive. "Attention, all Houses of Thalia. Any of your inhabitants that were on that prolong space journey to find the enemy report to Medicine. All Macas and Guardians, we expect and need full compliance."

"I think we best see what Papa has learned." Lorenz started the fliv and went upward. They were at the Maca's home in less than three minutes. They entered the backway and walked across the stone patio into the great room. They could hear Llewellyn's voice coming from the next room.

"Medicine, I need to ken why I would order all of my Warriors from that flight to report to Medicine. And have you determined whether Jarvis is the one who killed my lassie."

Marta, Guardian of Don, was on the screen. Her full face determined. "Llewellyn, Guardian of Flight, I seriously doubt if Jarvis went anywhere last night and if he did, he would have been too weak to have killed a Warrior like your Lillie.

"Jarvis has a neurological malfunction caused by a nay kenned organic compound. At this point we dinna if it tis from the original flight or from his last one. We have sent a crew to examine and scan the freighter he used to go to the asteroid, but we assume the one used on that flight has been thoroughly cleansed. If nay cleansed, I have requested the temporary Guardian of Ayran to allow my scientists and technicians to scour it with our scan probes. I realize the spaceship Jarvis captained when he discovered the Draygons has been cleansed at least twice, but I need your permission to send another crew there to examine it and scan in detail."

"Granted, I will alert the guards on duty at Flight to allow ye to proceed." Llewellyn turned to Lorenz.

"Would ye recall all my House members whilst I contact Ribdan, my Flight Counselor?"

"Aye, Papa." Lorenz pulled out his com.

* * *

The rest of the Maca's House returned to his home within minutes. Brenda's Benji had not left, but Ilyan had departed for Ishner claiming that her presence as a Maca was required.

Llewellyn looked at the assembled group. His shoulders were hunched and his hands clenched as he spoke. Brenda was not sobbing, but her face was sullen and swollen.

"Medicine does nay believe Jarvis was the murderer. I must ask ye to think a bit and remember who would hate my lassie enough to kill her."

Silence met that statement. Daniel shook his head. "Elder Fither, nay hated Lillie. Mayhap they could become upset over some of her recordings, but hate? I can think of nay."

"Someone hated her. Why else was my darling lassie killed?" Brenda's wail filled the room as deep sobs shook her body. "Medicine tis mistaken. It was Jarvis."

"My counselor tis correct. Think all of ye. Any incident that provoked harsh words. We need to ken. There had to be a deep abiding hate for a Thalian to kill a Thalian." There was a note of desperation in Llewellyn's voice. "She was our darling. The best of the new Thalians. It matters nay that Brenda may still have another. It tis Lillie we loved."

Brenda's sobs became wails and Benji moved to pull her into his arms.

Lorenz looked at the puzzled younger ones. "Kahli, during that flight, did Lillie quarrel with anyone?"

"Nay that I can think of or remember. There was nay dissension when we met with the Captain, nay was anything serious reported except among the idled Warriors and a brew usually settled that."

Lorenz took a deep breath. "Thanks, Kahli." He looked at his father.

"Papa, something is wrong here. Someone had to hate Lillie or ye or Brenda..." and his voice trailed away as a dead, flat look came over his eyes.

Daniel started to move toward him, but Llewellyn shook his head and raised his hand palm outward to stay him.

Lorenz's gray eyes came alive with anger. "Papa, that's it! Someone has hated you and Brenda for years and wants to destroy you both. I saw her. I'll kill her." He stood.

"First I need to prove it. We need Lettuce and her fliv scanner, but I know I'm right. It was Beauty taking her revenge." He stalked towards the door, his back rigid.

Llewellyn yelled after him. "She and her counselor are locked away."

Lorenz whirled around. "Aye, for one hundred years. Remember Stalag Luft 111? How long did it take them to dig their tunnels?"

The others were blank. His Earth words meaningless.

For a moment Llewellyn was struck dumb and then he remembered Anna's and Lorenz's kenning ways and his days on Earth.

"It took them about three to six months, but that was a huge group of men. Someone here would have seen the dirt and reported it. The ground around the home has nay risen that much." Llewellyn believed the logistics prohibited a tunnel.

"What if they carried the dirt to somewhere else rather than spread it around that home?" Lorenz asked.

"My House would nay betray me."

"Papa, other Maca's assign their enforcers or troopers for a month's rotation. It would not have needed to be done on a daily or weekly basis."

Brenda refused to give any credence to what they were saying and rose to her feet. "My sib would nay kill her younger."

"Well, she did." Lorenz's voice was vicious. "Coming, Papa?"

"Aye." Llewellyn turned to the others. "Ye will nay contact anyone till ye hear from us."

"Do ye wish me to go with ye?" asked Daniel. "Kahli still has to report to Medicine."

"If ye like," answered Llewellyn and the three were gone.

Chapter 23

Medicine

Lettuce piloted the fliv over the area of the prisoners' home. It had been built as a secure unit to act as a holding place for Beauty and her counselor, Belinda, after the Justine Wars and the Sisterhood were destroyed. The Justines refused to take them on the premise that the Sisterhood was a Justine institution for ruling Thalia. The Sisterhood had not committed a crime against the Justines, therefore they could not have committed a crime against Thalia.

After the home was built, the different Houses of Thalia had shared the guarding of the two for ninety-four years. This month the House of Medicine was suppling the Troopers guarding the two.

Llewellyn's mouth tightened as the scanning screen showed the tunnel running from the prison home to the home used for the other House's Troopers or Enforcers. The tunnel ran in a straight line to the home built for Beauty and Belinda. Another tunnel ran towards the edge of the Sector to stop a few yards from Lillie's Lass of Don's home. There was a statue over where the tunnel ended. He had directed his Enforcers to proceed towards the prisoners' home before they went aloft. He pointed to the padport at the side of the wall surrounding the prison home.

Once on the ground the Don Enforcers closed behind the four from the lift and they approached the two lilac clad Troopers at the door.

"Ye will step aside," commanded Llewellyn.

"We have nay such orders from our Maca or Guardian, and nay from the Guardian of the Realm," replied the Sergeant. The two Troopers from Medicine saw the weapons pointed at them and moved aside.

Llewellyn banged at the door. There was no answer. He touched the circle on the inset and the door swung back to reveal another lilac clad Trooper. She rushed at Llewellyn as though to stay him. He swept her out of the way with one blow.

"Arrest her with the others and search this place. Dinna forget to record all."

* * *

Marta, Guardian of Medicine, responded to the request of the Guardian of the Realm as soon as the Guardian appeared on the screen asking permission to land with those who accompanied her in the cairt, a flying vehicle that could hold as many as fifty beings.

"Why are ye bringing Flight Troopers here along with the Maca and Laird of Don?"

"There tis something ye need to see." Jolene's voice was calm as was her face.

Marta could think of no reason to refuse her. The fact that Medicine was overwhelmed with all the personal from the prolonged space journey did not matter to them. She had called in everyone with training in Medicine, science, biology, and any that had studied the physical and chemical behavior of metallic elements and their intermetallic compounds; and they were still searching to find any that matched the contaminants found in Jarvis.

Marta slipped on her purple sash to welcome the visitors. She had dispensed with it during the working day as a hindrance. She suspected the smile on her face was false as Jolene swept into her office followed by grim faced Maca and Laird of Don;

The ritual greetings were brief and Jolene open a small screen. The faces of eight Troopers from Medicine were there.

"These are the ones from Medicine that have been arrested for facilitating in the murder of the Lass of Don and for helping Beauty and Belinda to escape. We need to ken who assigned them and why. We also need to verify that those two traitors are nay hidden within Medicines walls or territory."

Marta stared down at the screen and back at Jolene. "Dear Gar, that canna be true. Why would ye suspect Medicine?"

"They kenned the two were nay there. They refuse to say who assigned them as they told us, 'That would betray our Sisters.' " Jolene's voice had become bitter, but she continued. "Medicine harbored the last of the Sisters that fought to restore Beauty. Why were the rest nay weeded out?"

"Mither kept all that supported her." Marta was stiff lipped. How dare they attack her Mither? "That was a time for healing, nay for causing more ill will."

"Marta, consider. Medicine and Ishner were the only two Houses that kept their own Troopers. The rest sent the Troopers to Army and used Enforcers."

"So why suspect Medicine and nay Ishner?" Marta kept her voice measured when she answered Jolene.

"We intend to visit Ishner if all tis well here."

"Then visit them first. We have enough to do trying to save your laddie and finding out if others are similarly infected." This time her voice was louder.

"Marta, Guardian of Medicine, I am most grateful for what ye are doing for my Jarvis. We are nay accusing ye. All ken that ye, your counselor, and laddie, Timor, suffered under the Sisterhood. All we wish to do is to question the one who assigned the guards for this month, and do a scan of Medicine to find any hidden places."

"There are nay hidden places. We have the only new buildings in most of Thalia. Lincoln, the Lad of Don, was involved with the planning, the drawings, and the construction when we were granted this island."

"We still need to question the Trooper that assigned them. Then we shall decide how we are to proceed."

We, Jolene, we? Who tis this we? I dinna see the Counselor of the Realm or the rest of the Guardians."

"Marta, be reasonable. Do ye really wish Beauty to escape?"

Marta closed her eyes and put her hand on the chair nearest her. She shook her head and opened her eyes. "Forgive me, Jolene. I am weary. We have been working straight through this morning and it will be well into the night before we are finished. I was too ready to take umbrage."

Marta touched a circle on her desk. "Captain Minta, would ye report to the Maca's Tower and my office. We need to verify something."

"Aye, Guardian, I shall be there."

The screen went blank.

"Would ye all like a brew while we are waiting?" The hospitality of Thalia must be observed.

Jolene and Llewellyn bowed. "I fear it might interfere with the rest of the investigation, but we will remember your generosity."

His com and Jolene's went off at the same time.

Jolene did nay hear the words from Llewellyn's com. What she heard from her com was, "Guardian of the Realm, one of Medicine's fighter flivs has taken off."

Chapter 24

Desperation

Captain Minta realized something was wrong when the Guardian of the Realm appeared with the Maca and Laird of Don and the Flight Troopers assigned to the Guardians of the Realm. Then came the call from Marta to appear.

Should she try to contact the Sisters on Don? Nay had reported in this morning. She paced in her office. What would be a reason to contact therm. Of course, the Guardian of the Realm arriving here. She pulled out her com and hit the circle that should have taken her to Sargent Mollie.

The face of Lettuce, Director of Don's Enforcers appeared. "Ye are noted." The face disappeared.

Minta gazed at the blank screen for a moment and ran for the one fighter fliv still allotted to Medicine. She would nay let them take her. She sped upward and headed for Ishner. They could hide her. She hit the circle that connected with a private screen.

"We are in danger."

The visitors in Medicine's Maca office ran for their cairt on the padport. The trooper left behind slid the door open. Llewellyn ran forward.

"I will pilot now. That one has the answers." He had to wait for all to be seated. He hit the circle for the House of Flight. "Lock onto my coordinates and send a fighter," he ordered Ribdan at the Guardian of Flight's office." They soared upward over the islands toward Ishner, but his cairt was not as fast as the modified fliv already receiving permission to land at Ishner.

Keeper Mira, assigned Medicine Keeper to Ishner, heard the warning from the secret line and touched the screen. Her warning would go to the other Sisters on Ishner.

"Minta tis landing here. She will betray us."

"Kill her," came the command, and the secret line from Ishner's Medicine quad to the Ishner Sisters went dead.

Mira swallowed and looked out. Captain Minta had landed in the First Center's padport and was surrounded. How could she get near her? Mira took out a minibot injector and slipped in Death. She did nay worry about contamination. For herself, she slipped a hard pellet into her mouth and ran outside towards those surrounding the Captain from Medicine.

Captain Minta broke free from the Director of the First Center and her scrawny assistants. She began running towards the harbor and the Medicine Quad. She was coming straight at Mira as though for protection. Mira dove and shoved the injector against the thigh, pressed the release, and rolled away towards the grass. She shoved the injector down through the grass and soft dirt and stood, making sure her boot stepped on the flattened grass.

As she started towards those pulling the sagging Minta upward, the cairt marked by the Guardian of the Realm symbol landed. Out stepped Jolene, Flight troopers, and the males from Don. Should she run? Should she take the poison now? She decided to walk towards those around the now dead Minta.

"Maca," Captain Ilmer was yelling at Ilyan, "she tis dead. We need Medicine."

"Stop all of ye." Jolene strode forward, her determination overriding her added bulk. "There tis nay reason for her to be dead." She turned to the Flight Troopers with them.

"Troopers, select two and devise something from Medicine's office here and take her to the House of Medicine and entrust her to Melanie, Lass of Medicine. Nay else."

"I am Medicine. I can examine her." Mira protested. "Ye nay need to bother those who are so busy."

"Just how would ye determine the cause of death of such a healthy, young Thalian? She tis nay more than two hundred years." Llewellyn pointed at Minta.

Mira swallowed. Minta was larger than most of Medicine and had been in superb condition.

Ilyan and her Troopers approached Jolene.

"Guardian of the Realm, what tis the meaning of this intrusion?"

"We need to ken if ye are harboring two fugitives. We do need to speak privately."

Ilyan's face and brown eyes were troubled. "That tis ridiculous. Who are these fugitives? Dinna ye need my Troopers to ken so they can begin any search that tis necessary?"

"Maca of Ishner, we need to be in a private place."

Ilyan found herself staring into the hard face of Jolene. She decided to use her hurt face and tone. Mayhap she should force a few tears. Her lip trembled as she looked at Jolene and said, "Forgive me, Guardian. I did nay realize I had offended ye."

"Standing here with all around us tis beginning to offend me."

"Oh, very well." Ilyan turned, "we'll use the Troopers' office."

"We will nay. We will use the Maca's office. It has a better chance of nay being watched or a troller installed."

Ilyan whirled on Jolene. "Ye canna tell me how to behave on Ishner or insult those who work for Ishner."

"My darling lassie, this tis nay time to be upset." Ishmalisa, her mother was beside her, stroking her back.

Inwardly, Ilyan was relieved. Her Mither was much better with those from the Houses who had survived the Justine Wars.

"Jolene, my friend, tis glad I am to see ye, but sad that a Thalian has died."

She and Jolene exchanged greetings and Ishmalisa started to turn towards JoAnne.

Jolene put her hand on Ishmalisa's arm. "There tis nay time for that. They ken. We must adjourn to the office."

Ishmalisa nodded and led the way. Ilyan was left to follow them.

Inside the aqua colored building, Ilyan decided to sit in the Maca's chair. "Please be seated."

The com erupted. "Maca, a Medicine Medvac asks permission to land. Tis Melanie, Lass of Medicine."

"Aye, permission granted." Ilyan responded.

Jolene raised her eyebrows. She didn't believe Ilyan was in charge. The woman was incompetent. She decided it was time to explain their presence.

"We have a problem. The two prisoners from the Justine Wars have escaped. We have determined they are either on Medicine or on Ishner."

Ilyan's stomach tightened. How dare they? "Who or what led ye to that stupid conclusion?" Rage shook her voice. She would make Jolene pay.

"Nay Thalian led us to this conclusion. We have the Troopers from Medicine who were to be guarding her. We have nay called in a Justine yet, but one of them let slip certain information."

Ilyan's mouth came open and her mind raced. What information? Medicine couldn't know about her. "Whatever it was, she must have told lies about Ishner!" Ilyan shouted.

"And how do ye ken it was a she?" Jolene asked.

"All of Medicine's Troopers are lassies as are mine."

"Exactly," retorted Jolene. "Ye kept the Troopers. They were Sisters. If there tis nay male Trooper, they remain Sisters. They will die before betraying Beauty and Belinda."

Ilyan hid her clenched hands under the desk. Her Mither should be refuting Jolene. She wanted to stop her ears and scream at Jolene, but that would nay stop her and Jolene's voice continued to pound at her senses.

"As Guardian of the Realm, I am ordering scans of both Medicine and Ishner."

The smile on Ilyan's face became sweet. "Of course, Guardian of the Realm. I am nay worried about that."

Jolene spoke into her com. "Commence the scan."

"Would ye both like a brew, Jolene?" Ishmalisa was certain they would.

"Nay, thank ye. This problem tis too serious." JoAnne, at least, looked a tad disappointed.

Melanie's voice came over the com. "She was given Death. Llewellyn has placed our Captain Mira in custody."

Jolene and JoAnne stood. "On our way."

Captain Mira was looking at the Maca of Don and his House. They towered over her and she almost bit down on the pill. Then she remembered what was in the Medicine quad. Had she remembered to close that circle?

"Mayhap ye would permit me to return to the Medicine Quad office for my personal items."

"We will nay. One of our Troopers will retrieve your items. They may or may nay be relevant to our investigation."

Mira bit down.

Chapter 25

A Thalian Funeral

The scanning of the continent of Ishner and the island that Medicine occupied had yielded no discernable, elaborately furnished hiding place. Someone could have hid them in their individual home, but such searches took Troopers and time: lots of time.

The Maca, the Laird, and the Lad of Don had returned to Don for the burning of Lillie. The entire population of the Houses of Don and Betron were gathered at Don's Byre Berm building, a round of blue glass and metal shimmering in the morning sun. JayEll was waiting for them at the doorway.

"Good morrow, Maca of Don and Maca of Betron." With the verbal greeting done, they all exchanged the Thalian greeting with JayEll.

"JayEll, it's a pleasure to see y'all. How did y'all get here?"

"My Elder Mither took care of things. That tis her way, but I am here for another purpose, Laird."

He turned to Llewellyn and Brenda. "I wondered if ye would like me, as the Martin, to say a few words from the Book of Gar?"

Brenda's face was becoming indignant. She could nay believe her ears when Llewellyn's words indicated he did nay consider this a breach of manners.

"Have ye studied enough to say words of comfort when we ken she has passed into the Darkness?"

JayEll gave a quick smile. "Aye, Maca of Don, and enough to ken it tis nay all Darkness. Much has been taken away from Thalians including Gar's comfort. I nay pretend to comprehend it all, but there tis enough to ken that we are loved."

"I would like to hear those words." It was Lorenz.

Llewellyn nodded. "When would ye say these words?"

"That tis up to ye. It can be ere the beginning or at the end."

"My love, have ye a preference?" Llewellyn asked Brenda.

"Let it be at the beginning." She stalked up to the door and the glass slid into the pocket opening wide to admit them all.

The seating was a semi-circle around the circular six-foot platform of blue stone. A blue metallic table was atop the platform and the body of Lillie, clothed in the blue of Don with a black Warrior's sash rested on the table. At the sight of her, Brenda broke into huge sobs. Llewellyn supported her to their seats.

They sat in the two middle front seats. The House of Betron sat on the side of Brenda and behind her. The House of Don were seated behind Llewellyn and to his left. JayEll strode forward, his red cloak discarded to reveal him dressed in a dark brown body suit, the color of Abania.

He bowed his head and then looked directly at Llewellyn and Brenda as he spoke. "In the beginning, Gar made all. When He realized that Thalians ignored what was written in their hearts he summoned Jerrod of Martin in the region Abania.

"Ye are to take my Word to those who dwell below. Ye will teach my Words to others. All who spread my Word will be called Martins. Ye are to tell them that I created them for this world until it is time they rejoin Me in the Light. That time is of my choosing. Sorrow will then be nay more. This ye must teach."

JayEll bowed again and left. Brenda was no longer sobbing, but tears were rolling down her cheeks. That madman had just said sorrow was nay more. Her lassie had gone to Darkness and her sorrow was deep. She turned to Llewellyn, but he looked oddly comforted. Had those years on Earth changed him?

An automated voice was heard. "From the beginning to the end."

The fire erupted on all sides of the pyre, the red, intense flame enveloped the body and subsided. The body was no more, nor was there any ash on the table. It was as clean as when they arrived. Brenda's hysterical sobs echoed through the building.

Chapter 26

The Hunt Continues

Llewellyn and Lorenz were meeting with Jolene for a report on any findings.

"It tis as we feared. The searching tis slow, and inhabitants of Medicine and Ishner are upset at being suspects. Nay has been found. Some have suggested we search the uninhabited parts of all of Thalia. That would mean Don, Troy, and Ayran. I doubt if there tis any part of Rurhran that tis nay in use."

"They might have fallowed some of the land," suggested Lorenz.

"What tis that?" Jolene knew mining, but agriculture was a mystery to her.

"They take part of the land out of production to let it rest or put it into native grasses. That way the soil can partially restore itself."

"Plus, there tis very little land left on any continent that does nay have someone traipsing over it even if they are nay using it," said Llewellyn.

"They must be somewhere and someone tis supplying them." Jolene banged her fist down to emphasize her words.

"True, but are the suppliers always sent the same way? Different House members could be suppling a steady stream of food stuffs to make it look normal."

"Laird of Don, ye canna believe so many in Thalia are traitors." Jolene snapped at him.

"It wouldn't take many," answered Lorenz. "Just a few dedicated believers in each House. It is a possibility like all the others that should be considered. Which House has something going on that is out of the norm?" Lorenz refused to back down.

"Guardian of the Realm," came a voice from the front entrance com. "The Guardian of Medicine tis wishing to communicate. She tis on Medicine's circle."

Jolene touched the circle. "Aye, Marta. What have ye discovered?"

The metallic molecules that built up in Jarvis are from the last three space trips that he took. The last two trips in the older freighters compounded those his system ingested in the search flight. If he had remained grounded as our text crystals recommend and the Guardian of Flight ordered, his system would have been cleansed of them. There tis but one other that has a slight concentration and we have place him on a restricted diet."

"What was restricted from his diet?"

"Brew, Jolene. Captain Pillar indulgences too freely at times."

Jolene smiled. "Tis my laddie healed now?"

"We intend to detain him one more day. He tis very remorseful at this point."

"What about your two troopers?

"Melanie's pronouncement of Death being administered to Minta tis verified. Mira tis the only one that would have had access to it. Mira also used Death rather than reveal anything about Beauty and Belinda." Marta's face became hard as she continued.

"I ken that this makes Medicine look like we are hiding them, but I swear to ye, I would have nay to do with their schemes. My laddie and I suffered under their rule. I want them locked into Darkness!" She signed off the screen.

Jolene took a deep breath and looked at Llewellyn and Lorenz. "Well, do either of ye have any suggestions now?"

"I still contend y'all should check out Rurhran."

"I have invited Radan, Maca of Rurhran here. Rocella will be with him as an advisor."

"Guardian, it tis the Maca of Rurhran and his Guardian Rocella." Once again the com from the front came to life.

"We are expecting them." Jolene released the circle and smiled at Llewellyn and Lorenz.

Llewellyn's brown eyes filled with amusement. "Ye see, laddie, this Guardian does look at all possibilities.

Jolene smiled at him and rose for the two visitors that entered. The Thalian greeting was exchanged by all and seats resumed.

"Ye ken the seriousness of the situation, but I did nay want my questions making the rounds of Thalia. I thank ye both for coming."

Rocella had removed her golden hat and looked at Jolene. "Are ye accusing Rurhran of hiding those two?"

"Nay, I wish to ken if ye had noticed extra shipments of produce going to a certain area."

"Of course, ye have already asked Don about meats and dairy products." Scorn was in Rocella's voice. Her younger might be the Maca, but he had just had his Confirmation Rite and was but thirty. She had been ruling Rurhran since her mither, the last Maca, had passed into the Darkness.

"Of course," came Jolene's placid answer.

Rocella rose. "I still say ye called us here to accuse us just as ye have accused Medicine and Ishner."

"Rocella, those are the two that harbored the most hardened Sisters."

"Ye ken my mither and I approved of the Sisterhood."

"But ye did nay approve of killing the male members or stripping a male Maca of his right to rule."

Rocella took a deep breath and sat down.

Radan's dark eyes looked at Jolene and the two from Don. "Since ye kenned that about my House, tis the other truly the only question ye had for us?" He was a tall, heavy Rurhran, and his voice was a pleasant baritone.

"Nay quite. We wondered if ye had detected any strange messages coming in or flights across your continent."

"We have detected nay. It was a surprise to hear they had escaped. We offer our sorrow again, Llewellyn."

"Thank ye."

"Have ye questioned Troy about any pina pod shipments?"

"Aye, he claims that nay noticed any. It might be the only product that two wanted and needed might be noticed if it were missing or a large quantity sent elsewhere."

"How could they keep it quiet as to supply deliveries?" Radan was puzzled. "That would require at least something the size of a fliv."

"They have been planning this for a long time." Llewellyn's voice was bitter. "They could have had a stockpile somewhere."

"What will ye do now?" Rocella asked Jolene.

"We will continue the search. We have almost finished with Medicine. Then we will finish on Ishner. To make sure there tis nay charge of favoritism, Ayran tis next, then Don, Betron, and so on. We ken they have nay left Thalia."

Chapter 27

A Vision Session

JayEll returned to the Shrine of the Kenning Woman once he finished at Don's Byre Berm. He had chapters and chapters of the Book to read, plus he was to meet with four young men interested in the study. He had turned down the females and regretted it. They could not be Martins, but one could have been another Handmaiden. He really doubted if his Mither would give up that role if a new Martin eventually served the Abs.

Lilith looked up as he entered. "Did it go well?"

"Aye, I wish it could have been longer, but I need to be further into the Readings before I do that. Have the students arrived?"

"Aye, and so has one of the lassies ye refused. She is adamant that ye are wrong and male kine headed."

"Mayhap she tis right." JayEll smiled. "I believe I was too hasty in refusing them. I shall welcome her. This tis all new to me. I'm sure Gar will be patient with us all." He went into the gym where he had had extra tables and chairs set up in semi-circle facing a huge screen.

Lilith followed him down. She intended to study the same material. After the greetings the first assignment was to read the first chapter. She was almost finished when the front door announced a visitor and Lilith returned to the front.

Brenda, Maca of Betron, entered. Her face swollen from crying, but her mouth set in a determined line.

"Welcome, Maca of Betron." They exchanged the greeting. "How may I help ye?"

"I have come for a vision. They claim my sib has murdered my lassie. I canna believe that. I want ye to determine the true killer with your visions."

"Maca of Betron, I canna promise that. A vision may come or it may nay. I have achieved my mission given to me by the old Kenning Woman. Soon there may be another Kenning Woman."

"Has one been born? They say a Kenning Woman kens when the new one appears."

"Ye are correct." Lilith admitted, "She has nay been born."

"Then I want your vision." It was a Maca's Command.

"There ye see the Book of Gar." Lilith pointed to the book set in the nook with the blue lume shining down on it. "We will pass in front. It tis customary to bow your head. Then we will go into my private alcove." She led the way into the hall and into a small room with a cushioned couch set against the far wall and a blue, velvet drapery to close off the space hung by the arched entry. There were no other furnishings.

Lilith sat and indicated that Brenda should sit next to her. When Brenda was seated Lilith took her hand.

"I ken your sorrow, Maca of Betron." The deep sorrow wedged in Brenda's body transferred through their hands and Lilith closed her eyes as she absorbed the grief.

For a few moments they sat like that and suddenly Lilith's eyes opened, but she saw nothing in the room. Her breath came in and out of her mouth and her eyes opened wider before she squeezed them shut and put both hands to her face.

Then she looked up at Brenda. Brenda had risen to her normal six foot four inches in height. She clenched and unclenched her fists. "Well," she demanded.

The Kenning Woman rose and pointed her index finger at Brenda.

"Ye and your House are in danger. Ye are hated for being the Maca of Betron and your laddie tis hated for being the Laird of Betron for from his seed will come the next Maca. If ye both are gone, then Beauty would be the Guardian of Betron. A Maca of Betron would nay appear again." Lilith dropped her hand.

Brenda stared at her in horror. "Are ye saying it tis my sib that killed my lassie and wishes to kill me and my Benji?"

Lilith nodded and in a gentle voice said, "Maca of Betron, she wishes ye, your laddie, and his counselor dead before a wee one tis born. Whether she kills ye or someone else commits the deed, she does nay care."

Brenda turned and stalked out of the home. Lilith sank back into the cushions and buried her face in her hands. Brenda had not believed the vision.

She could not intrude on JayEll to comfort her. He was busy teaching others the Book of Gar and trying to persuade the males to consider becoming Martins.

Chapter 28

The Fugitives

Ilyan, Maca of Ishner, had convinced Benji her counselor that she must return to Ishner after the turmoil that the searchers had caused among her Troopers. It was as good as excuse as any to be away from the gloom and darkness around him and his mither. There was also a ship that had a personal problem between two House members. She as Maca was needed to resolve the dispute. It was imperative for her to leave.

Benji, of course, cared nothing about the problems of Ishner. All he cared about was his mither and his table. What good had it done her to wed a huge Thalian? The man was a weakling compared to Daniel or Jarvis for bedding. Even the leader of the Sisters was more satisfying than Benji. She kenned how to treat a bedding partner. Getting Belinda out of the way was the problem.

Ilyan landed on the fishing vessel. It was the second largest troller in the fleet. She had tried once to take the largest away from Ishmael, but her Mither and Fither had protested. Ishmael and his sister, Issing, had endured the worst of the Sisterhood brutality against Ishner during the Justine reign. Their plum positions were their reward for their endurance. Others in Thalia would think it strange if they were not allotted some benefit for surviving in the Ab camp. After all, even Ilyan, as a child had suffered the Sisterhood's abuse.

"They are all that tis left of the House of Ishner besides us." Ishmalisa was adamant. "If we did nay have them in charge, the other Houses would wonder and mayhap question why we are in charge. We canna risk it."

Arguing with her parents was futile. She was Maca, but they ran Ishner so well that she did nay have to work in the Maca's office. She could enjoy life and her beddings and that helped her to forget what she did not wish to remember. The bad part of being wedded was the ending of her other pleasures.

Daniel had laughed at her for suggesting they continue their beddings. "If I summon ye now, my Fither and Elder Fither would toss me out of Don. The man ye wed tis the laddie of my Elder Mither. Ye are nay worth it."

She had attacked him and all he did was enfold her in his arms, ran one of his Maca's hands down her side, blow in her ear, and then heaved her away. She had begged him with screams and tears, and he had turned away.

Jarvis might bed her, but that depended on whether he was on Thalia or whether Lillie was available. She was relieved that Lillie would nay longer be a competitor. Jarvis would have to turn to her now.

The Captain of the ship greeted her as she stepped from the fliv. "Thank ye for coming, Maca. If ye will accompany me below, I will explain my problem."

Once in the Captain's office, the Captain unlocked the door leading into the next compartment. It was elaborately furnished with the green of Betron and the black of Warriors. The drapes quieted any noise coming from the rooms and the furniture was the finest in Thalia. The two sitting at the consoles looked up. One stood.

She stood six-foot-five. Her dark hair was cropped short, and muscles rippled down from her neck to her ankles.

"That will be all, Captain, I have business with this chit."

"Will ye need me for anything else, Commander?"

"Nay till I call ye," answered Beauty.

Ilyan cringed inside. Why would Beauty nay acknowledge how important she was? Belinda sat at the other console like the fat kine that she was.

Beauty watched the Captain leave and motioned to Ilyan to greet them. Instead of those two putting their heads on her shoulder first as her position as Maca required, Ilyan first put her head on their shoulders, acknowledging them as her superiors.

"Well, what news? Have they discovered anything?"

"Nay, but I thought ye might like to ken that the Kenning Woman has warned my Mither-by-Marriage that you mean to destroy her and Benji. I ken that tis laughable. She tis nay any danger to ye."

Beauty stepped closer, grasped Ilyan's arms and shook her. "I should have killed her years ago."

"Brenda?" Ilyan was shocked.

"The Kenning Woman!"

"The old one or the new one has located Gar's Book." Ilyan was puzzled.

Beauty glared at her. "There tis nay Gar. The old one when she prophesized the return of the Maca of Don. "Now what did this new so-called Kenning Woman tell my sibling?"

"That she and her House are in danger. Ye want them all dead."

Beauty allowed a tight smile, but her eyes were hard. "That would include ye if ye have been stupid enough to conceive."

"Nay, there tis nay wee one. Please ye promised when I brought ye news that there would be a bedding."

Beauty pulled her closer and began stroking her back and squeezing at the hips. She brought her leg up between Ilyan's thighs and rubbed.

Ilyan began moaning and moving back and forth.

Beauty looked over at Belinda who was glaring at the two. "Do ye think that was enough information for me to betray ye?"

Belinda stood. She was six foot-two inches tall, and softer than Beauty. Her hair was a deep brown and cut short, but it curled around her ears and at the neckline.

"She tis odious. How can ye stand her?"

"I can't, but she tis still useful. Aren't ye?" She grasped Ilyan by the biceps again and pushed her away. "Aren't ye useful to us, Ilyan? Ye will do as I bid ye, won't ye?" Beauty stroked her cheeks and her lips.

"Aye, aye, ye ken I will. Please, I need ye."

"How close are the Guardian's Troopers to finishing their scans of Medicine and Ishner?"

"They've finished Medicine. They are about half-way across Ishner and they are scanning any ship that tis in port or enters."

"And then where will they search?"

"They have nay confided in me."

Beauty slapped her and closed her hands on Ilyan's biceps again. "That tis nay helpful."

"Mayhap they will search the ships at sea."

Beauty tightened her grip. "When?"

"I dinna. Please, ye are hurting me. Benji is always nice to me."

Beauty laughed. "And that is why ye come to me. Ye canna stand the mewling man that tis my younger."

Beauty began giving instructions. "We need another refuge and it tis going to be built on Betron. Ye will "surprise" Benji with a get-away lodge in the forest close to the ocean. What part of Betron does Ishner consider too dangerous for fishing?"

"The rocks around Cape of Despair. We nay ever troll there."

"Tis there a suitable place to land?"

"Mayhap on a calm day on the other side in the cove."

"Excellent!" Beauty pulled her close and licked at her neck. Ilyan moaned.

"Ye dinna have to make the building grandiose. Just enough for a picnic and an overnight away from preying eyes. There will be a secret access to the bottom part that will have the gym and extra cushions. We need it within seven days or less."

Ilyan was shaking her head. "My mither-by-marriage would nay allow her Tris to build that and they would ken there was a hidden part."

"Ye are to have Ishner's Tris build it."

Ilyan flinched at the scorn in Beauty's voice.

"But they too would ken that there are secret rooms."

Beauty shook Ilyan again. "Are ye a complete fool? Ye will use your Troopers, but most or your Tris will be obedient if ye quarter their loved ones."

"Aye, but the Council of the Realm is suggesting that all Troopers become Enforcers or join the Army if they wish to be Troopers."

"May the Council descend into Darkness! Do ye wish your bedding or a beating?"

Ilyan looked up at her with adoring eyes. "I will have your get away built. Please, please. I need your arms around me."

"Then we will adjourn to the sleeping room and together we will plan the Tris and Troopers ye will use. Remember, if that tis nay built, ye will nay bed with me again."

Ilyan nodded her head, her body trembling in anticipation.

Belinda glared at them both as they walked towards the other door.

Chapter 29

The House of Ayran

JayEll found Lilith at the outside pool where she was lifting and throwing weights. Perspiration was running down her face and back. He stood for a moment to admire her body and stepped closer, grasped the weight, and lowered it before pulling her into his arms.

"What caused ye to work out in the middle of the afternoon?"

"She didn't believe me."

"Who did nay believe ye, Lilith?"

"Brenda, Maca of Betron. She was here seeking a vision as to the true killer of her lassie. I could nay give her more than tis known, but the vision said that she and her House are in danger. I had to warn her that her sibling, Beauty, wants her and Benji, Laird of Betron, dead. That creature tis gloating over the death of Lillie, Lady of Don and Betron."

JayEll stared at her. "Why does she nay believe that Beauty tis the murderer?"

"She simply canna believe her own sibling would do such a murder. Tis why she did nay believe me with the vision, but it tis true." Lilith almost shouted the last four words.

JayEll pulled her close. "Aye, I believe ye." He smiled down at her. "Since ye are so upset, why dinna ye come with me in the morrow? I must attend to certain things on Ayran since Jarvis was nay released from Medicine's clutches today. Then I must attend Elder Mither at the Guardians of the Realm quarters on Troy. JoAnne canna keep up with it all."

Lilith sighed. "There tis so little for me to do on Ayran, I would enjoy seeing the pina fields of Troy again. Plus, if we are together so much, people will say ye canna be Martin. Ye must give up all thoughts of being wed or bedding me again."

"From what I have read in the Book, that tis wrong. The first Martin was wed to the Kenning Woman. Others were wed to the different Handmaidens, or to those from House, or lassies from the Tris. They did nay eschew the wedded state or the right to bed. They did, however, rail against those who bedded without wedding. Something I am finding very strange. How can Thalians go for over eighty years or more without bedding? We are nay Justines."

Lilith's face went from puzzled to amused. "Ye are so funny, JayEll. When did the right of a Martin change from being able to wed to nay?"

"I dinna, but then I am but halfway through the book. There were Martins in every House and they are all were wed by the time they were in their forties or fifties. It seems we did nay live as long then, however, since being a Martin does nay prohibit bedding."

JayEll changed the subject. "Are ye coming with me?"

Lilith was smiling at him. "Ye are nay subscribing to the idea of giving up all beddings?"

"Nay yet, and ye as the Kenning Woman are nay giving it up either," he reminded her.

"My mission tis fulfilled. I found Gar's Book. When Thalia needs another Kenning Woman, she will be birthed, and, yes, JayEll, I will go with ye as long as I do nay have to descend into a mine. I will nay go into the ground again."

JayEll pulled her close and this time his Maca's hands awakened a response in her. They broke apart, both of them wide-eyed.

"What just happened?" Lilith was searching his face, seeking an answer.

"Ye my darling, recognized a Maca's hands. Mayhap it tis because ye are the Kenning Woman and there will be nay other as long as we are together. Did your original vision of me being the Martin show us together?"

"Yes, it said we grow old together."

"Then we shall ask your parents and my Elder Mither and Maca for permission to Walk the Circle."

* * *

The first person to greet them at the Maca's office was Jarvis. His face was taut and it looked like he had lost some of his weight. JayEll stopped at the sight of him, not knowing if he would be attacked again or welcomed.

Jarvis grabbed JayEll and pulled him close into an embrace before laying his head on both shoulders and making the "tsk" sound of the Thalian greeting in his ears. "JayEll, forgive me. I dinna ken what I was doing. Ye are nay an Ab. Ye are JayEll, my Elder."

JayEll smiled. "Aye, I kenned something was wrong. I hold nay grudge." The Thalian greeting was one that exchanged the emotions of two that had known each other as teenagers and both were caught in the brutality of the Ab world.

Jarvis's grin was wider, the gap in his wide teeth showing. "Thank Gar, ye are here. I needed to ken that there are nay grudges."

JayEll responded by laying his head on both of Jarvis's shoulders. "Aye, my Maca, ye are forgiven. I ken ye were nay well. When did Medicine release ye?"

Jarvis put his hands on JayEll's shoulders and smiled. "I was released this morning, and I thank ye for forgiving and arriving here. The crystal reports have piled up and all must be read. There are reports on the minerals I found on that new asteroid, and someone needs to go below and check on some water seepage. I am forbidden to be anywhere near where metal chips may be floating in the air. I tried to explain they would be encased in rock or earth, but it did nay good. On top of that, Medicine has grounded me for five, possibly ten years. Dear Gar, do they ken what that does to a Warrior?"

"Why so long?"

"To make sure that I remain on Thalia. They did say that after two years, they would test me every year to make certain that I am still clear."

"Where tis JoAnne?" JayEll asked.

"She tis at my Maca's home calming all the Directors and Keepers from the mines and from my home. With the murder of Lillie," and his face twisted in sorrow, "she had to remain at the Guardian of the Realm's office till now.

"It seems I managed to offend every Director and Keeper I came in contact with during my illness. JayEll, I dinna remember what I said. She will calm them down enough to start working again. That tis why the crystals have stacked up and why there tis water seeping below. The Directors of both mine and home were threatening to become Tris or Abs again. I still must apologize to Llewellyn for my words, and then offer my condolences for Lillie, and, JayEll, the last will be the hardest. If I had been able to be there that evening, Lillie would still be alive." Jarvis grimaced and turned away for a moment and then looked back at them.

"JayEll, she was a magnificent Warrior."

JayEll tried hard not to smile or show amusement. He had thought of all the years that Jarvis had humiliated him when they first joined Ayran as House. Nay had he ever seen him so contrite; nay even when he had had to apologize to Daniel, and the entire House of Don. Then he realized that inside Jarvis was grieving.

"Jarvis, I did nay realize she meant so much to ye."

Anguish swept across his face, and then Jarvis nodded. "I thank ye for that."

The com came alive with JoAnne's voice. "Jarvis, tis time to make your appearance. Tell JayEll and Lilith I will greet them soon."

"Aye," Jarvis responded and then looked at JayEll and Lilith.

"JayEll, ye might as well go below as I now must soothe all that worked for Ayran. Lilith, why nay come up to the home and use the pool or the gym?"

Their request to Walk the Circle was delayed.

Chapter 30

Frustrated Searchers

Jolene, Llewellyn, Lorenz, Ribdan, Daniel, and Lettuce were all listening to the reports of the scanner pilots. "We found nay on Medicine," reported Captain Tamar.

He continued with what they had not found. "There was nothing suspicious in the portions of Ishner that we have searched. The two ranges of mountains that cross Ishner are still to be scanned, but that will be a difficult undertaking. The caves hide in those mountains. There are trails that the Ishners have used for hiking or those that are made by the elbenors or other beasties. I propose the large pellet probes for there. The fishing populace of Ishner does nay care to use the mountains as a play area. They prefer the oceans. To them the mountains are for the wild beasties or any Abs that remain."

Jolene's mouth tightened. "Next ye will tell me the climate of our most northern continent tis nay welcoming."

"All those qualities make the mountainous area a sterling place to hide. If someone had been thinking about a hidden area, a deep underground hideaway would have been built. It would be difficult to detect such a place through all the rock." Llewellyn added to the conversation. "That tis how I hid the *Golden One* on the planet called Earth."

"Why would anyone on Ishner go to that trouble? Besides there were nay scanners in that primitive place." Jolene shot back.

"Do ye or anyone have a better solution?"

"I could go in on a horse-uh, zark and search the area, but that would take far longer than scanners. I say use the pellet scanners and use them now. After that we're left with Don, Troy, Betron, Rurhran, and Ayran. In the meantime, they would figure out ways to move them to an area that has been scanned." Lorenz gave his lop-sided grin. "Not really good solutions. I'm prohibited from using my mind or I would have found them." And killed her, he thought.

Jolene sat back. She had wanted to scream at him when he mentioned Ayran, but that would nay have been productive. "How do ye think they (whoever they are) would move them, Laird of Don?"

Lorenz look at her and wondered why the formality. He shrugged. "There are but two ways: by air or by sea. No one facility keeps logs of their own vessels if they come and go around their own continent and the small vessels from other continents are even less tracked. We can find out, but that too would take time and the quarry could be gone again."

Jolene nodded. "If we keep Troopers in the air or surrounding a continent, the Houses are going to complain. It tis nay their lassie that was murdered." She held up a hand to block Llewellyn interrupting.

"Ye ken it tis true, Maca of Don. I can keep the Troopers searching for now, but soon the complaints will come rolling into our office. Ilyan has nay objected yet, but that may be because she tis married to Benji and kens how upset the House of Betron and the House of Don are. I am in agreement with Lorenz. We continue the scanning of Ishner until finished. If we scan the individual ships, flivs, and carriers, the Houses will complain. That kind of repression ended with the Justines and the Kreppies."

"Y'all left out the Sisterhood," Lorenz mentioned. "They are trying to rise again."

"Two individuals does nay make the Sisterhood," Lettuce protested.

"It tis nay just two." Llewellyn's voice was as hard as his face. "Many Thalians were involved with the logistics of creating that tunnel and disposing of the debris, bringing in the equipment to shore up the walls, and providing the lighting. How many guards ignored the noise and the hauling out of dirt over the years? They also ignored the fact that both were gone. Now someone or several Thalians are hiding them. How many do ye think were needed to be that involved?"

Lettuce swallowed. Jolene looked glum.

"Ye are right, Llewellyn, but it does nay change what I said. The Houses will object. Rurhran louder than any. I doubt if the others would welcome such surveillance without a reason. We could reasonably assume Medicine as a possible hiding place because of the Troopers and Ishner because their Troopers and the boats sailing in the seas. Nay of those reasons are enough to accuse them outright. All of the Houses and their Tris have vessels that are large enough."

Jolene stood before continuing. "I shall order the Troopers to finish scanning Ishner and then I'll have them scan the ships. If they spot anything I will let ye ken. Tis that agreeable?"

Llewellyn and his House members stood. "It tis agreeable for now. If we discover anything in what was their prison home or in the tunnel, we will contact ye."

Chapter 31

The Best Laid Plans

"What are ye doing?" Brenda looked away from her screen and at Ilyan who had entered the room. "My Construction Keeper tis complaining that ye are ordering them out into the woods without adequate compensation from Ishner."

"Why would Ishner pay for something done on Betron?" Ilyan was puzzled. Nay on Ishner disobeyed or questioned her orders.

Brenda set her teeth. Why had her darling Benji married this silly creature? "What are ye having them build for Ishner?"

"I am nay having them build for Ishner. I am having them build that as a surprise for Benji. We can use that as an overnight get-away. Sometimes that tis important for a couple when there are always so many around in a Maca's home." She smiled at Brenda and tossed her long black hair.

"Surely, Mither, ye realize that ye as a Maca married to a Maca of another House, that we two would wish to be alone at times." Her tone grew sweet. "Don't ye ever want to be totally alone with him?" The thought of being alone with that huge Thalian was something that took her breath away. At night she fantasized she was with Llewellyn. Perhaps someday it would happen.

"We have responsibilities." Brenda's voice was firm. "And what tis this about bringing in your Troopers to finish the place?"

"They are nay Troopers. Remember, the Guardian of the Realm Council had an emergency meeting and declared the Troopers of Medicine and Ishner were nay more. To give my loyal Ishners employment, I made some of them construction workers. There tis nay much new building on Ishner and I noticed some of your workers were nay happy working in the wilderness. I thought it a good solution."

"They are still part of the old Sisterhood. I will nay have them on Betron." Brenda stood and towered over Ilyan. "Do ye hear me? They do nay cross into Betron. It was the Sisterhood that tried to destroy male Macas and male members of House."

"Of course, my Mither-by-Marriage." Ilyan's lips had tightened as she used the formal address. She bowed and left the room. That hideous woman had thwarted her plans. Nay would dare to do that on Ishner. She was Maca, wasn't she?

Brenda, however, was Maca here and now no underground compartment could be built under the lodge. All Betron would ken if Betron's Tris did the work. She stalked outside. Think, think, she told herself.

Then she remembered Brenda telling how the scanners were almost finished with the mountains and mountain passes of Ishner. She could start a hide-a-way there. Benji and she could spend one night at the completed woodsy home on the coast of Betron. After that Beauty and Belinda could stay there while the one in Ishner's mountains was built. Then she could see Beauty more often. As Maca of Ishner she could order whatever she pleased and go anywhere without questions.

Ilyan hit the com button to speak with Benji. He was with the Director or Head Keeper of the mills and he disliked being bothered. She would be brief.

"I must console those who have nay work to do here any longer. I shall return tomorrow or ye may join me at my Maca's home on Ishner."

Next she touched the circle for Ishner's Directors and pushed the one for Iolan, Director of Construction. The minute she saw Iolan's face, she issued her command. "Meet me in my office at the Maca's Tower.

She ran for her Ishner fliv and landed at the padport of her Tower in Iconda. Both her mither and fither contacted her by com.

"Welcome home, our darling lassie. Are ye staying long? Will we see ye this eve?"

Ilyan smiled at the two faces on the screen. Why upset them? They always favored all that she did. "I am nay sure. I must meet with the Director of Construction about soothing some workers. I will let ye ken later after I hear from Benji."

She walked into the Tower, nodded at the Tri Enforcer that rose to bow to her. "Tis Iolan here?" she asked.

"Nay yet, Maca. She tis on her way."

Ilyan walked into her office and sank into the aqua chair. The rounded windows gave a magnificent view of Iconda's clean streets leading to the harbor and the ocean. Such a soothing sight after staring at all those trees blocking one's view of the landscape during the day and the sky at night. Benji of course didn't ken. To him all that rain and green were beautiful.

"Tis Iolan." The com announced and the Director entered.

Ilyan rose to receive the Thalian greeting and acknowledgement of her status. That done, Ilyan motioned to a seat.

"I am sending ye on a building mission where the utmost discretion tis needed. I would like a secret hide-a-way in the Isomatic Mountains. It must be completed shielded from the elements and from scanners, yet be lavishly furnished and attended. Can ye complete such a project in less than a month?"

For a moment Iolan sat dumbfounded, red flushing her neck.

"Of course, nay." Iolan stopped when she saw the expression on Ilyan's face.

"Maca, dinna be upset. I just realized why ye would ask such a question. May I offer a temporary solution? That will give me time to pick the right workers and have all made perfect for two people."

Ilyan's eye opened wider. "Ye ken?" she whispered.

Iolan looked to the right and to the left as though there were others in the room. "There are those of us that ken the brave thing ye have done and are doing. We did nay ken how much ye believed in the Sisterhood. We would die for each other. The Guardians of the Realm's Troopers have almost completed their scans. Ye must get the cargo off the ship and into a safe place. I offer my home since it has been scanned. Your home tis too open to all as ye are classified as the Maca."

Ilyan stared at her. At least the Director was not using names. "The Guardian Troopers are most efficient. I ken another place for the moment. As soon as the Guardian Troopers are finished, I can bring the shipment here."

Iolan nodded. "That tis a wise solution. Can this be done without, upsetting anyone?"

"Aye. I would just need another day before the cargo can be transferred to the first location." She smiled at Iolan.

"Ye ken then, which people ye must choose to build this place?"

"Aye, Maca. How many rooms do I provide?"

"Well, it should be a place that offers all comforts. A gym would be needed."

Iolan smiled and rose. "It will be done. Let me ken when our guests arrive."

Chapter 32

The Trysting Nest

The submersible rose from the ocean and nosed towards the shore. At twelve yards away it stopped and a side door opened and two people emerged swimming towards the shore. Once there they stood and pumped their fists into the air. The submersible sank back into the ocean and returned to the vessel just over the horizon.

Beauty looked upward at the towering trees and took in a lungful of the forest smell: wood, rotting leaves, mold, and the green leaves emitting their own special odor to the air. Then she extracted a small lume from the pack strapped to Belinda's back and turned for Belinda to extract the stunner from Beauty's pack. They exchanged the equipment.

"Ye light the way."

"It looks higher and longer than what Ilyan said," Belinda complained.

"Of course, that twit has nay sense of anything, but this tis an improvement after being confined to that cabin. Dinna ye agree? Smell that fresh air." Beauty took several deep breaths. Belinda looked doubtful.

"Now," continued Beauty, "we will hike up to our new lover's nest. It will be a refreshing change. We will be able to go on long hikes and see the beauty of the trees again." Belinda remained doubtful, but held the lume so both could see the trail leading upward.

Belinda was a bit winded once they reached the top. Beauty looked at her. "I told ye that ye should have used the gym more."

Belinda did not answer but shone the light on the small, round home in front of them. The home had been wrapped in bralder tree wood. In the darkness it was difficult to tell, but where the lume illuminated the building, the reddish-brown of the wood was there. It was so different from the aqua colors of the rooms they inhabited for the past month.

"What if it tis locked?"

"Dinna fret, my darling, Belinda. Ilyan's technicians managed to incorporate my palm print in the module that opens the door before they were banished by my sib. We shall have a glorious time here." Beauty strode to the door and placed her hand on the pad by the right side of the door. It slid back into the wall turning on the lighting as the two entered.

They wasted no time and stepped over the threshold and Beauty placed her hand on the inside pad and the door slid back into closed position. They were in a pleasant circular room filled with green cushioned recliners and sofas. The screens were embedded in the wooden tables in front of sofas and the higher tables at the sides and by the recliner. One doorway led to a small alcove for eating and the other led to the sleeping chamber.

Beauty put her arm around Belinda's waist and led her into the sleeping area. "We shall investigate the place and the surroundings tomorrow."

"What if there tis nay food?" Belinda almost panicked at the thought.

"Even Ilyan would nay neglect that." Beauty smiled at her. "We shall be quite comfortable here. Captain Issaric will alert Ilyan that we are safely ensconced in the love nest." Laughter rumbled through her words.

Beauty was returning from her morning hike. The week with Belinda had been truly restful and restorative for mind and body. They did nay need to be hidden away from the eyes of the crew or a passing overhead fliv. There was plenty of food, although they would need to have it replenished within a few days. Betron's mountain air was invigorating after being closed away from the fresh air of the woodland for nearly one hundred years. This was truly their land and she, Beauty, should be its Guardian, not that overgrown, soft sibling of hers. Why had their Mither, the Great Beta, nay seen the folly of that?

Her resentment against her sister was cut short as a fliv descended from above and landed on the padport at the back of the home. She had nay been alerted to any visit from Ilyan.

The door slid open and Benji stepped down. He looked around and his mouth dropped open to an "O" when he saw Beauty pointing a stun weapon at him.

Beauty smiled and touched the trigger circle. The flame leaped out and hit Benji in the genitals and moved upward past his stomach area and seared off his face. The husk of what had been Benji's body collapsed; a burning hulk of partial flesh and bone. Beauty stepped around him and entered the home.

Belinda looked up from the screen as Beauty entered. "I saw the fliv land and didn't ken what to do. I pulled up the screen in case ye want it."

"Aye, I do," answered Beauty. She had pocketed the small weapon and strode to the table.

"Who tis it?" Belinda asked.

"It was Benji."

Belinda looked at her counselor. "Was? Does he ken we are here?"

Beauty laughed. "He kens nay and will nay ken anything again." She bent and touched the circle that meant pickup.

She frowned as the circle that negated the instructions lit. Then the circle for the other location lit and went dead to disappear into the screen.

"What?" Belinda gasped. "Ye killed your younger?"

"Aye, and I will kill Brenda if I ever have the chance. She betrayed us. Dinna ye remember? Your mither died because of traitorous Sisters like her."

"It was LouElla that killed Mither. She claimed she did nay belong to the Sisterhood."

"She started it." Beauty snapped.

"But she denied it." Belinda was confused.

"That does nay matter. We must leave. I'll pack the food that tis left and ye pack us a change of clothes. We'll grab the sleeping pads on our way out. It will be a pleasant walk to the next pickup point. Ye need the fresh air anyway.

Chapter 33

A Secret Divulged

Belvin, Director of the Woods, knelt beside the burnt remains of Benji and realized that ants were crawling over and through the cavities. He jumped up, his stomach lurching and pulled out his com.

"Medicine, ye are needed at these coordinates."

He walked next to his own fliv and began to vomit. Nothing in his life as a woodsman on Betron had prepared him for that sight. Death was entry to the Darkness, but it was clean, coming with the end of a person's decline. Thalians do nay kill Thalians, the old truism ran through his mind. Yet, four Thalians had been murdered in less than a month.

"Belvin," the commanding voice came over the beeping com. "Answer me. Why tis Medicine needed and at those coordinates." It was his Maca. He could nay refuse her.

"There has been a terrible deed done here, my Maca." He forced the words out. "Your laddie tis down." Dear Gar, she had suffered so much.

"Benji?" Her voice quavered.

Belvin eyed the com as though it were the one speaking. How to delay her?

"Medicine tis coming now." He pushed the circle and snapped the com shut and stuck it in his pocket. The com began a strident beeping that Belvin ignored as he ran to the arriving Medvac.

Two Medical personal jumped out. Medicine had not realized that the injured was House and had sent the regular Tri staff. One was a Keeper with a purple sash running over the one shoulder and the other was a male Medical Tri in a lavender suit.

"Who tis down?" The Keeper had her medical kit slung over her shoulder. "Do we need the hover gurney?"

Belvin pointed to the body. "Tis the Laird. He has been murdered." He hid his face in his hands.

The two ran over to the body to ascertain whether his statement was true. They stopped in complete shock. Who could do such a thing? The Keeper recovered first. She whirled on Belvin and his bleeping louder and louder com.

"Have ye informed your Maca?"

"I dinna kenned the words to say."

Mavis glared at him and pulled up her own com and hit the circle for the Maca of Betron's Tower. "We have a downed Thalian. I must speak to your Maca. Be aware she will be devastated."

Brenda's voice interrupted her. "What has happened?" Fear was in her voice. "Tis my Benji all right? My Director said he was down."

Mavis took a deep breath. "Maca of Betron, it tis my duty to tell ye that your Benji has entered the Darkness."

There was silence for a moment and then the screams began. Mavis heaved a sigh of relief when the voice of Llewellyn came over the com.

"Tis what she tis screaming true? Tis her laddie truly gone into the Darkness?"

"Aye, Maca of Don. We are attending." She looked over at Malroy who had transferred Benji to the gurney and had it at the door of their Medvac. "We are taking him to the Byre Berm of Betron."

"Dinna touch anything," Llewellyn commanded. "We need to see the scene as it happened."

"Those instructions are a little late. We must attend." She pushed the circle. Her commands came through Marta, Guardian of Medicine or Marita, Maca of Medicine. Of course, Marita preferred the fields of Troy.

* * *

Llewellyn hit the circle for the Guardian of the Realm. Jolene's full face appeared on his screen. "Have ye heard? Someone has murdered Benji and Medicine tis moving the body. Tell them to stop. I must console my counselor. Get Lorenz to look at the ground."

Jolene's mouth opened, then closed, and she swallowed. "Dear Gar, what next? What do ye mean not to let them move the body? Our instruments can scan quite well and tell us all we need to ken."

"Nay, it will nay," he shouted. Llewellyn was growing desperate. He could hear Brenda still screaming. "I must go. Stop them from destroying any evidence." He pushed the circle and ran into Brenda's office. His office at her Maca's Tower had been created close to hers.

She was sitting in her chair hands over her face, rocking back and forth. At times it was moans and then screams. "My Benji, my Benji," was being repeated over and over again. Her Director of Affairs, Beldona, was trying to hug her and offering futile words of meaningless condolences to the distraught woman.

Llewellyn bent down and pulled her up into his arms, holding her close, and taking her grief into his system. It was almost overwhelming when he realized it was grief for both Lillie and

Benji. She had lost two children in less than a month. It was too much for one being to comprehend.

"Shush, my love," he murmured, but shush she would not. He did nay realize that Beldona had been absent for a period when she reappeared.

"I have summoned Medicine. Tis more than my Maca can bear."

He nodded at Beldona and continued to hold Brenda, upset that he could not be out there trying to run Beauty down. Nay else mattered in his mind now. People on Thalia did nay ken how to investigate a murder. Thalians do nay kill Thalians was a bitter joke. Beauty was not only killing Thalians, she was killing the members of her own House.

"Beldona," he said, "ye need to bring in your enforcers. Your Maca tis in danger also."

Surprise, then realization that this was true, spread across her face. "Aye, I shall do so." She ran to the front. She soon returned with Marta, Guardian of Medicine.

Marta swept into the room and pressed a thin, purple tube against Brenda's arm. Brenda slumped against Llewellyn and he picked her up.

"Shall I place her on the couch here or shall I take her to home?"

"Home would be best, Llewellyn. She will need to rest and have her House around her until the arrangements are made. From what Mavis, my Keeper at the scene said, it will take the personal of the Byre Berm some time to create the hologram to reimage his body. She tis in nay condition to see him as he looks. Ye must keep her consoled. There tis very little that Medicine tis able to do for grief."

"Surely, the thought that she tis still young enough to conceive another will help."

Magda tried to repress a frown, but she could not hide the surprise in her eyes at that statement.

Llewellyn stared at her. She tis two hundred and seventy-eight. It tis possible. Most House members can conceive three times." He stared at Marta who had looked down by pretending to arrange things in her bag.

"Your face and your actions tell me that I dinna have the information ye have. Why can my counselor nay have the third child?"

Magda picked up her bag, slung it over her shoulder, and started for the door. "Llewellyn, ye are my friend and my counselor's friend, but I am Medicine. I canna divulge what I ken from my position in Medicine."

"Did she deceive me about one of ours?"

"Nay, Llewellyn, ye canna think that. This was before Benji was born and before ye returned."

"I thank ye, Marta, Guardian of Medicine." In his heart and in his stomach a knot grew. Brenda had deceived him. She had had an abortion.

Chapter 34

Thwarted

Lorenz arrived at the crime scene seconds after the Guardian of the Realm and her Troopers. Just why Jolene had decided to join the hunt puzzled him. She could devise all sorts of schemes and knew the history of this planet and its metals and resources better than others, but tracking down a killer was not something she had ever dealt with before. He hoped it would occur to her that this killer might be as clever and ruthless as she was.

When he stepped out of his fliv the Guardian of the Army, Captain Pillar, greeted him. "My Laird, it tis good to see ye." Pillar gave the Thalian greeting.

Lorenz gritted his teeth, but realized he would have to greet Jolene the same way. The politeness of Thalian Houses always annoyed him as damned unnecessary. What was wrong with hello and a handshake?

"Captain Pillar, good to see you again. Where did the murder occur?" It would do no good to tell the man to quit calling him Laird. All those who had been part of the rescued Tris when they were young continued to honor him with his title.

"There, my Laird." Pillar pointed to a spot in front of Benji's fliv.

"Let's take a look. Do ye know when it happened?"

"Aye, Laird, it happened yesterday morning about eight-thirty according to Medicine. The entire front part of the body was burned away: face, torso, and genitals."

Lorenz took a deep breath. "Son-of-a-bitch. They've had at least thirty hours to get off this continent. Does anyone have any idea which way they went and how they did that?"

"Nay, Laird. The scanners have picked up nay and the people at Betron's Maca Tower's Ops Room are going over the reports of any nay authorized flights, but so far they have nay."

"Has my father been informed?"

"I did nay inform him. That tis for the Guardian to do. She tis examining the home now."

They stopped by the fliv and Lorenz looked down. Too many people had trampled there. He began to circle the area.

"What are ye doing, my Laird?"

"Trying to find out which way they went and all these people milling around here sure as hell haven't made that easy."

Pillar swallowed. He remembered the Primitive Training that Lorenz had taught and could still hear him telling cadets just how green and inept they were. He had not spared any. Not even his own laddie. He followed well behind Lorenz.

Lorenz had circled about fifty yards away when he went into a duck walk, sometimes using his hand to pick up a leaf or a twig to examine it. After about five minutes he stood and began walking at a steady pace, then looking down at the ground and nodding. He stopped at the top of a tree covered hillock and looked down and outward.

"Pillar, aren't there two small coves or inlets to the Southeast of here and one to the Northeast?"

"Aye, Laird, I believe that tis correct. I did a scan of the area when I brought the Guardian of the Realm here."

Lorenz pulled out his com and hit the circle for Jolene. He did not waste time with long-winded titles. "Jolene, have Betron's Tower Ops check for a fliv or boat landing within the Northeast one-quarter corner of Betron. There are three small coves spread out over the area. Beauty and Belinda left by way of one of those coves. They should also check for a larger boat in the surrounding waters. They would have sent in a smaller one for a pickup."

"Are ye sure?" Jolene asked.

"Their trail leads that way. They were walking steady and with a purpose. They knew someone would meet them."

"The scanners showed ye that?" Doubt was in Jolene's voice.

"I didn't use a scanner. I used my eyes and the footprints told me there was no hesitation. They knew which direction to go and they were in a hurry to get there."

Silence greeted that statement.

"That sounds like a wild guess to me," Jolene snapped.

"Wild, hell, I had the best tracker in the West teach me. Those two killed my sister and y'all are wasting time. Have their Ops check that area."

Lorenz snapped the com off and put it in his sidepak. "Let's go back," he said to Pillar. "They are long gone and I'll bet anything someone sent in a low flying fliv or a small boat. Now I'll have to argue with Jolene about what continent or what else they can scan since they have finished with Medicine and Ishner."

"But, Laird, the Maca of Ishner was wed to the Laird of Betron. That would be a terrible affront to their own Maca."

Lorenz looked at him. "If ye were involved in killing off so many Thalians are ye going to worry about offending your Maca?" He yelled the last and realized his temper had flared again. He fought the red anger down. This was no time to make others upset or angry.

"Uh, I dinna, Laird. I would nay ere make any affront to my Maca."

For a moment amusement rose in Lorenz's grey eyes. "Y'all are right, Captain Pillar. No way would I make my fither angry for any reason. Let's go back. Maybe they'll have something by the time we get there."

What they had found confirmed that Lorenz was correct. The scans showed that Beauty and Belinda had spent time at the love nest built for Benji and Ilyan. They had left in a hurry, but had taken bedding and some of the food with them as though expecting a long walk or a long wait.

"Mayhap they were planning to stay in the woods and mayhap shoot an elbenor," Jolene speculated.

"They wouldn't have known how to properly cut off the gland, skin it, or butcher it." Lorenz looked at her. "Y'all kenken as well as I do, those two did nay have the full Warrior's training. They grew up under the Justines and the Kreppies."

Jolene sighed and nodded.

"Did the Betron Ops find anything along that coastline?" Lorenz was persistent.

"They did nay. If it was a fliv and it flew low enough, they would nay have detected it as there are nay logging operations in that area. The same holds true for a small, swift boat. It could have come in and returned to a larger ship. There was a fishing troller returning to Ishner from the waters of Troy, but there was also a pleasure craft from Rurhran with a Director of Grains and his family aboard. I have sent a request to each Maca to conduct a scan, but the Maca of Ishner is in deep mourning and hysterical. She tis refusing medication."

"Do ye ken where my fither is?"

"Aye, Lorenz. He tis with Brenda on the chance she awakens. If she does nay, she will sleep till noon tomorrow and should be through the worst part of the grieving. Your fither said for ye to take care of his Maca schedule for today. He will try to stop by his Tower office this evening if there tis something ye need to discuss."

* * *

Lorenz had shouldered all the appointments that did not require a Maca and reset those that did. Most were piddling (in his mind) disputes easily settled. He went to his home for dinner, but decided to meet with his father and headed back to the Maca's Tower.

His entrance was unheralded as his palm print and eyes opened all doors. He stepped through the office door and saw Llewellyn staring downward at a screen showing the face of a woman smiling, her grey eyes alive, and curly, white hair cascading downward.

Llewellyn looked up, touched a circle, and rose as the screen slid from view. He opened his arms for the Thalian embrace.

"Ye have discovered my secret."

Lorenz looked up at his adopted father and embraced him, feeling the sorrow and confusion that weighed the man's emotions.

After the greeting, Llewellyn stepped back and spoke. "There are times when I need your mither's counsel. She canna speak, but I think of how she reacted to all things. She would nay have ever dreamed of deceiving me. It was I who deceived her."

"What the hell are you talking about?"

Llewellyn gave wry smile. "When she lost our first wee one, I dreaded losing her. So many women in your land died during a pregnancy or birth then. I wanted nay more, but she insisted. After Mina was born, I took the dosage from the *Golden One* that stopped my seed. I did nay tell her. I feared she would have a Thalian sized lad or lassie. There were nay real Medical beings there."

"Mama never suspected?"

"Why would she? There were long years between the children of her first marriage and she did nay to stop any birthing then."

"I don't believe my Justine biological father did as much bedding as what a Thalian would do."

Llewellyn turned and looked out the window towards the Bay of Donnick. "True, but that did nay occur to her, or if it did, by then she was of the age when it tis more difficult for an Earth woman to conceive."

He turned back to Lorenz. "She might have been angry if I had told her, but I did nay lie to her. I simply deceived her. Now it tis payback time. I am the deceived one, and it hurts far more than I thought it would. Nay because of the deception itself, but because there will nay be another lassie or laddie with my counselor."

Lorenz looked at his father. "You are saying that Bernice knew she would not have more than one when you two wed?"

"Aye, the Sisters had aborted an earlier male pregnancy. They let her keep Benji for fear that too many abortions would end her ability to conceive. There was nay way of kenning what the Justines or Kreppies might do. Her deep grief now is for her lassie and laddie, but also she kens her Maca line has ended. There tis nay way for the title to go to her descendants as Benji and Ilyan were nay expecting."

"There's always Tamar. He comes from that line, doesn't he?"

"Aye, but it tis another branch. The other tis Beauty and I fear she will go after Brenda next. Do ye have any good ideas where they might be?"

"Papa, I still think they are being protected by Ishner or Medicine. If we didn't have to keep our promises about not using our minds, I'd know. How likely is it that the Council of the Realm will permit that?"

"Nay likely."

"Then they better come up with a better way to monitor low level flights."

"Lorenz, there are other ways. Thalians have nay used them. We do nay monitor what someone does on our own continent."

"That woman isn't flying around for pleasure. Why not put troopers on a continental watch. Y'all could say it was training for monitoring the Dragons or Krepyons if that becomes necessary."

"Tis a thought, but it would need the approval of the Guardians Council of the Realm."

"Why? They let y'all do all sorts of training."

"Aye, as I keep most of it over or in Don, Betron, or Troy. Betron and Troy's Macas have nay objected as it tis nay months of long training exercises."

Lorenz looked at his father. "Doesn't the Council want them caught?"

"Of course, they do. The Macas are angry because we might scan or stumble onto a plan they have for a secret tryst or a maneuver to outdo one of the others. They are nay angels."

Lorenz shook his head. "They are all acting like spoiled brats. I'm going home, Papa." They embraced and the door closed behind him.

Llewellyn looked down at his desk. "I must leave ye hidden, my love." He turned and headed for the door.

Chapter 35

Safety

"It was amazing." Ilyan was describing the burning of Benji to Beauty and Belinda. "They had the features and his body outlines perfect. When the flames started, it was like the real body was consumed into the Darkness."

Then she added, "At least Brenda did nay allow that odious JayEll to speak about Gar."

Beauty stood and paced around the front part of the cave's one room. The cave had been hastily hollowed out to provide enough space for a bed and dining area. The power was generated by a portable unit. It was doubtful that Ilyan would be able to have more work done here unless they boarded another troller and Beauty was sick of the sea. She wanted the green forests of Betron back.

"Do all the Houses' Byre Berm workers have the ability to create holograms like that?"

"I dinna," Ilyan replied. "It tis possible since there were those that died in wars and it was the Byre Berms that were in charge of all preparations and presentations."

"Why do ye ask, my beloved?" Belinda was looking at Beauty with puzzlement in her eyes.

"I have been thinking. If they can create one to surround our faces, we could walk the streets of Bretta again."

"But how would we get there?"

"That tis easy enough, Belinda. The trollers of Ishner still deliver the rake sail there, do they nay, Ilyan?"

"Uh, I believe so. Mither takes care of all the details, especially since I wed and spent so much time with Benji. Both Mither and Fither have been most accommodating in allowing me time alone since his death." She smiled at Beauty.

"Tis this nay what ye wanted?"

"It tis nay." Beauty roared at her. "This tis primitive in the extreme. Heating decent meals tis a problem and it tis damp in here. We need decent power generation. Do ye want the rest of the list?"

"The time was so short. My troopers worked as hard as they could. There was so little time. What if they saw ye?" A noted of desperation crept into Ilyan's voice.

"They are loyal to us. What tis the matter with ye? Arrange a work party when ye have the materials. My Sisters are loyal to me, nay ye." Beauty glared at her before continuing.

"What I want tis a hologram that will fit over or around my head, yet let my eyes see. The eyes and mouth must move in unison with my own. In fact, there needs to be two different faces on the same belt or ring that circles around my neck. There must also be a way to turn them off and on if I am discovered. Ye are to find out if your Byre Berm Director or Keepers can do that and make another one for Belinda. Then report back to me. Ye also need to find a way to put us into more comfortable lodgings till this tis finished. Do ye ken that? Bretta would be preferable, but a home in Ishner would be acceptable."

Ilyan's face filled with dismay. The Captain of the ship that brought them here was upset. She realized who the two were. If the danger of retaliation from the Sisterhood had not been so high, she would have turned them over to the Guardians Council of the Realm. Captain Issaric was the one Ishner captain and crew that remained part of the Sisterhood, but Captain Issaric and her crew had been off on leave celebrating a successful season. It had been a risk to send them on the other vessel, but there was nay other available. Ishmael would have given them over to the Guardians Council.

"It is too soon for another voyage. Ishmael is Director of the Fleet and he might become suspicious. He hates the Sisters. He did nay object to any of the scans and helped them find any place they may have missed."

"Then fire him."

Ilyan swallowed. "Then I would have to appoint Issing and she hates all connected with the Sisters too."

"Ye are Maca. Ye can do as ye wish."

"Aye, but it will take time to craft the hologram faces ye wish. Ye just canna go into Bretta. Something could go terribly wrong." Ilyan desperation was growing. If it went wrong, she would be implicated.

Beauty's face began to redden, and Belinda reached out and touched her arm. "Usually, that creature kens nay, but today she tis right. Ye must ken where Brenda walks and when. She tis sure to have a different routine now that she tis grieving. Someone can find out for us while the holograms are being built."

"Why would she still be grieving? One was but a male and the other a Justine-mutant mix. Why would Brenda grieve so long for them?"

"But she tis." Belinda assured her. "Beloved, do you remember how I grieved for my mither? When the Darkness takes someone ye love, it does nay matter what others think of them."

Beauty looked at her and her and ran a hand over Belinda's face. "Ye are correct. I am too impatient."

"Plus the Maca's Tower of Betron tis placed on a hillock so that the Maca tis able to view trees instead of the far away harbor. If ye try to go up that way, all would see ye. My Mither's home tis but a few yards down the hillock, but I dinna if it remains or if it tis empty. Someone might notice if we were there for a lengthy stay."

Beauty considered. What Belinda said was true. Betron was the only House that was nay on the harbor for an ocean view. She turned to Ilyan. "How likely tis it that someone will scan for us here?"

"There should be nay danger. "I can arrange some more cushions and the food will be brought in. Ye have to stay safe. At least ye can hike here." Ilyan looked at Beauty with hope in her eyes. Benji was dead. She needed a bedding.

"Arrange it then and send some weights for exercising, plus a few bars to bend. We need to keep fit. Start tracking Brenda's movements and find out if the home of Bobinet tis still standing. It was the home for an important House member. Also, let me ken when the holographs will be ready." Beauty waved her hand in dismissal.

Ilyan looked at her. "Tis that all the thanks I am to receive for all the risks I have taken?"

"Aye, for ye promised comfort. This tis nay comfort. It tis confinement. Have ye nay eyes?" Beauty's voice rose in volume. "I'll nay upset my counselor for so little. Make good on your promises of a sumptuous place to stay and a decent eating area. If Thalians weren't such chatterers, we could be lodged in your home. See if that isn't possible during the darkness of night. If such arrangements are made. We shall consider 'a thank ye' then."

Chapter 36

Interruption

Jolene, Llewellyn, Lorenz, and Captain Beni, a Warrior from Betron, were in Jolene's office going over options for more futile scans of possible hiding places.

"They could be anywhere," Beni stated. "Ye dinna ken how many of the younger ones have been drawn to the philosophy of the Sisterhood."

"How tis that possible?" Jolene snapped. "They nearly destroyed Thalia. What is there that could attract any Thalian?"

"There tis the fact that they would be superior to all males and the Maca system would be nay more, there would be nay House members, Tris, or Abs. All would be one."

Captain Beni had their attention, but Jolene and Llewellyn were more puzzled than Lorenz. To him, a Maca was a fancy euphemism for King or Queen no matter what claims were made about a Maca's hands. He could visualize a system without a Maca, House, Tris, or Abs. Just why his father couldn't was puzzling.

"And why do they wish to do away with Macas? I had nay heard that before." Llewellyn felt it was something he needed to ken.

"It was nay mentioned during the months after ye arrived. The Sisterhood fought to retain their hold on Thalia after ye destroyed the Justines. They were fighting the rebellious Macas that would need to be taken down. The Guardian of the Realm can tell ye that my words are true." The Captain looked at Jolene.

Jolene shrugged. "Aye, ridding Thalia of Macas was among the tenets of the Sisterhood. I always believed Beauty wanted the Macas gone so that she could be named the Guardian of Betron rather than let Brenda continue in power. It galled her that Brenda was Maca by right of birth after Betron's Maca died. She may have said, 'destroy the Maca system', but it would have been but a ploy to put herself in charge of all Thalia. Rurhran, of course, was in disagreement about ending the Maca system and had stayed away till ye started taking their kine. Why the others wanted to be rid of the Maca system baffles me. Even some of the males supported that tenet."

"That position is easily explained."

They all stared at Lorenz.

"Come on, people think. Papa once told me he wasn't a king, he was a Maca. He may be dubbed Maca, but for all intents and purposes the title Maca takes the place of King or Queen in my world. It's an inherited power and no one else ever has a chance to sit on their thrones unless they are so physically strong they are able to issue a challenge to the death. There are people, excuse me, beings that chaff under such a restrictive system. As for most House members, they lord it over the lesser Tris and Abs. All should be equal under the law."

"Lorenz, we are nay trying to start a revolution or change the way Thalians govern. We are trying to stop a murderer, plus there tis more to being a Maca than just heredity."

"Fither, I'm not starting anything. I'm giving you a reason for their thinking. As for Beauty, if she weren't such a damned aristocrat, she would let her hair grow longer and throw on the brown clothes of an Ab. Who would even look at her?"

Jolene shook her head. "Why would she do that?"

"To disguise herself. She could fire a flame or something else at the target before anyone would challenge her. I'll grant that as long as Brenda has her Enforcers around her, that eluding capture would be difficult. If Beauty has someone else willing to die for her, that method could be used."

Llewellyn stood. "Damn it, laddie, why do ye think of such things?"

"Because I have a devious mind, Papa. Y'all told me that a long time ago. Who even knows the names of the Abs that are out there anymore? Jolene was probably one of the few that once did, but I have a hunch that even she may have forgotten or doesn't know any of the younger ones."

"I have nay forgotten the ones I kenned. The younger ones, or mayhap land Abs that I nay ever met, ye are correct. I dinna ken them or their names." Jolene was glaring at him. She disliked people knowing what she knew and didn't know.

"I have nay been involved with the day to day operations of the mines since I have been Guardian of the Realm."

"Exactly, Jolene, and ye were the only one smart enough to recognize them, call them by name, and keep track of how they were doing. I'm guessing once they were sentenced to Ayran, they never bothered stealing from y'all."

Jolene nodded her head. "There was always one, but the rest did nay. How did ye ken?"

"I ran a ranch on my world, station, according to your lingo. The pay wasn't that good for ranch hands, but if they were treated right, they'd work their butts off."

Llewellyn looked at Captain Beni. "Tis there any chance that Beauty would disguise herself as an Ab?"

Captain Beni shrugged. "It may depend on how desperate she tis. If she waits for Realm Day this winter, nay would recognize her in Ab clothes, but few Abs appear for that. They scorn the Council."

"Captain Beni, y'all are a Betron. Did y'all ken Beauty before she was condemned?"

"Nay, as I am from a Tri family. From the gossip, however, the Sisters were her fervent followers during the Justine occupation. It was afterwards, when the Sisters waged war against the Macas that many of the Sisters deserted Beauty."

"That's when she would have lost control of things. Papa, how well does your counselor know her sister?"

"They must have been close at one time. That tis why she tis so desolate now. She finds it hard to accept that her sib could murder her own House. I fear that she might even initiate contact to prove that it could nay have been Beauty."

"Then I suggest you assign Captain Beni to help guard Brenda. The Enforcers are good, but someone like her from Army would be better."

"Guardian of the Realm, we have received a request from Captain O'Neal of the Golden One. Shall I connect you?"

Jolene looked at the screen. Why this interruption now? "Aye, put Captain O'Neal through," she replied.

O'Neal's face was on the screen. His red hair was combed back and sideburns framed his face. The copper eyes with the Justine golden circle around the pupil were dancing with amusement.

"Hullo, Guardian of the Realm. I have two passengers that wish to disembark and remain on Thalia in the House of Don. I have another one that wishes to visit with the House of Don, and a load of rare earth minerals from the asteroid that Jarvis hasn't returned to for the scheduled pickup. I also have orders for Rurhran's brew and for Betron's timber. This Captain would also like to visit with ye." His grin became a wide slash.

Jolene caught her breath. She couldn't let the others see how eager she was to meet with him. She did permit a smile. "Welcome, Captain O'Neal. Jarvis has developed a space sickness and

163

could nay make that scheduled flight. Thalians do welcome the trade ye bring. Who are our visitors?'

O'Neal's smile grew wider. This was an easy way to irritate Llewellyn and Lorenz. That didn't happen often. "Oh, just some of Don's kin. I'll see you in thirty minutes." The screen went dead.

Jolene looked at Llewellyn. "What members of your House were ye expecting?"

"I was nay at this time," there was annoyance in Llewellyn's rumble. "I suspect one tis my youngest, Ardith, as she said she would do a medical turn on the *Golden One*, but I canna say if the other members of my House that were studying at the Justine Refuge intend to visit or arrive to stay."

"What about Beauty and Belinda? Where do we search next? I still say they are either on Medicine, Ishner, or on one of Ishner's ships." Lorenz drove them back to the search.

"Why leave out Rurhran when ye mention fanatical sisters?" Llewellyn asked." Rocella has become more outspoken since her parents died."

"Rocella just makes noise," Jolene snorted. "Tell me one time that she ever fought in the Arena."

Llewellyn nodded. "Ye canna discount her words."

"Rocella believes in the Maca system." Jolene smacked her hand on the table.

"Let's not argue about it. We can do prelim scans of all the continents and then zero in on the one that we think will be the most promising." Lorenz spoke as he rose from the seat. "Besides we have to be ready for our guests."

Chapter 37

The House of Don

Jolene stood at the front of the welcoming stand when the Scout from the *Golden One* landed. The hastily called gathering of the Guardians of the Realm to welcome the visitors meant that not all attended. Brenda had managed to be there with her counselor, Llewellyn, to welcome Don's guests.

Diana was resplendent in her suit of Don's blue with the blue sash covering the front and back and a deep, blue cape as a covering against the fall wind. Lorenz had his arm around her waist and was waving at the four people disembarking.

Captain Jeremiah "Red" O'Neal removed his hat and bowed with a flourish.

"Welcome, Captain O'Neal. Ye have nay visited Thalia for some time." Jolene smiled. The Captain was one of her bedding favorites. Then she, like the others, fastened her gaze on the other three. One of them they recognized as Ardith, acknowledged youngest of Llewellyn. Her blonde hair and blue eyes no longer startled them, but the man walking beside her in a one piece suit of Don's blue was as much Thalian as any in the welcoming stand. His muscles rippled as he walked with the same rolling gait of a Thalian. The other was dressed in the strange clothes of Earth beings.

Jolene led the way down the stairs to welcome the group. Captain O'Neal embraced her heartily while giving the Thalian greeting, and she returned the hug with equal enthusiasm. She could nay wait for their private conversation, but she must.

Lorenz as usual dispensed with formalities. He was shaking hands with the Earth being and then threw his arms around the man and hugged.

"Welcome to Thalia, David. What took so long?"

David Krampitz, had grown to six-foot three like his Great-great grandfather, Lorenz, when he swallowed the Justine mixture to restore his cells to youth. The Justine genes had been overruled by the rapid maturity of Earth beings, but once set in motion, they completed the growth of a Justine.

"Myra lived to be over one hundred. I couldn't leave her. Then it was a long wait for the Golden One to return. Priscilla came also, but she stayed at the Justine Refuge."

"David, you will have to greet my counselor and the rest like a Thalian if y'all are planning to stay. Are y'all planning that?" There was hope in his voice.

David grinned. "I know. Ardie reminded me of the drill. I'm surprised she hasn't dyed her hair black. As for staying, Paw-paw, I haven't decided. I guess it will take looking at things here."

Jolene was glaring at Llewellyn who had preempted her with the huge Thalian male and his youngest Ardith. That was nay the way a proper delegation was met. She was Guardian of the Realm. It seemed Llewellyn was as heedless as Lorenz with Earth beings.

Llewellyn smiled at Jolene and approached with the two, his arms over each of their shoulders. "Guardian of the Realm, ye have met my darling Ardith."

Ardith stepped forward. It was always startling to realize that this blonde, blue-eyed Earth being was as Thalian as any. She was as tall as Jolene and far more muscular. They exchanged the traditional greeting.

"And now," Llewellyn's deep voice continued, "I wish ye to meet another of my youngest. This tis Jerome, and he tis Ardith's elder sibling."

Jerome stepped forward, put his arms behind his back and bowed. Then he stepped closer and put his head on first one and then the other of Jolene's shoulders and made the tsk sound in the ear. His hug was powerful and Jolene felt his joy at being here. When the greeting finished, she looked up into his eyes and gasped. They were as deep blue and as disconcerting as Ardith's blue eyes.

"It is a pleasure to meet you, Guardian of the Realm, and an occasion I have been anticipating for some time. I hope you'll forgive me for visiting with other members of my Eldest Fither's House at the Justine Refuge. It had been a lengthy time since I had had that opportunity and pleasure. Thalia will be a grand learning experience as I am planning to settle here for the rest of my life. There may be a visit or two to my home planet to see youngers." His voice was as deep as Llewellyn's and the words poured forth.

"Jolene, if ye would be so kind," Llewellyn interrupted him, "to announce to the rest of Thalia that one of our visitors tis Jerome MacDonald on Earth, but here he tis Jerome, Lad of Don. He will assist in our various businesses. He will be able to co-ordinate all the various enterprises. Ye may even be interested in his skills."

"That would be splendid, Eldest Fither." Jerome started to say more, but Llewellyn shook his head.

"Guardian, I would also like ye to meet another of my youngest, David Krampitz, on Earth. I dinna if he plans to stay or nay."

David bowed, stepped forward and performed the Thalian greeting. Jolene felt the hug was impersonal and nay rewarding. This man had nay the Thalian abilities of emotional transfer. It was as impersonal as a Justine greeting.

"I fear our celebration of their arrival will be a bit somber, but ye are welcome to join us this eve, Guardian of the Realm."

"Llewellyn, I would nay impose upon your House. Will I see ye tomorrow?"

"Aye, I will be there after the lunch hour to go over plans." They nodded at each other and Jolene and Captain O'Neal walked toward her office. Ardith noticed, but assumed it was about trading.

"Lorenz and Diana, will ye be joining us now or later."

"David and I will be later, Papa. I want to show him our cattle operations. I also want to let Lesta know that we need to add a barbeque and mayhap a pie to your celebration. I'll let Daniel and Lincoln ken they are to join us." He turned to his counselor.

"First ye must greet David, Diana. He is my youngest through my laddie Kendall." Lorenz grinned at Diana.

Diana's eyes widened, but performed the welcoming hug. As they stepped apart, she had to wonder if David would be a threat against her laddies? She was irritated that Lincoln showed no interest in the kine, or in being a Warrior like Daniel.

Lorenz didn't notice her distress, and had his arm around David. He was leading him toward the fliv.

"Did y'all have something y'all wanted to see first, or are y'all willing to let me show y'all the operation?" His Texas drawl was thicker than it had been in years.

"I think just looking will be good enough. There will be time to inspect things later. Will we need to change for tonight?"

Lorenz grinned as they boosted up into the seats. "Yeah, I'll have to have Linan run up a Don suit for y'all. Mine won't fit as I'm not as bulky." The belts snapped across and they were airborne. "The coordinates for the ranch on the prairie are there." Lorenz pointed to circle he had touched.

"Did y'all fly one of these things at the Justine Refuge?"

"Yes, Pawpaw, I did, but why did Grandpa Mac say it would be a somber gathering?"

"Two of the most dangerous of the Sisterhood escaped their prison. One of them killed Lillie the night she left."

"Lillie? Grandpa Mac's daughter? When?"

"That happened about six weeks ago. When we were closing in on those that helped them, one of the so-called guards was killed, the one that did the killing was killed, and it is a tossup if another one died by murder or suicide. Beauty, Lillie's murderer, and her counselor disappeared. We had to get permission from the Guardians of the Realm and then the Macas of the more obvious continents where they might be hiding. What held up the initial investigation, most of Thalia including Papa and his counselor thought someone else had killed Lillie."

"Can't you use your mind to find them?"

"No," Lorenz's voice was harsh. "Both Papa and I had to promise not to use our Justine abilities while we live here. Don't use yours either. You might decide you like it here." He pointed below.

The fliv was over the tops of the Skye Maist Mountains and onto the plains. "Take a look. Some of that grass is virgin, un-fenced prairie just like what the land on the Rearing Bear once was like."

David sucked in his breath. "My God, can you ride horses there?"

"They call horses zarks here, but, yes, you can ride for miles and the wind will sweep away all your cares. There are some fishing settlements on the coast, some Ab villages in the far North, one vacation city complex in the South, and the town of LouElla is at the western foothills of the mountains. It was all prairie when I arrived, but agriculture and the towns have been expanding. The town of LouElla and the coastal settlement of Bitwo each have a distribution center, a school, and a Center Director."

Lorenz headed the fliv downward. We'll look at the ranch headquarters here. I'd like to live here, but Diana prefers the main station. That's what they call ranches. I'll show you the main station next. It's filled with pens for the kine and the various buildings for processing and distributing like the butchering and distribution centers for Don's meat, dairy products, and disposal of the by-products. Laten is the Director and his wife, Dolo, is the Head Keeper.

They stepped out on the padport by the round house and walked to the door. It slid open at Lorenz's touch and they entered the foyer.

"Y'all can see the kitchen there." Lorenz pointed to the right. It and this hall will open onto the dining area and the back patio and pool. The great room is the last to the right. Directly in front of us is the door to the gym and on its left the door to the office. The other doors on the left lead to bedrooms and private cleansing rooms. Sometimes a director is here, but mostly it is me. The other personal are out in the individual homes. Remember houses are called homes here."

He led David to the office and touched the circle on the desk to pull up a large viscreen. Then he touched Linan's circle. The angular face of the Director of the First Center appeared.

"Aye, Laird?"

"Hello, Linan. This is my youngest-youngest David Krampitz, soon to be David, Lad of Don. Could y'all send a complete set of Don's clothes for him and send them to the Laird's Station?"

"Aye, if he would remove his shirt and shoes so that I can have the correct dimensions."

Lorenz grinned at David. "Go ahead. He isn't like Medical and ask for a complete disrobing. Not that that matters to Thalians."

* * *

The House of Don's gathering was more somber than usual. Lorenz had explained the killing of Lillie and Benji, and the bottleneck of getting permission for more scans after they had finished on Medicine and Ishner to David.

Brenda greeted everyone and presided at the opening of the food presentation and excused herself. The bitterness at the size of Llewellyn's Earth House was gnawing her insides. There were even more living in Don from his Earth/mutant Andrew youngest. Somehow these newest were also part of Llewellyn's House. They should nay be so many when her own sibling was accused of killing her darlings.

The evening became more strained when Ardith asked, "Where's Red?"

"He tis, I'm sure, still negotiating with the Guardian of the Realm." Llewellyn smiled at her. "It tis his usual way. It seems to guarantee a successful trading session."

Ardith's blue eyes hardened. "And do these sessions continue all evening?"

"They have since the time of my mither's passing into the Darkness."

"The hell! That son-of-bitch! I'll wring his lousy neck."

"Really, Ardith, our parents would be shocked at your language at one of our Eldest Fither's celebrations. It tis nay like ye; nay the way we were raised." Jerome stopped when he realized his sister was about to throw something at him.

"Jerry, for once keep that rumbling voice of yours inside your mouth." Ardith set the vase down and stomped off, but turned at the door.

"Does Red come here for breakfast?" Her eyes were still hard.

"We may nay see him till we are at the Guardian's office. That tis his usual way, but, Ardith, ye canna be upset over his behavior. Red has never considered being with a woman permanently. Tis nay his way."

Ardith clamped her lips tighter and disappeared down the hall.

Chapter 38

Decisions

Ardith arrived at the Guardian of the Realm's office complex in Bretta early and was waiting at the back padport when Jolene and Red O'Neal appeared. Jolene smiled at her, which to Ardith looked like she was smirking.

Red, however, realized that Ardith's blue eyes were as hard as her Great-great Grandfather Herman Rolfe when the man was intent on killing. He tried to put a smile on his face, and instead found it necessary to shift his body weight and put up his right arm to fend off Ardith's first swing. Her next one caught him square in the stomach and the next hit his left temple as Ardith twisted to miss any blow he might throw at her.

Captain Beni, the assigned Army Trooper to protect Jolene, tackled Ardith and they both went down, rolled, and began trading blows. Llewellyn had landed and ran towards them. As the two rolled to their knees, he reached down and swung Ardith up into his arms and moved away.

"Stop it all of ye! We have enough problems without fighting each other," Llewellyn roared.

"I was but protecting our honored guest." In Beni's mind, anyone with the Guardian of the Realm was an honored guest.

Jolene had her hands on her hips. Red was retrieving his hat and wincing at the effort. Ardith was flailing her arms and legs.

Llewellyn set Ardith down, but did not release his hold and asked her, "Why were ye fighting one of our Warriors?"

"I wasn't fighting her. She interfered while I was having a dispute with that two-timing, skunk-assed Texan and she jumped me."

"Ahh," came out of Llewellyn's mouth. "Ardith, I thought ye kenned the way of Thalians."

"Thalians, yes, but he isn't Thalian."

"Have ye calmed down?"

"Uh, Mac, part of this may be my miscalculation. I assumed since we were both off the ship..." Ardith's voice cut him short.

"Assumed, hell!" Ardith raged at him. "You went right back to your lying, cheating Earth habits, you son-of-misbegotten Justine."

"Ardith, if you will give me enough time to sign the contracts that were agreed to last night, I can meet up with you and explain."

Ardith's laugh was shrill and Llewellyn caught himself grinning. Nay in his long life-time had he ever expected Red to offer an explanation to any woman.

Llewellyn turned Ardith to face him. "My dear, I ken your anger, but, ye are right. Captain O'Neal returned to his old habits. We, however, have more problems than just trade and freighting. If ye would be so kind, ye will permit us to accompany the Guardian of the Realm to her office and complete what needs to be done so that we can return to looking for a murderer. I suggest a good round in the gym."

"Very well, Eldest Fither." The words were as stiff as her lips and she stalked off.

It gave Llewellyn a certain satisfaction to see Red's face almost the color of his nickname.

* * *

Red walked down the steps of Guardian Complex and pulled out his com and pressed the circle for his Medical Officer. The screen remained blank. He used curse words he hadn't used since leaving Earth the last time. Somehow they seemed appropriate. As he started to put the unit back, it beeped.

"I'll be taking the Scout back to the Golden One to get my things. You can visit with any bawdy broad you want."

"You can't do that. You are the Medical Officer for this flight. If you desert, I'll make sure you never work a spaceflight again." Soothing Adrith was not possible. Why try now?

Her mouth snarled out words. "Why not hire one from Thalia's Medicine? Thalians like to bed."

"Thalian Medicals don't know Earth beings like you do, nor do they have Medical training for any Kreppies, De'Chins, or Ayanas we might have on board. We have a contract. You can spew at me all you want, but business is business, darling."

"Don't you darling me, you two-timing piece of bovine excrement."

"Will you be joining me in the Scout?"

There was silence. "Very well." Her voice was ice. His stomach was one huge convoluting gut at the idea that their interlude was over. It was more than the fact that she was the best looking female on this flight. Damn it. Why was he still angry enough to hit someone? She had never exhibited that type of proprietorship before. Because you were an ass and let yourself slip, he told himself. Why the hell had he told her he loved her? She would be impossible to placate.

The bile in his mouth worsened. He knew he wasn't being honest with himself. He had told her he loved her because he did love her. He wasn't drunk that night. Space captains can't afford to be drunk. He had spent his sex life on Earth with whores until he met LouElla, Llewellyn's mother. She had ignited his appetite for Thalian women. Try facing this one, Jeremiah O'Neal, he told himself. You've missed LouElla and Ardith is the first one to replace her. Ardith not only replaced her, she wedged herself right into your life and into your heart.

He let out a deep breath. Now all he had to do was convince Ardith. He saw her landing and walked towards the Scout.

Ardith stepped down. "I've changed my mind. You'll have to hire a Thalian Medical."

Red stopped in front of her. "Ardith, I was wrong. I still love you and no way do I want to lose you. Can you calm down long enough to understand that? For some reason, I believed you were so Thalian, it wouldn't matter."

Ardith put both hands on her hips. "We bedded more than three times more than one night. Remember? Don't you know what that means to a Thalian?"

Red's face grew blank. "Uh, no, I haven't been enlightened."

"Well try this. It is the same as a marriage proposal. I thought you knew that with all the times you bedded my Eldest-eldest Mither. That is one of the favorite bits of gossip on Thalia."

Red swallowed. In the back of him mind something stirred. She was right. LouElla had never permitted more than twice in the evening or morning. "She never mentioned the reason for limiting the number of times."

"She must not have wanted to marry you." Ardith's words were almost a taunt.

"If you must know, she didn't. She remained in love with that Warrior Jason. His picture hung in her office and in her bedroom. She made no excuses for her feelings. Like all Thalians, she liked beddings. Hell, I didn't even need to explain to her why I had two hearts. It made things a lot easier for both of us on Earth. You weren't even born then." Red shook his head.

"Ardith, as it is, I will probably outlive you by a thousand years. Then what do I do for a companion? Do you have any idea of what it is like to be alone for most of your life and think that's fine and then you suddenly discover you have been lying to yourself all those years?"

Ardith looked at him, doubt filling her blue eyes. "Red, do you know why it is so hard to believe you?" Before he could answer, she continued.

"You tried to put your own sister in a nunnery." She held up her hand when he started to protest.

"You have lied to my Eldest Fither about some of your trade dealings, and who knows how many times that was or continues. You knew what the Kreppies were doing before anyone else, but did you bother to warn anyone? So why am I supposed to believe this sudden outburst of confession and declaration of love?"

"Because, dammit, it didn't make any difference what I told Mac about my trade jaunts. Those were for the MacDonald Corporation and for profit. When it came down to survival of the Justine League, I risked my neck the same as everyone else. That is something I never did on my own planet." He looked at her for a moment. Then he bowed.

"As you wish. Just remember, we did bed three times in one night more than once." He started to turn and Ardith grabbed his arm.

"Don't you dare walk out on me!"

"I thought you didn't want anything to do with me."

"Red O'Neal, you have ruined all my plans for marrying a nice Thalian male and if you walk out of here without us having my Eldest Fither marry us, I am going to start that fight, oh, hell, Red, why are we fighting? We have to stop him and Lorenz before they leave, and get whoever else in the House must be invited. Then we have to keep Jerry from spewing words. He could delay us for hours." Both sprinted for the lift to take them back to Guardian of the Realm's office where Llewellyn was with Jolene and Lorenz.

* * *

Llewellyn came out of the Jolene's office with a puzzled look on his face.

Red gave him a stiff bow, but Ardith jumped up into his arms. "Eldest Fither, ye must wed us ere we leave."

Lorenz had to keep biting his lips to stop the laughter during their ceremony. David found it hard to believe that his cousin, Ardie, had finally decided to marry anyone, and Jerry was disappointed. He wasn't allowed to give a speech until after the nuptials.

Chapter 39

Nay Convinced

Llewellyn returned to Brenda's Maca home in the afternoon. Jolene was locked in negotiations with the other Maca's of Thalia over scanning. None would concede that Beauty and Belinda could be hiding in their bailiwick. His mouth was in a straight line and inside he seethed. He was as frustrated as his laddie, Lorenz. He could nay use his mind to find them and without finding them there was nay justice for his lassie. He was as ready as Lorenz to wrap his hands around Beauty's neck.

Blaine, the Director of Betron's Maca's Home, opened the door as he approached. "Welcome. Maca of Don, mayhap ye would care for a brew?"

"Aye, in a bit. Where tis my counselor?"

"She tis out by the pool, Maca. Should I page her?"

"Nay need." Llewellyn smiled at the man. "I believe I can walk there."

He went through the hall and the great room. All were decorated in various shades of green. This was the week for their stay on his continent, but Brenda was reluctant to leave Betron. She seemed to believe that by staying here she was closer to her dead lassie and laddie.

Brenda was sitting in one of the side chairs, a mug of brew rested on the table beside her. She was wearing her thong and strap, but if she had been in the pool, it must have been some time ago as her dark hair was dry.

Llewellyn bent and put his arm around her. "Nay was accomplished today except to argue with Rurhran and Troy about scanning. It did nay good to assure them that Don and Betron were being scanned too."

Brenda sat as though chained, her hands closing into fists. "Your investigation tis folly!" She stood and looked at Llewellyn.

"When will Medicine retest the rooms? Why weren't ye negotiating for that?"

"All of which rooms, my love?"

"Lillie's room and those thee rooms at the cottage where Benji was slaughtered. That tis the only way ye will find the true murderer." Her eyes were hard, the tears gone.

"My love, Medicine kens what they do. They analyzed everything that was there. It was your sibling at Lillie's and both she and Belinda were at the cottage. Ilyan and Benji were the only others there except for the listed workers. Why do ye keep denying this?"

"Tis nay denial." Her eyes took on a wild look.

"Jarvis was the one that was going to visit Lillie, nay Beauty. His elements were there in the room, and it must have been some stray Ab that killed Benji."

"Brenda, be reasonable. Medicine could determine how old those DNA markings were. Jarvis had nay been there for over three months. There tis nay Ab that would have a stunner with that power. It would be against all they believe."

"Bah, Llewellyn. Ye are the stubborn one. There are nay any true Abs left. They all ken and use technology. They should all be moved back to Ayran and Ayran renamed Abania. As for Medicine, they are in conspiracy against me. They dinna want their part in my shame to get back to ye." Brenda's voice was becoming hoarse from yelling at him.

"What shame, my love?"

Realization of her words spread across Brenda's face and she re-clenched her fists and turned towards the door before spinning back to face him, bitterness and hurt lacing her words.

"Dinna pretend that ye have nay heard that I canna have another wee one. They took my first one because he was male. They left me with Benji for fear that all I could bear was male and Mither forbade another abortion. She was Guardian of the Realm and head of the Sisterhood. She commanded then. Now ye can accuse me of lying to ye and leave me with an empty House."

Llewellyn felt like he had been slugged in the stomach. His reason for marrying here was to increase his House. Anger started and suddenly the words stuck in his throat. She had not lied, she had but deceived. He had not even asked if there had been another wee one besides Benji.

He swallowed and then considered whether to hold her or leave until she were calmer. He decided on the latter.

"Brenda, ye did nay lie to me. The number of children that ye could bear did nay arise during our courtship. We were too busy fighting the Sisterhood which Beauty was directing, nay your Mither. Your Mither heeded your Maca's Call. Your sibling and Belinda did nay. Neither would acknowledge ye as Maca then and they do nay now. Beauty killed our lassie and your Benji, but there tis one member of your House left besides Beauty and Belinda."

"Ye are wrong." Brenda screamed at him and raised her fist

He caught her wrist as she swung. "Ye need to rid yourself of this anger. Then we will continue this discussion. Ye are wrong about my intentions. I will nay leave ye for another. I dinna give my word lightly."

He loosened his hold and walked out of the room.

Brenda was left with her chest heaving, her features determined. She entered the home and went to her desk to pull out a com. There was but one circle on it. She stared at it. This was the one way she could resolve all the doubts in her mind and heart. She pressed the circle and Beauty's face appeared.

"I must ken the truth. Meet me where Benji died." She closed the com.

Chapter 40

Siblings

Brenda stood in the glade waiting. Perhaps she was foolish, but she had to ken or the doubt and grief would continue to eat away at her core.

Captain Beni, however, had refused to let her out of her sight and it was necessary to tell Captain Beni where she was bound. Brenda had done so after extracting a promise that Captain Beni would nay follow her for at least thirty minutes. The Captain had warned her to have her weapon ready.

She saw a lift rise from the ship sailing in the Baffin Sea. It stayed low and headed for the glen. Brenda was standing not far from where they had found Benji's burned, mutilated body.

The lift landed and the door opened. Beauty appeared in the open door and Brenda realized she was holding one hand behind her back. Why? Because ye fool, her mind told her, she tis holding a weapon.

A grin slashed across Beauty's face, but there was no welcome in her eyes. She jumped from the lift, her weapon swinging towards Brenda when she realized Brenda's weapon was already trained on her. She pointed hers upward.

"Did ye arrange this just to kill me?

"Nay, if I had done that, ye would be into the Darkness already. I need to ken if it was ye that murdered my wee ones."

"Why would ye care? One was but a male and the other a misbegotten mutant cross being."

Brenda's face crumpled and anguish spilled out of her mouth. "Ye killed your own House!"

Beauty pulled her lips back and her teeth showed as she yelled.

"I challenge ye to the death! A mewling weakling like ye has nay right to be Maca."

"That challenge must be given in public."

"Bah," answered Beauty. "In the eld days it did nay. We are close enough in age and weight. We can both place our weapons on the ground and step away. Do ye dare, or are ye the sniveling weakling I think ye are."

"Ye have destroyed our House!" Brenda was still shouting.

Beauty's hard eyes never wavered. "Fight me or we both die and our House with us."

It was true, Brenda realized. If they both fired, their House line ended. The thought brought the rage of the senseless deaths of Lillie and Benji to the forefront.

"Very well, we will put down our weapons. This fight will be to the death."

The two sisters bent, put the weapons on the ground, and stepped away. Beauty leaped though the air at Brenda. She did not bother to shed any of her garments. Brenda had just time enough to whirl away, turn and face her, and send her fist smashing into Beauty's face.

Both began raining blows at each other, neither noticing anything around them. They aimed for the face, the chest, the lower section, or any portion of the exposed body. Beauty driven by the hatred of a sister that outranked her and had won their Mither's approval. Brenda was driven by the mad anger and grief of a Mither who has lost her children. Sibling ties were forgotten.

The bout became an endurance marathon. Both were six-foot five and both weighed over three hundred pounds. Their bodies were honed to perfection from hours in the gym and practiced bouts. Brenda did have the advantage of having Llewellyn as her opponent while practicing. They continued to smash fists into the other's body, landed kicks, and attempted body holds. They were able to break the other's hold just as they had done when younger and practicing in their Mither's gym.

Beauty whirled, jumped one more time and closed her legs around Brenda's. They both crashed downward, Brenda's ribs landing on a rock. She ignored the pain and rolled, sending Beauty's arm onto a rock. Brenda smashed her fist down on Beauty's arm and the arm bent at a grotesque angle.

For a minute the two massive forms went still, both dragging in huge breaths of fresh air, using their Warrior techniques of breathing to drive back the pain. Then Beauty twisted her torso towards Brenda, reached upward, and grabbed Brenda's throat with her good arm and hand to close off Brenda's windpipe.

Brenda's arm shot outward and grabbed Beauty's throat. This hold gave Brenda the advantage. Her hand was larger. Both were beyond feeling the pain of broken bones and they rolled side to side to bang the other's head against the rocky, forest ground. Blood was seeping from abrasions, flowing from cuts, and both succumbed to the lack of air. Again both figures were still.

Belinda ran out from the lift. She reached down and grabbed Beauty under the armpits. The beeper from the sea had warned her of incoming craft. She paid no attention to the gagging and gasping sounds both Beauty and Brenda were making. She looked upward and saw a black speck in the distance. She pulled Beauty into the lift and seated herself at the controls. She did not bother to strap Beauty into a seat. She simply fled back to the boat headed for Ishner.

* * *

Captain Benj landed and ran to her Maca. She hit her com circle for Medicine. "Send a Medvac to these coordinates. My Maca tis down."

She then touched the Guardian of the Realm's button. "Suspect has been at these coordinates. Alert Llewellyn. My Maca tis gravely injured." She knew there would be a reckoning for letting Brenda out of her sight.

Medicine landed a fliv within five minutes as though they had been waiting for a call. Two lilac clad Medicine Tris emerged. They ran towards Brenda and stopped, looking around as though confused.

Captain Beni stepped forward and pointed her stunner at them. "If my Maca dies, so do ye. Where tis the Medvac I ordered?"

The two Tris looked at her, then at Brenda. "We will transport her to Medicine."

Captain Beni had her stunner aimed at them as the Guardian of the Realm's fliv and the Maca of Don's fliv landed.

The Medicine Tris nodded at each other and moved towards Brenda.

"One of you dolts get the oxygen!" Beni commanded.

Llewellyn was beside his counselor and looked at Beni.

"Where tis the Medvac?"

"It did nay come."

Llewellyn pulled out his com and hit the circle for Marita, the Maca of Medicine. "Where tis the Medvac ordered for here?"

"They insisted there was an error and changed to a fliv."

"Whoever they are, they lied. The Medvac tis needed."

Jolene had made it over to where the Medicine Keepers were looking down at Brenda. "If she dies, ye two are in the mines of Ayran for the rest of your miserable lives."

One ran to the fliv yelling, "I'll get the oxygen."

The other knelt beside Brenda to run a scan. She looked at Llewellyn and put out her hand as though to massage the throat, but Llewellyn caught it. "First I have a question for Captain Beni.

"Captain Beni, how did this happen?"

"I obeyed my Maca's order to leave her side for thirty minutes instead of obeying the orders from ye or the Guardian of the Realm."

"Ye ken that means a demotion."

"Aye, Guardian of Flight."

A Medvac appeared and lowered itself besides the Guardian's fliv. The door flew open and Marta leapt down guiding a hover gurney. Two lilac clad Tris followed her with equipment. As they ran, Melanie followed her sister with more personnel and equipment.

Marta ran to Brenda. "Llewellyn, stand back. I will attend my friend." She ran the scan while the one Tri placed the oxygen over Brenda's nose and mouth. She touched the button that initiated the breathing process, the air returning from the lungs forced out a different tube.

Melanie was right behind her sister. She sent a Tri running back to the Medvac for another stabilizing devise. This was placed around Brenda's leg and the Tri's were inserting the webbing under Brenda and the other stabilizer around her torso. Some of the abrasions had been sprayed and they were healing. Once the webbing was under the length of Brenda's body the Tris and Marta lifted Brenda onto the hover gurney.

"May I accompany ye?" Llewellyn asked.

"Nay, we leave now. Ye may come to Medicine, but I will nay let ye into the Healing Room (HR) till I believe all tis well."

Llewellyn bent to give the Thalian embrace, but Marta stepped away. "Ye may do that at Medicine." She and the others started towards the Medvac.

"What of these two?" Jolene asked.

"Put them to work in your mines."

The two Tris gasped. "We but obeyed our Maca."

Marta spun on them. "My Marita told ye nay Medvac?"

"Aye, Ilyan had called her and said it was just one down."

Shock registered on all their faces. Magda spun to Jolene. "Ye, as Guardian, will need to sort this out. I need to follow Brenda to Medicine."

Jolene nodded and looked at Llewellyn. "Aye, I ken."

His eyes were anguished and he looked at Captain Beni. "Why did ye nay tell us?"

"My Maca forbade me. She asked me to follow her, but to give her time alone with her sibling. Her hurt was so deep, Guardian of Flight, that she could nay bear the pain of believing Beauty had killed her wee ones. Nay could dissuade her. Surely, ye ken that that tis true. At least I was in time to keep Belinda from killing my Maca. I will accept any punishment ye decree." She bowed to Jolene and to Llewellyn.

"That can wait till we have time to discuss this. Did ye at least see where Beauty came from or went?"

"Aye, Guardian of the Realm, the lift that brought Beauty and Belinda here returned to a fishing troller of Ishner."

Jolene nodded and looked at the two from Medicine.

"Did ye hear Ilyan's voice when she spoke with your Maca?"

"Nay, Guardian of the Realm. We were at the Medvac when our Maca appeared and said she had heard from the Maca of Ishner that there was but one down, slightly injured and nay for a Medvac. A fliv from Medicine was all that was necessary."

Jolene's mouth tightened and she turned back to Captain Beni.

"Captain Beni, any punishment for nay communicating what Brenda was planning will come from the Guardian of Flight. Right now, I want ye to take these two to the Guardian of the Realm's complex at Betron. We will question them there." Jolene looked at Llewellyn.

"Do ye agree?"

"Aye, but I need to follow Medicine."

"First we need to speak privately." She nodded at Beni.

"Captain, take those two now. Ye can tell the troopers there that they are to be held for questioning. Nay charges at this time." Jolene then ignored the three and turned to Llewellyn.

"Llewellyn, we may need to arrest the Maca of Ishner. What do ye propose?"

Llewellyn nodded. "Ye definitely need to question her. She kens far more than she has said. My counselor and her laddie were misled about why this home was built." He pointed at the forest home. That will weigh even heavier on Brenda. If we just go charging in there, however, they have the right to take the entire matter to the Council of the Realm before we have a chance to prove anything. Proving that the lift landed on the troller will nay be easy."

"That tis my thought. I shall need to present all of this at the next Council meeting and those territorial Macas may still refuse us."

"Aye, that tis true, but I must go to Medicine. I need to be there when they release my counselor. She will need me."

"As soon as she tis back at her home, let me ken and we will arrange our next move."

Chapter 41

House of Betron

"Do ye need me to stay with ye?"

Llewellyn had accompanied Brenda back to her Maca's home from Medicine. She had spent overnight at Medicine as a precaution. Her voice was still a tad hoarse. While the medicines of Thalia had healed the broken rib, the bruises and scrapes, they could do nothing for her spirit.

"Nay, I am fine."

"Your tone tells me that ye are nay fine."

"Llewellyn, my House tis depleted. The only other blood line to the old one before the Justine War tis Belinda. She will nay conceive another child. When we die that tis the end of the House of Betron."

"That tis nay true, my love."

Brenda stared at Llewellyn. "What do ye mean? My Lillie, my Benji, they are gone." She hid her face with her hands and started to turn away.

Llewellyn stepped closer and held her in his arms. "Think, Brenda. Tamar tis Belinda's laddie by the seed of Troyner. He tis of your House. It was Belinda and Beauty that tossed him out. Troyner could nay take him at that time. Once Troyner bedded and then wedded Marta, he could nay take him as it would have made Marta angry. Tamar should have been Laird of Troy.

It was Lamar and your elder, Beatrice, that provided for him. That Tamar should have also been Lad of Betron was one of the reasons that Lamar did nay claim him."

Brenda was licking at her lips. "But he tis called Lad of Don."

"It tis a complimentary title for he was a fine laddie and has grown into a worthy adult. He prefers the growing of trees to raising the kine and sheep of Don. Logan tis becoming jealous of his success with the brool trees from Devon, the coffee trees imported by Lorenz, and the state of the tobacco hydro units. Logan insists the latter nay ere be planted in good ground."

"Are ye saying that Tamar is more Timber or Agra than Warrior?"

"Aye! He really prefers trees. Mayhap ye or Belvin can find or create a space for him. I am told that he has been able to sell coffee to the beings at the Justine Refuge, also to some of the pastry shops here on Thalia, and to the Ayanas. It seems the Ayanas developed a taste for that brew when they lived near Earth." Llewellyn shrugged. He had not liked the coffee of Earth and preferred the pina tea of Thalia.

"Tamar would be permitted to bring the coffee trees, but the brools are another matter as they are from the ones found at Devon. I fear Logan will insist they must be kept as one of Don's unique foods to trade with others."

"Betron has brools. If he can better what we raise, we will see who does the trading."

Llewellyn grinned. "Ye see, my love, ye have increased your House. When shall I tell Tamar to meet with ye?"

Brenda considered. "Tis he free now? Would he consider a name more suited for Betron?"

"That question, ye must ask him."

* * *

After the formal greetings, Tamar took a seat in the Maca of Betron's Tower Office. As usual, he kept his face bland and his brown eyes had a guarded look. The summons had not been expected and he was curious. He could see Brenda was studying him, and seemed to swallow before speaking.

"What do ye think about returning to Betron as the Lad of Betron, which tis your lawful title, and claiming your birth mither's home? They are both your birthright."

Tamar's eyes widened and his mouth open a fraction of an inch. He pulled in a big rush of air before trusting his voice.

"What would I do here? I have my position in Don and when necessary as a Warrior of Thalia for Flight. I nay felt welcomed here except when I was with Beatrice and Lamar."

"Llewellyn tells me ye have been quite successful with the two plants brought from his laddie's planet and that ye are experimenting with the brool trees of Don. Could ye nay bring those project's here? There tis also a point of land that overlooks the Baffin Sea that nay who loved and worked under my Benji wish to go near. Ye could plant some of those crops there." She set her lips and her eyes moistened, but she kept her gaze on Tamar. "Ye would also have back your birth name of Beaudon."

Tamar sat back in the chair, his eyes alive. "Maca of Betron," he began.

"Why do ye call me that? I have always been Brenda to ye."

Tamar smiled, his eyes filled with warmth. "I called ye that as I thought this was nay but an official visit. If this is to welcome me back into my true House, I still need to call ye that and put my head on your shoulders as a true Betron."

Brenda smiled. "It tis both. What tis your answer?"

Tamar stood. "I am nay sure about the name as I have been Tamar as long as I can remember. As ye ken, they stripped the name from me when I was too young to even speak. Lamar and Beatrice I remember from my earliest days and it tis Beatrice's home on Betron that holds my memories, nay that place owned by my birth mither.

"If I could dwell at Beatrice's home, then, aye, I wish to return. I am nay a part of the House of Don and all ken that, although, their kindness has been beyond belief. I would also remain a Warrior on call to defend Thalia."

Brenda stood. "Then when I make the announcement, and I shall name ye Beaudon, Lad of Betron." She opened her arms to him.

"I shall accompany ye to my sister's home and rename it the Lad of Betron's Home. Ye will be introduced to all at the next Council of the Realm. It will give me great satisfaction when ye choose to wed."

Tamar smiled. He already had a lassie in mind.

Chapter 42

Revenge

"We know where they are. Why haven't you sent in the troopers?" Lorenz demanded. They were gathered at the Guardian of the Realm's office to plot their next move.

"Ishner and Medicine are still refusing to let us rescan if we dinna scan the other continents first," replied Jolene. "Ye should be able to ken that."

"The hell I do. It is a big waste of time and that woman is now plotting to kill Brenda. The Medicine renegades have healed her by now. Plus, Ilyan should have been arrested, not just questioned and let go when she started crying."

"Brenda kens how serious the threat from Beauty tis. The information she was able to whisper when rescued tells us that Beauty was probably in as bad as shape. We dinna if Medicine sent someone or the Medicine Keeper at Ishner has healed her."

Lorenz looked at each one. "Just tell Ishner we are going in to retrieve her."

"We do nay have their Maca's permission."

"Arrest her too."

"Laird of Don," Jolene gritted the words out, "ye ken we canna do that. If we break the laws of Thalia, the other Houses will object. At first Rurhran refused to be scanned, but has now relented. Both Don and Rurhran are huge continents and it takes time to do a proper scan and satisfy all the other Maca's that we are nay accusing them."

Llewellyn stood. "I agree with my laddie. This has become a farce. My lassie and Brenda's laddie cry out for justice." His voice and eyes were hard.

The Guardian's com came to life. "Guardian, their tis a call for the Maca of Don. It seems there tis a bit of a crowd waiting for him at the Maca's Tower. It tis his day for any of Don's populace with a grievance to petition him. They are nay happy that he has missed the last two."

Llewellyn bent and hit the circle. "Tell them I am on my way." He mouth was still in a tight line as he leaned over and gave the courtesy acknowledgment to the Guardian of the Realm. He turned to Lorenz.

"Are ye coming?"

"I'm a fifth wheel on a wagon, Papa. They don't want to see me."

They watched him leave and Lorenz stood. "Nothing is going to happen today." He smiled at them and like Llewellyn bid them goodbye. Once outside he headed for his Laird's Station and the boathouse. His com came alive as he left the fliv.

"Laird, do ye need one of us?" It was his Director of the Station, Laten.

"Nay, this morning. I thought I take the boat out for some fishing. I need to be alone for a while."

He opened up the doors to the boathouse, climbed aboard, and released the mooring with his com. He checked the back. The small emergency lift was there and he engaged the motor and headed out of the bay and westward.

He opened the com and called Diana. Their Director Lesta's voice came on. "I sorrow, Laird, but Diana tis at the Warrior's Training this morn."

"We won't bother her then. Just tell her the fishing isn't too good right here. I may stay out all night. I need to think." He cut off the communications and closed all links.

He used the sea lanes to head northward and skimmed the tip end of Don and avoided the ice floes as he neared Ishner. At the northern tip where the rivers flowed down from the mountains, he pulled around a point and anchored the boat. The com on his boat screen kept flashing, but he ignored it, grabbed the stunner, belted on his knife, slung a rope over his shoulder, and climbed into his lift.

Lorenz, like all the rest on the Guardian's team of investigators knew where the landing for the flivs and carriers had been created in Ishner's mountains to bring in certain materials. He also knew where the trails were that led down to the floor of the small canyon. He had no doubt that the trails led down to Beauty's hiding place. He was aware of where there was a smaller clearing in the forests climbing the sides of the canyon carved out by the river in ancient times. He kept the lift below the scanners of Ishner. He assumed that they had lowered the range to prevent anyone from entering or fishing illegally. If Beauty and Belinda were spotted by some young flyer or fishing boat, Ilyan would have to explain why she was protecting two fugitives.

Once he stepped out of the lift, he stood and listened. He let the forest, the wind, and the scents talk to him. He could hear the birds that flew or nested in this cooler climate. The breezes swept down from the mountains told him that Thalian beings must be to the East. There were no scents in the breezes but that of flora and fauna and the musk smell of his father, Llewellyn.

Lorenz whirled and faced an almost nude Llewellyn. All Llewellyn wore was his thong, light, supple shoes, and a tight smile on his face.

"I kenned what ye were up to the minute ye refused to go with me. Killing Beauty tis my duty and right, nay yours."

Lorenz stared for a moment, nodded, and asked, "How did y'all have time to do such a damn good job of hiding a lift?"

"I had planned this for some time. I also ken where she walks." He turned and hurried downward.

Lorenz shrugged and followed. Both would pause every so often to listen. It was Lorenz that heard the shuffle of small stones and a twig bending. He reached out touched Llewellyn's arm, and laid his finger to his lips when his father turned. Then he pointed to the bend ahead.

Beauty rounded the trail at a jog. She was dressed in her black, Warrior's suit. The sight of the two men stopped her and she reached for the small stunner at her side.

Lorenz trained his stunner on her. "Pull it and ye die the same way Benji died." His voice was as flat as his gray eyes.

She halted her movements and looked from one to the other. "If I drop it, ye will still kill me with that."

"He will nay." Llewellyn's deep voice rumbled out. "I intend to use my fists and my hands. Ye can disrobe or fight me as ye are after ye unbuckle the stunner and step away from it."

"Do ye really believe I will let ye have another chance to force me to spread my legs for ye?" Rage was in her voice.

"I do nay wish ye for a bedding. Ye are far too polluted and stained."

Red flushed over her features and the belt and stunner slipped to the ground.

"Better hurry, Papa. The flivs are coming in for a landing."

Llewellyn looked upward and Beauty jumped at him. He twirled away and came back at her with outstretched hands.

Beauty swung at him and landed first one and then another blow, but his long reach meant his hands were around her neck and he was squeezing the life from her the same as it had left his darling Lillie. The blows and kicks became less and her hands were at his trying to dislodge them from her neck.

Llewellyn did not see Belinda running towards them with a drawn stunner, but Lorenz saw and the bolt from his stunner took off Belinda's forearm. She fell forward and remained prone. In the sky the flivs let down ladders for the troopers to descend in this narrow terrain. One fliv landed on the trail.

Llewellyn continued to apply the pressure even as Beauty's hands dropped and her legs dangled uselessly.

"Stand away, Maca of Don." One of the Guardian's Troopers stepped forward, his stunner rising towards Llewellyn's back when Jolene knocked it away.

"Llewellyn, ye have accomplished your goal. Ye are magnificent and a fool." Jolene's voice showed her irritation. She did not relish arresting the Maca and Laird of Don. "Ye are both under arrest."

Llewellyn dropped Beauty turned, and placed both hands on his hips. "And what, Guardian of the Realm, tis the charge? We are guilty of apprehending two fugitives." He nodded at Belinda being tended by two of Medicine's Tris. "I am the only one guilty of killing the murderess Beauty. That I should have done long ago. Then my lassie and Benji would still be alive."

Jolene winced. "Ye are both charged with violating Ishner's airspace and landing without permission. Ye will also be questioned as to whether either of ye used your Justine minds."

"Tis but a small stipend for that offense of violating Ishner's spaces. There was nay need to use our minds. All kenned where they hid. Ye also need to question the Maca of Ishner as to why she hid these two."

"How dare ye defame my lassie!" Ishmalisa stepped out from behind the group of troopers and Ishner's enforcers. "Ye canna believe that she tis involved with any of this."

Llewellyn bowed his head towards her and pointed down the trail. "Their hide-a-way tis but a few steps in that direction. If ye have someone search there, I am certain they will find nay but goods and furnishings from Ishner. Where tis the Maca of Ishner if this tis such a dreadful breach of Thalia's laws?"

"My lassie tis still despondent at losing her counselor."

"Bah," slipped out of Jolene's mouth. She, like the other House Thalians, kenned that Ilyan had been seen laughing and talking with others in her age group.

Two troopers came from the direction of where Llewellyn had said the cave was located. "Guardian of the Realm, permission to report."

"Aye," snapped Jolene. She did not like being in the middle of two Houses glaring at each other.

"Your surmise tis correct. The furnishings are all Ishner's. We have the crystals from there. If there are more they will be found while the Guardian's Troopers continue to remove everything and do a scan."

Jolene nodded. "All will return to the Guardian's Compound in Betron. Notify the Maca of Ishner that she is to be there also." She then turned to Llewellyn.

"Ye are a magnificent Thalian Warrior, Llewellyn, and a pleasure to look at when nay clothed, but I insist that ye be clothed when ye arrive."

Llewellyn's smile was grim as he bowed to her.

Chapter 43

The Conspiracy

Brenda met them at the padport of the Guardians of the Realm's compound with Llewellyn's clothes. Before handing them to him, she threw her arms around him and they clung to each other.

"It tis over," she murmured.

"Nay quite, my love. There will still be an inquiry by the Guardians of the Realm."

She nodded and turned to Lorenz and embraced him while putting her head on his shoulder first. "I thank ye. I dinna ken till now how deeply ye cared for our lassie and laddie."

Lorenz returned the greeting and smiled. "They were family."

Brenda shook her head at his Earth words, and handed Llewellyn his clothes. "We need to go to Don's unit at the Guardians of the Realm's compound. Jolene has called for an immediate Guardians Council of the Realm."

Immediate meant that it took almost an hour for all to be present. The Maca of Ishner arrived under protest and wailing. Her parents, Ishmalisa and Illnor, arrived with set faces. They glared at Jolene standing at the head of the procession for filing upward. Ishmalisa rushed up to Jolene, her anger lashing out at her with harsh words.

"How dare ye send Warriors after our Maca like she tis nay but an Ab? Do ye ken what a breech this tis against our Thalian laws?"

Jolene glared back. "Do ye nay ken how your lassie, the Maca of Ishner, has thwarted our laws? If nay, ye shall."

"How tis she able to take her rightful place? Your Warriors insist she remain below. It leaves Ishner without a full vote on the Council."

"Then she best hurry and appoint ye and Illnor as Guardian and Counselor of Ishner." Jolene turned her back on Ishmalisa and signaled for the trumpet blare.

The Guardians and Counselors of each continent, plus those for Flight, Army, Trade, and Manufacture split to take the two stairs leading up to the grandstand above the visitor area. Like all architecture in Thalia, the building was round, the seating area for the ruling Council was in a semicircle and the visitor area in a semicircle facing the Guardians and their Counselors.

The news had spread across Thalia that Beauty was at the Byre Berm in Betron, Belinda at Medicine with a missing forearm, and an emergency Guardians Council of the Realm had been called. The visitor section was filled with House and Tri members, their colors making a rainbow hue across the area.

Jolene pounded the gavel when all the Guardians and Counselors were seated. Ilyan continued her hysterical wailing for her parents and for her dead Benji.

"Ilyan, if ye do nay be silent, ye will be placed in a cell till called," Jolene announced. The wails subsided to gulps and sobs.

Llewellyn and Lorenz were among those standing below. Diana and Lincoln had been appointed as Guardian and Counselor of Don. Llewellyn had appointed Ribdan and Daniel as Guardian and Counselor of Flight.

"Guardians and Counselors of the Realm, I thank ye for your quick appearance. I now intend to dispel the rumors and relate what has occurred. Llewellyn, Maca of Don, and Lorenz, Laird of Don, did nay wait for the approval from Ishner to enter their continent. They landed and tracked down Beauty. Llewellyn and Beauty fought their final battle and she tis dead, the air gone from her body the same as from Lillie, Lady of Don and Betron." Jolene took a deep breath.

"Now it tis up to the Council to determine if those two have broken their pledges and used their Justine minds to accomplish what all of us wished done and over."

Silence fell for a moment. Marta, Counselor of Troy, stood. "How can we determine that? All of us had deduced where those two were hiding. Llewellyn and Lorenz are guilty of carrying out revenge, but we would need someone in agony with a headache and nay other injury. In Belinda's case, any headache would be from her arm injury if she were conscious. She tis nay, and she will nay wake till morn as the shock will have worn off her system by then." Marta sat down and silence once again descended.

Ishmalisa stood. "What do ye mean that all kenned where Beauty and Belinda were? The Council also wished to scan the other continents and rescan Troy and Medicine first."

Marta sat straighter as she lashed back. "They did nay request to rescan Troy. It was Medicine. That tis because the two would have fled between Medicine and Ishner. The traitorous Sisters among our Houses have helped hide them. The Sisters are well hidden, but nay as well as before." She pointed at the two Ishner Troopers clad in their aqua uniforms standing with the others in front of the Council's rostrum.

Ishmalisa's face went white, then red. "How dare ye make such nay founded charges?"

Jolene banged her gavel. "Enough. We are voting on the first question." She turned to Army.

"Guardian and Counselor of Army, what say ye?"

Pillar of Don looked straight at Jolene. "My Maca does nay lie. If he says they did nay use their minds, I believe him. Nay guilty, and my Counselor agrees."

Jolene nodded. She had expected that answer. "Ayran, how say ye?"

Jarvis stood. His outward physical recovery complete. "The Laird of Don and the Maca of Don dinna lie. The Laird taught the Primitive course for Flight and for Army, and he can hear the wind. Nay guilty."

"Nay guilty," responded JayEll. He wanted this done so he could return to the study of Gar's Book.

Jolene looked at the set faces of the Guardians and Counselors for Betron and Don. "We shall bypass Betron and Don." She then looked at Flight. Llewellyn was Guardian of Flight and his chair was occupied by Ribdan, Lad of Rurhran, the Counselor's chair by Daniel, Lad of Don. She wondered if Rocella had influenced Ribdan or the young Maca of Rurhran for that matter. She knew how Daniel would vote.

"Guardian of Flight, how say ye?"

"The same as everyone but what the Guardian and Counselor of Ishner will say. They are nay guilty. Any that took either Warrior course can tell ye how the Laird and the Maca of Don are able to maneuver in the wilderness. Be done with this and try the real criminal: Ilyan of Ishner."

Ilyan's screams erupted again. Both Ishmalisa and Illnor were on their feet trying to shout him down and Jolene was banging her gavel.

It took several minutes before order was restored and the voting proceeded just as Ribdan had said. Even the newly created House of Trade sided with the two from Don. At that point, Jolene banged her gavel again.

"Ye two are adjudge nay guilty. Please take your seats as Guardian of Don and Guardian of Flight. There is a slight rest while this tis accomplished."

Once they were seated and Lincoln and Daniel back in Don's section, Jolene looked down at the two Troopers. "Ye two are charged with knowingly helping to set up Beauty and Belinda in the man-made cavern in the Isomatic Mountains. If ye are clever enough to plead guilty, name the others who helped, and tell what plans were being developed, ye will avoid being Abs for life. Well?"

Illa and Ilma looked at each other and then at their sobbing Maca. It was as though they both knew that Ilyan would not defend them or anyone but herself. They bowed to the members of the Council.

"Guardians and Counselors of the Realm, we are the Sisterhood. Ye may sentence us, but our beliefs will continue and someday, the rule of the Macas will die. Our Sisters will rise to defeat you."

"Take them to the mines of Ayran," snapped Jolene. That this was in essence slavery would not be mentioned by any of the Houses. Those two were criminals and they fortunate to remain alive.

David was in Don's section, his head swinging between the action above and below. "What is this?" He whispered to Daniel, "A governing event or a trial?"

Daniel laid his index finger on his lips, but whispered, "It tis both."

Now all eyes were focused on Ilyan and she seemed to shrink.

"Ilyan, Maca of Don, ye are accused of aiding and abetting a murderer and helping two fugitives escape from their punishment. There are those that believe that ye are partially responsible for the death of Benji, Laird of Betron."

Ilyan looked up at them and fastened her gaze on her parents. "I loved Benji. They threatened to kill my parents. I was forced to do what I did."

Jolene hit the circle that went to the visual and audio control. "Play the crystal."

The screens behind the Council and the visitor's tier came alive. On it appeared the Tri workers from Ishner working on the cave, the furnishings being delivered and Ilyan inspecting the cave. It was apparent that someone was playing snippets from the crystal, but the fact that Ilyan was there and directing events could not be disputed.

The next scene showed Ilyan entering through the hidden cave door, laying her head on Beauty's right shoulder and then on the left. In response Beauty slapped first her right cheek, then the left.

"Now beg," commanded Beauty's voice.

Ilyan could be heard saying, "Please, I need ye to bed me. I'll do whatever ye say. Please, Beauty, please."

Beauty was laughing at her and slapped her again. "Bow to me and then to Belinda."

Once again Ilyan obeyed.

"Stop this," screamed Ishmalisa from her Council seat. "Ye have damaged her and Ishner forever. Let us take our sick, wee lassie home and we will see to it that she stays there forever."

Jolene had her finger on the circle and the image remained on screen and did nay move. "Ishmalisa, your lassie tis nay a wee one. She tis over one hundred years of age." Jolene turned to the rest of the Council.

"Have ye seen enough?"

"Aye," rumbled Llewellyn's voice. "It tis enough to turn everyone's stomach. Tis it possible for Medicine to cure such an affliction?"

Marita, Maca of Medicine serving as Guardian, looked at her Mither, Marta, seated beside her wedded counselor Troyner in Troy's Guardian and Counselor chairs, and then she looked at her elder Melanie, seated as Counselor of Medicine. "I dinna ken any such technique, but I still have much to learn. Mayhap, my Mither or Elder can answer that question."

Marta leaned forward. "Ye will recall the Justines destroyed much of our learning, but nay all. We, however, were so devastated by the Justines that controlled our minds that nay of us wished to pursue any studies that altered the mind of another or entered it to rearrange how the neurons would connect, transmit information, or affect the emotions. The only ones we have improved upon tis when someone has been over indulging in our brew or the alcoholic drinks from other planets. We are forbidden to do anything that changes the mind patterns." She gave a quick frown in Lorenz's direction as the alcoholic beverages from Earth were potent. "It tis be possible to do scans and a study with her, but that tis nay a guarantee that we can cure anything."

Jolene nodded. "Then we are left with a Maca who tis guilty of hiding two escaped fugitives and who continued to help hide them after one of them also murdered her own counselor. We dinna have a place to contain such a one. Our attempt to detain House members was a complete failure. We will have to ask the Justines if they would hold her in exile. There she would nay have any visitors or see any but the Justines. Until then, we need another method of detaining her."

"Nay!" Ishmalisa had risen again. Illnor rose and put his arm around her as though to steady her or protect her, and it was he that spoke.

"Guardians and Counselors of the Realm, the first suggestion my counselor gave ye was a true one. We will take our lassie home and keep her away from all. She would be secure and nay would need worry."

"Bah!" Contempt was in Jolene's voice. "Ye would accede to all of her requests and wishes just as ye did when she was a wee one."

Jolene looked down at Ilyan. "It seems, we must sentence ye to being an Ab for the rest of your life and to the mines."

Ishmalisa struggled in Illnor's arms. "Ye have nay right!"

Ilyan had raised her head. If she went to Ayran, Jarvis, she believed, would rescue her. "Mither, it tis all right. Everything will be well once I am there."

"Wait, Guardian of the Realm. She tis a Maca. She tis House. How can ye justify that among the rest of us? I believe we should vote, or at least have a discussion." Rocella, Guardian of Rurhran, until the new Maca, Radan, had his Confirmation Rite, was horrified. Her hair was graying, and she was still a secret member of the Sisterhood. Radan was sitting as Counselor.

"How does being a Maca and a member of House make her eligible for a lesser punishment?" Lorenz asked.

There was a moment of silence. "House members are nay Tris or Abs," Rocella answered. "They have been trained. All have the Maca's hands, and they are better educated."

"That means they should behave in a more civilized manner." Lorenz said and then exploded. "What the hell is wrong with y'all? Weren't y'all listening to that Ishner Trooper? The Sisterhood wants to end the Maca system. As long as House Thalians protect the Sisterhood member and permit the Sisterhood to continue to sow the teachings and dissent of the Sisterhood, Thalia is in danger of a revolution. That means more deaths by killing. The only reason they haven't pulled in more adherents is the fact they have no clear governing method to replace the current system. It would be a change to a different name with the same power system. Once they are smart enough to figure out a new way, you will see more atrocities."

"Are ye saying we are wrong to have Macas? Jolene was glaring at him.

"No, I'm just stating the problem. Most Thalians prefer the Maca system, but as long as the Houses keep protecting those of the Sisterhood, their dissent will continue."

"Ye are saying ye are nay Thalian." Rocella hurled the accusation at him. "If so, ye have nay right to be sitting there and interfering."

"I am Thalian as long as I live here, just as I was a Texan as long as I lived in that state of my country. I will, however, outlive almost everyone in this building. I will leave when that happens just as I left Earth, but it doesn't change the fact that I was born in the United States of America and that is my land until my last dying breath.

"This, however, isn't about me. It's about the Sisterhood in Ishner, in Medicine, and, I suspect, in Rurhran. You haven't quelled it. You have let them live and continue to draw others into their group."

"Some are members of our House, but they have nay broke our rules. For what could we punish them?" It was Marita, Maca and Guardian of Medicine. "We canna accuse them of wrong when nay tis done."

"Two of Medicine's citizens are dead because of the latest killings. Four are imprisoned, and another one has been condemned as an Ab for a year for nay following protocol and sending the Medvac. Just what the hell do ye call wrongdoing? Do ye really believe those younger ones weren't recruited by the older Sisters at Medicine and Ishner?"

Jolene had to restrain a smile. The Laird was as blunt as usual. She knew she had to take control again.

"If any can suggest a way to keep her imprisoned other than the mines of Ayran, I would like to hear it."

The Guardians and Counselors shifted and looked at each other. All kenned the futility of sending her to Ishner and none wanted her in their land. Silence filled the spaces.

"So be it. Troopers, take her to the transport for the flight to Ayran."

"Nay! Nay! She tis my baby," Ishmalisa was screaming. Illnor collapsed in his chair while Ishmalisa ran down the stairs toward the departing trio of two Troopers and Ilyan. They were out the back door before she could reach them and the door had closed and relocked. Ishmalisa beat on it with her fists and turned to face the Guardians and Counselors.

"My counselor and I are leaving now. We will nay return." Tears streamed down her face. Illnor made his way down to her. He did not speak as he took her arm. Together they walked to the

Ishner box where members of House could sit. They continued through the room for Ishner and out the back door.

The Council watched them depart and then Jolene addressed the Guardians and Counselors of the Realm that remained.

"The rest of the crystals taken from the cave on Ishner will be available to any who feel they have a right to request viewing to make sure that nay of their Tris or House members were involved. That means it tis either the Maca, Guardian, or the Director of Enforcers from that House."

Jolene banged the gavel down. A bad taste was in her mouth. Damn the Laird for speaking the obvious and she could think of no way to root out the rest of the Sisters.

Chapter 44

The New Martin

JayEll stood in front of the First Center of Don. The streets radiated out towards the harbor, the Maca's Tower, the Academy for the wee ones, and the Shrine of the Kenning Woman. He was dressed in the red of one from the House of Ayran, and the heavy scarlet cape flapped in the wind. A black pouch with strange bulges hung at his side. He had eschewed the staff that all expected a Martin to hold.

He looked at the busy streets. His timing was perfect. The cool fall was now slipping into winter. People were busy preparing for the coming season and the festivities of Realm Day, the celebration of when all the Houses had been united under the Guardian Council of the Realm.

"People of Thalia, hear the Word of your Gar. It tis nay Darkness that awaits ye at the end of life, but the joy and Light of our Creator." A few of the people stopped to look and stare. A Martin had been absent from the scene since the death of the Ab that pretended to be one. That had been over eighty years ago. The Handmaiden had appointed someone else, but all ignored him.

They had heard of the recovery of the Book, but why was this Lad of Ayran proclaiming like a Martin while still dressed in House colors? Had he lost his senses? Wasn't the Martin supposed to be an Ab? Of course, none would have listened to an Ab.

"We have been lied to over the years, or the original Words of Gar have been forgotten since the Justines destroyed the crystals. The complete Word of Gar is now in our possession again. Ye are once more able to read or hear the Words. Ye can spread the news that the crystals containing the Word of Gar are available from the Shrine of the Kenning Woman in Don, or wherever I am. I have them now for any who would wish one. If nay now, come to Don's Shrine of the Kenning Woman now or tomorrow afternoon. We have begun the studies of Gar's Word again."

"Our Creator loves us and appointed the first Martin to train others. There were nay Abs then and the Martins did nay have to be Abanians. That there be but one Martin was another enforced rule of the Justines working with the false Martin, It was a lie on top of a layer of lies. There can be more than one Martin and more than one Handmaiden. The Kenning Woman tis unique until another tis appointed by Gar. The old Kenning Woman will ken who she tis and what her mission will be." The people continued to listen and JayEll continued to speak.

"If any here wish to learn more, or kens someone that does, I have the crystals of Gar's Book with me. If ye prefer, ye can send any that are interested to the Shrine of the Kenning Woman in Don. Crystals of Gar's Book are available there. As I said, this afternoon starts the study and discussions. Remember it tis light and love that awaits us, nay the Darkness."

JayEll bowed to those listening. Some half-way returned the bow and left. Some were shaking their heads. Some wondered if another member of the House of Ayran had gone mad.

JayEll watched them with disappointment lining his face. Nay had asked for a crystal or asked what he had meant by the Light instead of Darkness. He returned to the House of the Kenning Woman and Lilith greeted him with a warm hug.

"That did nay go quite as I expected." JayEll looked at her. "Mayhap I should ask ye for a vision of what I should be saying."

Lilith smiled at him. "Any vision would tell me again that ye are the long-lived Martin and must proclaim Gar's Word."

"And if nay students show this afternoon or tomorrow?"

"Then ye must go out again. Nay just in Don, but in Ayran, Betron, Ishner, Medicine, Rurhran, and Troy. I dinna need a vision to tell ye that."

"And what makes ye believe the other Houses would permit that?"

For a moment she stared at him, her dark eyes blank. She closed her eyes and the scene was before her eyes. JayEll would leave her and here. Nay House of the Kenning Woman existed there. Her body swayed for a moment and she shook her head before opening her eyes and drawing a deep breath. "They will all permit it at least once, but Ishner needs ye the most. They are hurting and bleeding without a Maca. The Sisters are wrong. Thalia's continents have always been ruled by a Maca. Tell me, JayEll, since ye kenned Ilyan when ye where younger. Does she have the Maca's hands?"

"I dinna. Ilyan always avoided me after the time she urged Jarvis to anger Daniel. She tried to stop me from warning Daniel, but I moved her hand away and ignored her."

"Bah, she touched ye. Did ye feel a Maca's hands?"

"Nay, but all were in a hurry, and she was young then."

"Dinna ye ken, JayEll. She felt your Maca's presence."

JayEll stared at her for a moment. He too drew in his breath. "Then who tis the Maca of Ishner?"

"The vision did nay show me that. First ye must try to have the classes here, but in the coming days request to go to Ishner."

"And if I am refused how would I proceed." He smiled at the thought. "Ye must go with me. We shall request walking the Circle first. Gar kens the needs of Thalians."

Lilith threw her arms around him. "Will your Maca approve?"

JayEll smiled. "Oh, aye, right now he tis still feeling guilty over behaving like a crazed spacer."

The com circle that alerted the inhabitants that someone was entering the Shrine pinged. They turned as the Hand Maiden to the Abs walked in. JayEll stared. His Mither had nay been anywhere near him since the Laird of Don had rescued him, Daniel, and Kahli some eighty plus years ago. She had scorned him at the one meeting of the Council of the Realm she attended.

The Handmaiden's blocky body moved toward them. Her thin dark hair hung in strands and the brown Ab gown looked thin and in need of replacing. Her feet were encased in the heavier leather that the Land Abs tanned. Her mouth was set in a straight line and her dark eyes looked angry.

JayEll had read through most of the Book and he knew how he must greet this woman who had abandoned him to Martin's condemnation and the mines of Ayran. Gar's rules about honoring one's parents were clear and he turned to her with open arms.

"Welcome, Mither, it tis good to see ye." He stepped closer as if to lay his head on her shoulder, but she shook her head.

"Do ye now proclaim that I am nay the Handmaiden of Gar?"

"Mither, ye are the Handmaiden to the Abs. Ye have cared and comforted them through the years. The work ye did and still do tis your calling from Gar. I did nay say ye were nay a Handmaiden."

"Then who are these other Handmaidens ye are going to choose?"

"I choose nay. Gar does that. A Handmaiden tis the one that comforts and feeds the distressed. From what I have read there may be one for each House and perhaps more, but I am nay certain about the latter. A more careful reading will tell me whether it is one for each House or for each continent as some continents have two Houses with Trade or Manufacture. The one that was

Martin to the Abs lied about everything or he had nay kenning of the true Words."

Jaylene raised her hand as to slap him, but JayEll stepped out of her reach.

"Mither, if ye dinna believe me, join Lilith and me for lunch and stay to study. Ye can also join the group every afternoon. Ye need to read Gar's Words to ken what I am saying is nay a lie."

"I am female. It tis forbidden to read Gar's Word."

"Nay, Mither. His Book tis for all. Ye will read in there that the Handmaidens and Kenning Woman can wed if they wish or they can remain without a counselor. It tis their decision. Will ye stay? Mayhap even give your approval for us to Walk the Circle."

The Handmaiden stared at them both.

"Ye are heretics!" She turned and walked out of the Shrine.

Chapter 45

Who Has The Maca's Hands

The Ceremony for Daniel and JoAnne was still weeks away when JayEll and Lilith Walked the Circle. Neither JayEll nor Lilith were that high in the ranking of the Houses and all they needed was the approval of their parents and the Guardian of their House. Out of courtesy they had also visited their Macas.

The one difference was the huge celebration at the town of LouElla. It was here that the old Kenning Woman had anointed Lilith. The Great LouElla had made special trips to the town to endow it with sculptures and equipment for their Center and Gym. Few Tris had ever been so honored. They could repay the House of Don by this extravaganza. Ishner refused all invitations and forbid any from Ishner to attend. Ishmael sent his regrets and stayed away to protect his sibling Issing.

JayEll had only visited the town to meet Lilith's parents. Her parents had welcomed him then and now the people had prepared the best that their small town could offer. Lilith's brother stepped forward to welcome him after he and Lilith had greeted her parents, Menden and Laci.

"This tis my brither, Larmine," said Lilith with a huge smile. "And his counselor, Lava."

Larmin put up his arms and put his head on JayEll's shoulder as a proper Tri and then on the other. JayEll returned the greeting.

JayEll saw a male about six foot tall with the more slender build of someone from Medicine or Ishner. The muscles were more like them also rather than the bulky mass of Don's Tris. "Ye look to be from Ishner or Medicine."

Larmin looked at JayEll and then at his fither and back to JayEll. "It seems our fither fled our House during the Justine rule. How tis it ye have a Maca's hands?"

"I am Martin." JayEll replied. "There must be some authority for what I say and do. Lilith tells me that there tis but twenty-seven years between ye and her. Tis that true?"

Larmin shook his head. "I dinna see what difference that would make."

"Nay do I, but one nay ever kens in such matters as a Kenning Woman."

Their conversation was interrupted by the arrival of Daniel, Joanne, Kahli, and Lania, and Jarvis and Aretha. All of the new arrivals were proclaiming their greetings and congratulations to the couple in loud voices. Everyone gasped when the Laird of Don and his counselor Diana followed them into the Center's great room.

"Someone needs to start up the music," Lorenz grinned at them all. "It is what we would do on my world."

All questions about Houses were forgotten as Lorenz swung out his guitar. "Who has a request?"

* * *

The ceremony was performed the next day by Jarvis as the main members from the House Ayran and the House of Don watched. Jolene was almost simpering and her comments verged on bawdy as she toasted the couple with fresh mugs of beer.

"Where do ye two intend to hibernate with each other?" Jolene asked after directing the Keeper where to place the fresh, baked pina pod chips.

"We are nay going to hibernate. We, or rather I, have the work of a Martin before me. I have decided to concentrate on Ishner as they have ignored all the requests for the new Martin to enter and preach the message of Gar."

"Bah! Ye both need to relax and enjoy each other," was Jolene's retort.

* * *

Before JayEll sent another request to Ishner, he decided on a private visit to his Elder Mither. Jolene always had the ability to make him think deeper or see what he had missed, and he must have missed something if he could nay proclaim Gar's Word in Ishner when all the other Houses had permitted him to speak at least once.

Jolene rose from her desk and her arms encircled her younger. At different times he had served as her Counselor of Ayran, Counselor of the Realm, and Director of the Mines. His mind was more acute than Jarvis's mind, and his disposition far superior to his mither's.

" Welcome back and why did ye sound so mysterious in your request to meet?" Jolene asked him.

"I did nay mean to sound that way. I had hoped to hide the reason I came to question ye."

Jolene smiled. "Oh, it was good enough to fool all the others who bothered to listen to our words. Anything they spread in Thalia will be distorted. Did ye wish to share a brew?"

"Of course, Elder Mither, but ye are right. I was being mysterious as I need to probe your memory and I dinna wish others to ken my questions."

Jolene motioned to the cooler cabinet and waited for JayEll to fill the mugs. She took a huge drink and said, "There, that tis better. Drink well and ask."

JayEll smiled and took a swallow. "Elder Mither, my Lilith has had two visions. She said that Ishner is bleeding because they have nay Maca." He saw the frown on Jolene's face and he hurried the other words out.

"They are bereft of a Maca and have been for over two hundred years. If that tis true, Ilyan could nay have been the Maca. I dinna believe Lilith's visions are false."

Jolene sat wide-eyed. Her tongue flicked out at her lips and she frowned. "Nay Maca? The old Maca died in the Justine War. There was nay birth from one of his descendants until Ilyan. Ishmalisa did nay have any other wee one before her or afterward. The Sisterhood forbid it, but they lost power. For some reason Ishmalisa and Illnor did nay have more." She suddenly drew in her breath and held up her hand to silence JayEll.

"I am thinking. It was the Sisterhood and the Justines that appointed Ishmalisa after the Justines won the war. The Maca, the Laird, and the Lady of Ishner were all downed in the space fight between the Justines. The Laird's and Lady's older children and all their wedded counselors were with them. There was a younger one from the Laird of Ishner, but he had been left as the Director of Ishner as he was nay yet old enough for the Confirmation Rite. I was but a wee one and am nay certain of names and dates. It was whispered that the Mac of Ishner had had an Ab child with an Ab female years before, but nay cared other than to whisper. If that Ab child was his first born, then she or he technically would be the Lady or Laird of Ishner. That one could have birthed the Maca. Nay ken if the Justines killed the Maca during the sky fight or if he lived longer. There were those that did and were nay returned. The Justines had the Kreppies and Sisterhood destroy all the old records of the Houses. Thalia was fortunate that the Directors and Keepers of most Houses were able to hide so many crystals. Medicine did a superb job of hiding crystals that held the blood lines. It did nay occur to those overlords that those of lesser standing could be so loyal when hearing a mere suggestion that it was a pity that such and such could nay be saved."

"'Tis that how ye saved Gar's Word?

Jolene smiled and nodded and JayEll continued.

"That means all the Houses have their ancestry records so why would Ishner nay have one?"

"JayEll, use your mind." Jolene snapped the words out.

"Was nay Ishmalisa descended from the Maca?"

"How would one prove she was or was nay if nay crystals were found after Llewellyn and LouElla defeated the Justines and the Sisterhood? That was more than a century after Thalia had lost to the Justines. Betta, Raven, Rollo, Magda, Bernice, and Lamar were the ones that would have recalled and they have gone to the Darkness. I canna be certain why Bernice would nay have said anything except to protect Lamar. Why the others kept silent tis mayhap for the same reason. Lamar did nay care if it did nay pertain to being a Warrior and his own House. The rest might have preferred what the Sisters had done when they were first in power and did nay care later. Ishmalisa and Illnor were appointed long before Llewellyn arrived. A scan and a simple test at Medicine could prove or disprove Ilyan's descent. That tis, if Medicine has the records of the people of Ishner."

"Someone in Ishner must have kenned where the crystals were and destroyed them. That way there could be nay to claim that they too were from the last Maca or that Ishmalisa and Ilnor were nay that important in the House of Ishner." JayEll's voice was grim. "That means there could be descendants from either the Laird or the Lady of Ishner and nay ken who they are."

Jolene smiled at her younger and drank from the mug.

Chapter 46

Visits

Jarvis looked again at the report from Medical. The diagnosis remained the same. He was still susceptible to inhaling the minute particles that could float in the air of the mines or a spaceship. As long as he was on land and there was fresh air, there was nay danger. Recommendation: Patient to remain on Thalia for five to ten years. He slapped the circle and closed the screen and sat back, a scowl crossing his face.

The door chimed and opened. Jarvis looked up as JayEll walked in. He stood.

"Ye canna ken how glad I am to see ye. I dinna ken all these names, tables, and alloys."

"Where tis Jada? Tis he nay helping ye?"

"Jada claims to be busy with he own division." Jarvis's voice was stiff and harsh. "Plus, Ilyan has been insisting I meet with her, and Jada sneers out the request like I am a traitor and will honor it."

"Ye two have nay quarreled? He kens all that happens here. Surely they ken ye would nay go against the Council of the Realm."

"He has nay but contempt for a Maca that does nay ken the true operation of the mines." Jarvis ran the fingers of his right hand through his hair in frustration.

"I canna believe that. He has always been most helpful."

Jarvis shrugged. "JayEll forget him. Just take your chair and look at the screen and bring some sort of order to this mess. Jada wanted the analysis on the new minerals three days ago, but I was still woozy after leaving Medicine. To top that, I've had a call from Mither claiming that the MacDonald's *Golden One* brought requests from the Kreppie's, Ayanas, and Draygons for the minerals or raw materials they lost in the War. I dinna ken which ones they are or if they are allowed or nay allowed by the treaty."

"Jada would."

"Forget Jada. I need ye!"

"Jarvis, I told ye. I am the new Martin. I came because I ken ye may still be ill. I can help out in the morning, but there tis still much to study in Gar's Book and I have a class to teach each afternoon."

"What? What class? When did ye start teaching a Warrior's class?"

"I am teaching about Gar's Word and for those that may become Martins or just wish to learn more."

"There tis only one Martin and he tis Ab," roared Jarvis. "When have Abs ever studied a book of any kind?"

"Jarvis, from what I have read (and I am reading it again), there can be any number of Martins spreading Gar's commands and assurances of love. Nay were they Abs. They came from all levels of our society. The Martin I'm reading about now is from Abania."

"There tis nay Abania."

"Jarvis, calm down. Ye are getting that same look in your eyes and on your face as when ye came for me."

Jarvis looked at him and saw nothing but concern in JayEll's eyes. He turned and took a deep breath and turned back.

"Ye are right. They warned me not to become too agitated. For Gar's sake JayEll, I need the help of a true Ayranian here, nay the words of a Martin."

JayEll smiled. "Jarvis, I am here to help. It tis why I came. I can stay until midday and then return tomorrow morning. JoAnne will serve as Mither's Counselor of the Realm until she decides she wants either ye or me to replace JoAnne."

"Ye are refusing to stay all day then."

"Aye, I have promised others that I would hold that class about Gar's Book. There are seven enrolled." He held up his hand as Jarvis started to explode. "They will nay all be Martins. Some are there just to study, but it looks like there are at least three that have heard the call. Some of the lassies are angry as the Martin is always male and there tis but one Handmaiden for each continent and one Kenning Woman for all of Thalia. The Kenning Woman canna be a Handmaiden as the old Martin said."

Jarvis was shaking his head. "Wait, are ye saying the old Martin was lying about that too?"

"I canna judge if he was deliberately lying or if he was just making up things. Since I have finished reading the Book, I dinna think the man ever read one word from it."

Jarvis nodded. "I need ye to check the metal analysis. I am nay sure if ye can do it all by what our labs have found or if ye need to do certain procedures again." He ignored JayEll's raised eyebrows. Once again the com interrupted his day and Joven's voice flowed into the room.

"It tis Ishmalisa, Guardian of Ishner again."

"Tell her I am needed down in the mines now." Jarvis looked up to see JayEll still standing there.

"Jarvis, how often does she call to request to see Ilyan?"

"I dinna why she calls now. Usually the request is to see me. I refuse to speak to her again. She will wish something like ye just said, or she will want me to release Ilyan. All such requests are to be directed to the Council of the Realm. It would be a wasted visit. It's bad enough that half of those reports from the foreman will be one or more complaining about Ilyan's attitude, lack of work, or her constant demands to see me."

"Mayhap ye could help me."

"What?"

JayEll smiled. "The Kenning Woman says that Ishner needs a new Maca. Elder Mither has told me enough hidden history to suspect that Ilyan tis nay the Maca. Ishmalisa tis refusing to let me even speak as a Martin on Ishner. It is important for me to determine what the situation really tis and if any would care to learn more about Gar. I do have a question for ye. Did ye ever feel Ilyan's Maca's hands?"

Jarvis sat back in his chair. "I dinna recall."

"As many times as ye two bedded, ye canna recall?"

"They were beddings; nay else." He shrugged and looked down at the screen with numbers from the mines below and the sequence of the foremen that had reports, and swung back to JayEll. "Nay have ever commented about her lack of a Maca's hands, but, ye are right. I nay felt them at all."

JayEll nodded. "Jarvis, let me handle all of those reports. Just contact Ishmalisa and offer to let her visit ye while I visit Ishner. It can be in the afternoon when I do my work as a Martin. I can go any day, but today."

Chapter 47

Ishner Visits Ayran

Ishmalisa guided the official Ishner fliv to the padport in front of the Maca of Ayran's Tower. She was upset that she had to permit JayEll to speak, but if that was how she could plead her case to Jarvis, she accepted the bargain. Illnor, her counselor, tried to dissuade her. "It will do nay good. He canna change what the Council of the Realm has degreed."

"I canna even get through to the Guardian of the Realm. Nay will put me through; nay at the Guardians of the Realm Complex and nay at her home. Where else can I plead our lassie's plight?"

And for that he had no answer.

They entered the Tower and were bowed into Jarvis's office. He had set out the mugs of cold brew for all.

After the greeting, Ishmalisa and Illnor removed their capes and sat in the chairs across from Jarvis.

"Ayran tis warmer than Ishner in this hemisphere." Ishmalisa was trying to make small talk.

"Aye." Jarvis's voice grated on her ears.

"Ye must ken why we are here. Our lassie tis a Maca and House. She has nay ever done physical work. That was always done by our Directors and Keepers. She will die in your mines."

"My dear Guardian of Ishner, I am a Maca and I do physical work. The Maca of Don and Betron both do physical work. Being a Maca does nay negate strength and ability."

Ishmalisa looked horror stricken. "Jarvis, ye have loved our lassie. How can ye be so cold? Ye must ken how delicate she tis."

"I submit that someone who tolerated Beauty abusing her is nay quite as delicate as ye are claiming."

Both Ishmalisa and Illnor blanched. They had seen the start of the crystals recording. How much had this man seen? Ishmalisa tried again.

"Jarvis, all we ask is that ye excuse Ilyan from any hard, physical labor, and that ye give her a warm safe place to bed, and to be served."

"Ishmalisa and Illnor, I canna change what the Guardians and Counselors of the Realm have decreed. Ye must believe me and take your pleas to them."

"How can ye be so cruel when ye two almost Walked the Circle?"

It was Jarvis's turn to be dumfounded. "Guardian of Ishner, that remark tis nay true. I was absent from Thalia for years. We did bed ere I left Thalia on my assignment for a lengthy voyage and full crew of Warriors to search for the enemy. We did nay discuss Walking the Circle as she was too young. When I returned she was old enough to be wedded and was wedded."

Ishmalisa fought to keep her emotions out of her face. How dare this man lie to them about their darling lassie?

"My dear, Jarvis, we ken how hard this all must be for ye, but it would be so simple for ye to take her as your bedding woman. All ken that the Guardian of the Realm, or ye, have been using the Abs from the mines to warm your beds."

Jarvis shook his head. "I canna do that. All would say I had made life comfortable her. It would nay be a punishment."

"Of course, it tis punishment if she tis dressed like an Ab and canna leave Ayran. That tis punishment enough."

"I assure ye, Guardian and Counselor of Ishner, many of us regard Ayran as a pleasant place to dwell."

"For Gar's sake, Jarvis, at least get her out of the mines and that hideous cell below. Let my darling see the sky again and live like House. Ye are Maca. Ye can do that."

Jarvis stood. "I am sorry, Ishmalisa. but I can nay do that. I would be going against the Guardians of the Realm which is the same as going against my Mither. That tis nay something I have nay ever done and dinna plan to do now. My Mither has a remarkable ability to take down any opponent and her ire against one should nay be raised."

Ishmalisa and Illnor rose. "So ye refuse to help our defenseless baby. How can ye be so cruel?" Their faces were as stiff as their bodies.

With those words Ishmalisa led the way out of the Maca of Ayran's office and Tower. Why had she ever agreed to let JayEll and the Kenning Woman visit Ishner? Would there be retribution for that?

Chapter 48

The Martin at Ishner

JayEll stood on the windy streets of Iconda dressed in his Ayranian red suit and a brown cape flapping backward in the breeze. In his left hand was a staff. His wife, the Kenning Woman stood beside him dressed in the blue of the Don Tri's. Her cape was snug around her, but wisps of dark hair floated around her face.

"People of Ishner, listen to the Words of Gar. Ye are loved and ishes joy for all people, nay Darkness. Come and learn how the Darkness has been banished." His words caught the attention of several passing Tris dressed in lilac. They looked at the two and one man stepped closer.

"Did I nay hear that ye and the Kenning Woman have Walked the Circle?"

"Aye, but that has nay to do with the Words of Gar."

"Yes, it does." The man was yelling. "Ye are a fraud. A Martin canna wed and he canna be House."

"If ye would but read or listen, ye would learn that those are myths put out by the Justines and the man they named Martin."

"Just how do we read something that ye have secured in Don?"

JayEll fished out a crystal from the pouch at his side. "Here, I have made copies. All are welcome to one. They are free. If anyone wants one after we leave, all they have to do is request one at Don's Shrine of the Kenning Woman." He dropped the crystal into the man's hand and looked at the people crowding around and others hurrying by on their morning errands. Most seemed to draw away and avoid eye contact. Their mood was as gray as their skies.

"If the words make ye confused, why nay come to Don's Shrine of the Kenning Woman in the afternoons or early evenings to discuss Gar's Words with others. Thalia has been without the Words of Gar for a long, long time. All need to hear and learn them again."

A harsh voice from a woman broke into his speech. "How can ye say the Darkness tis banished? Ye lie and ye ken it. My counselor has passed into it. He can nay longer see the sun and I canna see the light in his eyes when he looks at me for he tis gone. Day has become Darkness." She strode down the tarmac, hurrying to be away from his hurtful speech.

The adults weren't looking at Lilith, but a child pointed at her and said, "Look at the Kenning Woman. She tis shaking and her eyes are closed." JayEll turned to look at her as did the others.

Lilith opened her eyes, but they were like glass. Her breathing was returning to normal. She looked around at the people of Ishner, pointed her index finger at those standing near, and intoned, "People of Ishner, ye are bleeding. Ye have nay Maca. The false Maca tis gone. Ye must start your search for your true Maca north of here where once the Maca of Ishner had a home. Thalia. Some of his House preferred that wild place on the coast. One that lived at the edge of Iconda made a perilous journey across the seas to escape pursuit. Another made the journey to escape the Justines, the Kreppies, and the Sisterhood. Someone, somewhere kens who your Maca tis and any that do ken where the Maca tis may be in danger." She took a deep breath and looked around. She remembered her vision and what she had just said. She looked at JayEll.

"I sorrow. I ken we must leave now." She turned to the people staring at them, but stepping away as if they were contaminated.

"Dinna forget what I said. The Justines and the Sisterhood have deprived you of your true Maca."

The crowd stared at her. Someone cleared a throat and someone in the back yelled, "Who tis our true Maca if what ye say is true?"

"The vision did nay show me that. Whoever the true Maca tis, she or he will be the descendant of the previous Maca. I saw two blurry figures driven from the isolated shores on the edges of Iconda at different times. One by a crowd, and one by the Justines, the Kreppies, and the Sisterhood. The Sisterhood did nay and does nay wish to have a true Maca. They want a figurehead that they can control."

The crowd had grown larger and Lilith was speaking in a loud voice to project her voice to the people that had gathered. JayEll noticed the Ishner Enforcers marching towards them, and he grabbed the Kenning Woman's arm to pull her away.

"We must leave now." They hurried to their fliv parked on the padport a few feet behind them on the green. It was JayEll's red one from Ayran and clashed with the colors of violet and purple on the common padport. As soon as they were secure, they were aloft. Lilith looked downward and saw the Enforcers shaking their fists at them. She realized that they kenned her words to be true.

* * *

Isabelle snapped off the screen, her dark eyes deep and angered, her hands clenching and opening. "Did ye hear that, Mither? The Kenning Woman says that Ishner tis bleeding for its true Maca."

Itillian looked at her lassie. "She also said whoever kens who and where the true Maca might be tis in danger. We canna risk that. Nay after all these years."

Isabelle looked at her mither and charged out of the home. She ignored Itillian calling her back. Enough was enough. She hurried to Idana's place and ran to the back where he was working on the netting for small boats. They were Tris, but they were allowed to fish for the specialty sea creatures that could nay be trolled from the high seas. They would nay be wealthy, but they could at least afford the products from the other Houses.

"Have ye heard what the Martin and Kenning Woman had to say?" She demanded.

He looked up from his work, shrugged and looked back down, his mouth in a tight light. "Careful, ye are upset."

"Careful, my backside. Tis time we gather our 'friends' and visit certain places. We ken where the Sisters are congregating. How can our true Maca return if they guard the coasts and the ports?"

"And their quarters and compounds are well guarded. Our group tis nay large enough. Ye must be patient."

Chapter 49

The Guardian's Visit

Jolene arrived at Don's Shrine of the Kenning Woman just as the discussion of Gar's meaning centered on death, Darkness, and Light had become heated. It was so heated that none noticed that the Guardian of the Realm was watching and listening.

"How can ye say there tis nay the Darkness with Death. That tis what Death tis!" One Don Tri bellowed his defiance.

"According to Gar's Word that we just read, death tis the passage from here through the Darkness. Then we will be in Gar's Light." JayEll stood behind the counter and pointed at the words on the screen.

"Our bodies are burned to a teaspoonful of ashes. What tis left for any light? We canna see, hear or sense anything." The protester was adamant.

"That tis why ye need to read more of Gar's Word, Leftan. According to the Book that part of beings that kens right from wrong, the essence of our being is taken into the Light when we walk in Gar's love and forgiveness. It tis called the spirit of life."

"Forgiveness for what?" One of the female Tris from Betron interrupted. "There was that list of 'Do not dos and Do dos, but really, what Thalian tis going to miss their First Bedding or wait till they are almost one hundred years of age before bedding when they wed? That tis foolishness."

"It would be a difficult task to complete," JayEll admitted.

"Difficult?" Leftan was laughing. "Nay would qualify. Nay ye, nay our Guardian of the Realm, nay my own Maca. And how many of the wedded ones remain true to each other after the bliss of the first twenty years or so wears off? Shall I name names?"

"Well, that tis an interesting insight. Just who has the Maca of Don bedded since his arrival other than his counselor?" Jolene had had enough, but this was something she might pursue if Llewellyn was less than faithful to Brenda. She usually kenned all of Thalia's rumors and she had nay heard this one. Had Don's Tris kept it silent to protect their Maca?

The entire room turned their attention to the Guardian of the Realm. The Tri speaker was left with his mouth open.

"Well?" Jolene's question was a demand. "Does your Maca have a favorite or does he dabble with all?"

Faces froze and no one ventured a word.

Lilith appeared behind Jolene and the lone Trooper from the Warrior's Academy assigned for this week as an attendant. No guard was really needed now that the threat of Beauty and Belinda was ended and the Trooper was listening to the conversation rather than guarding Jolene.

"Welcome Guardian of the Realm. May I be of assistance?"

Jolene turned to look at her lassie-by marriage. "Why are ye being so formal? Tis that how ye greet someone that who has welcomed ye into House?" Her words snapped out. She was annoyed that she had nay answer to her question.

Lilith swallowed and stretched out her arms to give the official greeting. Jolene's tone was enough to warn her that the Guardian was nay in the best of moods.

Jolene looked at JayEll once the greeting was over. "I do need to speak with ye both now. These people," she waved her hand at the assembled five, "may stay if ye have a private place to speak."

"Of course, we do, Elder Mither." JayEll bowed to her. "Lilith take her into the Kenning Woman's alcove and I will be right there." He looked at those who were still in shock at seeing the Guardian of the Realm.

"I suggest ye continue reading. We have just covered the first eight chapters and there tis much more to learn. I ken the meaning better with each reading." He bowed to them and hurried after Lilith and his Elder Mither. The guard remained stationed at the hallway entrance.

Once he entered the alcove JayEll greeted Jolene. "To what do we owe this pleasant surprise?"

"To the two of ye upsetting Ishner so much they are ready to file charges against ye for trying to start a riot or overturn their governance. What did ye say? Ishmalisa was too hysterical to make any sense of her words, and Illnor simply agrees with her." She snorted.

"I sorrow Elder Mither, but I had a vision. I canna stop the words from flowing when that happens. We were in Iconda close to where I once saw a scene from an earlier vision."

"What was this vision?" Jolene was annoyed. This was like trying to get water out of sponge that had been out of the oceans for days.

"The vision told of a laddie and a lassie from the last Maca's House. They both had to run. It looked like the lassie may have left before the Justines arrived, but the laddie ran from the Justines and the Sisterhood. They were both shrouded in the fog of Ishner. The laddie had time to bid farewell to someone shrouded in the fog. I could nay see whether male or female. Then the Lad of Ishner left in a boat, but I have nay vision of where either went. It may be that their laddie or lassie tis the true Maca of Ishner." Lilith stopped to take a deep breath.

"Dear Gar, did ye say all this on the streets of Iconda?"

"Yes, there were several of their Tris around us. Some did have teal sashes, but I did nay see any House member. I believe that

Ishmael and Issing are the only other true House members. The appointed Directors and Head Keepers would be House, but nay of the last Maca. It tis a continent that tis hurting without their Maca."

Jolene stared at her and then shook her head and turned to JayEll. "And what did ye say then?"

"I said nay to anyone, Elder Mither, and neither did Lilith. I saw Ishner's Enforcers moving toward us and I took Lilith's arm and hurried into the fliv. We left immediately."

"Ishmalisa tis in a rage. She intends to charge ye both at the Guardians Council of the Realm for trying to incite a revolt in Ishner. She also expects an apology from ye both and a retraction of Lilith's words."

"I canna retract what the visions say. If this tis a true vision, it will come again and again till the true Maca rules in Ishner."

"I will have nay choice but to call ye both in front of the rostrum when Ishmalisa makes her charge. It will be necessary to let the Guardians and Counselors discuss this and to vote on it."

JayEll smiled at her. "Elder Mither, I ken the workings of the Guardians of the Realm, and I also ken they can make us both Abs. What they canna do, is stop the message of Gar's love and make the Kenning Woman a mute."

Jolene looked at him in horror. "Ye are the one that tried so hard to be Ayran."

JayEll nodded. "Aye, I wished someone in my House to love me and cure the hurt of my mither's rejection. Ye did that Elder Mither. For that ye have my love. I am grateful and will honor ye all my days. I do nay ken or care to ken the name of the Ab that forced my Mither."

Jolene closed her eyes and shook her head and then she straightened. "Ye canna believe that your mither did nay ken who forced her if anyone did. I think she deliberately told a falsehood to hide what she had done. She, as the Handmaiden, kenned every Ab in the Ab's Quarter on that continent."

"But, Elder Mither, all said that she had been forced."

"All Abs said exactly what that Martin or Handmaiden told them to say." Jolene interrupted him. "The only Ab she took into her bed was Diana, who was the Kenning Woman, at that time. Even then all realized that magnificent body had to come from a House. Then Diana left her for Rocella. Having a wee one was a way for the Handmaiden to get even, but I ken her. She would nay have bedded a male Ab after all the times she berated me for doing so."

"I have another House?" JayEll was in shock.

"Ye will recall that at that time many of the so-called Abs were House members. The Sisterhood and Justines had forced them out or food was so scarce that only the Abs were being fed. From the looks of ye, I would say it was one of the slender Houses like Medicine or Ishner. They made sure none of the males in those two Houses remained. They were condemned as Abs or driven out of the Houses' homes."

"I am surprised that ye took me to House if ye kenned all that."

"JayEll, ye were but a youth, but I kenned ye were clever and more like me than your mither or Jarvis. Now ye have finally decided how ye will run your life and nay do the bidding of others. I dinna fully approve, but I am proud of ye."

She put out her arms for the Thalian goodbye.

"Ye have given me much to think about Elder Mither." He put his arms around her for the farewell.

Chapter 50

Attack and Counter Attack

As Lilith prepared for bed that evening her body froze and her eyes glazed over. Her breaths were short gasps. JayEll could do nay for her, but stand there and watch. Her eyes flew open and Lilith whirled towards the com.

"I must warn them," she screamed and hit the circle for her parents' home.

JayEll was not sure she was still in the vision or if she was back to this world when her fither, Mandril, appeared on screen.

"Ye must flee!" Lilith was screeching at her fither. "The Sisterhood kens where ye are. Leave that home immediately!"

Mandril's sleepy face and eyes suddenly became alert and he severed the connection.

Lilith stood there moaning while she swayed back and forth and her hands covering her face. JayEll's arms were around her and he pulled her close.

"Do ye really believe the danger was so imminent?"

Lilith looked up at him. "Aye, I must go to The Town of LouElla now to find out if they escaped."

"Sweet one, let us turn on the screen. If anything so violent occurred it will be on there. The Sisterhood tis dead, nay could they so easily destroy something in Don."

"They killed Lillie with nay problem. They have drawn in others. The Macas and Guardians were too lenient."

JayEll shook his head. "Why would other Thalians wish to destroy what has been built up since the Justines and the Sisterhood were beaten?" He reached down and hit the symbol for the screen. It came up on the wall totally black.

"There, ye see, there tis nay about an attack on any urban area in Don."

"The Town of LouElla tis nay urban."

"Then call their personal com and assure yourself that they have suffered nay."

Lilith was still shaking and her eyes were opened wide as though the vision was still upon her. "I canna do that. It may put them in more danger. Why, JayEll, why would they be after my fither or mither. Both are but Tris from Don. They have nay power."

The screen behind them came alive.

"People of Don, there has been an attack on a Tri home in LouElla. All must remain in their homes. We are tracking any movement. When more tis kenned, there will be another announcement. If any are visiting or enjoying a brew hall, receive clearance ere ye leave for home or work. This announcement will be repeated every fifteen minutes till all tis clear."

"I shall go there in the morning. All will ken I am going to check on my kin and my childhood home."

Lilith's plans to fly to LouElla were thwarted in the morning by the arrival of the Guardians of the Realm's Warrior Troopers.

"Lad of Ayran and the Kenning Woman, ye must excuse our intrusion, but Ishner has issued a charge that ye deliberately tried to start a revolt in their city of Iconda. They claim they have the recording of your words. The Guardians Council of the Realm have called a special meeting for tomorrow eve, but till then ye are forbidden to leave Donnick except under escort. We are to accompany ye to the meeting in Bretta."

* * *

Jolene's face showed nay emotion as she called the Guardians Council of the Realm to order. She looked down at her younger JayEll dressed in the scarlet of Ayran and Lilith in her blue Kenning Woman's cloak and the blue of Don's Tris. This canna be happening, she thought. There should be nay charges and Don should nay have been attacked.

To make everything more surreal, the Tris and House section for visitors was full. The tension of nay kenning why Thalians were still trying to kill Thalians and why would anyone bother to destroy a Tri home in an obscure town? Was the Sisterhood just trying to prove they could do it? Was it really the Sisterhood? And why was the Lad of Ayran carrying a metal book while facing such a serious charge. The buzzing in the visitor group quieted as the Guardians and Counselors took their seats. It was whispered that one of the Houses was manufacturing the mechanical stinger. Was it Ayran or was Ayran helping those that tried to do murder. Would that be revealed this eve?

"Guardians, Counselors, and Thalians, I thank ye all for coming." The amplifiers carried Jolene's voice throughout the round building. "We are here tonight for two reasons. First we will address the charges brought by Ishner against my younger and the Kenning Woman. The second is the horrifying attack on the innocent people of Don. I have sent the Guardian of Flight and the Troopers from the Army after them."

Jolene looked down at the screen built into the area in front of her. The charges brought by Ishner were read:

The Lad of Ayran and the one who calls herself the Kenning Woman, did urge the people of Iconda and the rest of Ishner to find the True Maca of Ishner. The Kenning Woman gave a show of having a vision after the Lad of Ayran had condemned the way all Thalians lived and urged them to turn away from their government and ask forgiveness from Gar. Both should be

238

condemned as Abs and apologize. The false Kenning Woman must be forbidden to have any more such visions."

A murmur ran through the crowd. This was not like the way the new Martin had spoken when they heard him. Jolene ignored the murmuring and looked at all the assembled visitors before continuing.

"This tis the recording that JayEll made of the incident. She slipped the small, personal crystal into the slot and pressed the circle. The voices uttering the words of that afternoon played out. There was silence as it ended.

Jarvis, Maca and Guardian of Ayran spoke first. "Guardians of the Realm and Counselors, as ye heard, my Elder, JayEll, made nay mention of revolt against any Guardian, Counselor, or Director of Ishner. His words were about the rule of Gar. I submit all charges against him are dropped. As for stopping a Kenning Woman from having a vision, that tis preposterous. It was she that saw where the Book was and she was correct."

"He tis trying to protect his elder," Ishmalisa protested. "Her visions are false. Ask the Old Kenning Woman what the mission for this Kenning Woman was and if the fate of Ishner was included."

Jolene shook her head. "Guardian of Ishner, ye are looking for excuses." She turned to face the Thalians in the audience, knowing her face was on the huge front screen and the screens of anyone not attending.

"Guardians and Counselors, ye have heard the crystal. Do any besides Ayran have comments on this situation?"

Brenda, Maca and Guardian of Betron hit her speaker circle. "This tis a waste of our time. JayEll tis absolved by his own words and nay can keep the Kenning Woman from having her visions. I did nay believe her when I asked for a vision, but she was correct. Free them both and be done with this."

"Nay," Ishmalisa yelled. She was on her feet.

Before Jolene could call for order the screen in front of her and on the wall behind the rostrum replaced her and her Counselor's faces with that of Llewellyn.

"Guardians and Counselors of the Realm, I am interrupting ye to ask permission from Ishner to investigate those who bombed one of my Tri's home. Our scans show the debris from the stinger is metal from the shipyards of Ishner. The Sisterhood must still have a compound or complex where they can manufacture something that kills Thalians. If permission tis nay granted, I intend to gather more evidence and go in anyway. I will deal with the charges later."

Silence, then murmurs filled the hall. That sound was broken by Ishmalisa screaming, "Nay, ye have nay right. Denied." Illnor was standing beside her as though to hold her steady.

"Llewellyn, the Council of the Realm gives ye permission." Jolene closed down the screens. Her head was held high and she addressed all.

"As Guardian of the Realm, I have the right to initiate an attack against those that would destroy Thalia. The rest of ye, now have the right to select a new Guardian of the Realm if ye disagree with me."

"Ye have violated the space and rights of Ishner." Ishmalisa's voice was raw.

"Why do ye and Llewellyn name the Sisterhood as the guilty ones?" It was Troyner, Maca of Troy.

"We have been following them since the attacks on Lillie and Benji. This tis more than just revenge against Don and Betron. These members of the Sisterhood have become imbedded in Ishner and Medicine. Medicine has screened most of them out, but Ishner welcomed those that fled Medicine. We are nay sure of their agenda, but doing away with all Macas and any power for the male Thalians is the core of their beliefs. They wish to subjugate all Thalian males. It makes me wonder why Ishner is so eager to protect the Sisterhood. Does anyone really object to our Warriors pursuing the Sisterhood?"

The eyes of all gravitated towards Rurhran where Rocella sat as the Counselor of Rurhran. Radan had claimed the Guardianship since his Confirmation Rite, but Rocella was still his trusted advisor.

Rocella, Counselor of Rurhran spoke, her dark eyes flashing. "Guardian of the Realm, it tis nay secret that certain aspects of the original Sisterhood were attractive to me and to my Mither, Raven, Maca of Rurhran, before she passed into the Darkness. This group tis even more fanatical than those we destroyed. They wish to destroy all Macas, and all of Thalia's House males. That endangers my House and my younger. Why are we even discussing this? Dismiss us now and call us again when Llewellyn tis ready to give us his full report."

Ishmalisa continued to stand. Her lips were white. "I dinna ken why ye wish to destroy Ishner. My House and I will leave now."

"Ye will sit down till we hear from the Guardian of Flight!" Jolene roared as she banged the gavel down. "Nay will leave for Ishner till then."

A light blinked on the screens and Jolene reactivated them. Llewellyn's voice rumbled out. "We have destroyed their headquarters and the Troopers have landed." The screens went dark again.

"We will now resolve the issue before us. Who here wishes to vote that JayEll, Lad of Ayran, and Lilith, the Kenning Woman, are guilty of starting a revolution on Ishner?"

"Guardian of the Realm, why dinna ye just dismiss the charges? Nay will vote to convict them but Ishner." Jarvis's voice raised in volume as he continued. "This tis a waste of our time." Inside he was seething. He had nay been selected to go with the Guardian of Flight. The fact that Daniel, Lad of Don was also missing was almost too much to absorb. Damn them all. He should be with them. He was a Warrior.

Aretha, temporary Guardian of the Army, stood. "Guardian of the Realm, my Counselor and I declare them innocent and agree with the Maca of Ayran."

Jolene could see that all wished done with this. "Very well, all those wishing for dismissal say Aye."

The Ayes rippled forth.

"Those opposed?"

The voices of Ishmalisa and Illnor responded, "Nay."

"This session of the Guardians of the Realms tis dismissed. I will have Llewellyn broadcast his report and if any see a need for another meeting, ye can request one. Otherwise we will meet next month on the continent of Rurhran."

Chapter 51

The Trail To Ishner

Lorenz guided his fliv to The Town of LouElla. He had cleared it with their Selectman that he would be landing at the padport and needed a zark and supplies for a couple of days. The Don Enforcers had determined that nay had been killed in the blast that hit Mandrin's and Lata's home. Mandrin and Larmin had disappeared. Lata was at the home of Liken, the current Selectman, and Lolan, his counselor.

The Tris of LouElla had nay wished to give up the office of Selectman and their Select Council after the Maca had restored Don and Thalia. They liked having their own officials rule on the small matters that arose among Thalian Tris that remained and farmed in the area. They did nay ken it was the Earth exile their Maca had endured that allowed him to realize how beneficial this arrangement would be.

The Thalian greetings were exchanged and Liken led Lorenz to the saddled Zark and the one with two days' supply. Lorenz looked at the supplies and realized they could last him a week. He turned to Liken. "Would it make any difference if I questioned Lata about where they went?"

"Nay, Laird. We ken they headed upward into the Skye Maists, but we believe they must have returned to the prairie. There tis nay water in the mountains this time of year."

"There is if y'all ken where to find it, but ye are probably correct. They would return to what they ken."

"Mandrin kens a certain amount of fishing too. They probably headed to the Valiant River or the Hurin River, or mayhap the ocean."

Lorenz considered. "How much fishing does Mandrin ken?"

"He tis always successful when he goes on an expedition. That skill saved us from severe starvation after he arrived here and before the Maca and his Mither returned."

"He was nay one of the Tris that fled from Donnick?"

"Nay, Laird, he arrived about five years after we had set up our Town of LouElla."

"Was he dressed in Tri blue?

"Nay, Laird, he was dressed as an Ab, but it was clear from his speech and his kenning that he was nay an Ab by birth. It was the Justine and Kreppy rule that made so many of the Tris Abs."

"Did he ever mention where he was from?"

"Nay that I ken. He asked for refuge and offered to work and help build our defenses. We needed all the hands we could muster in our early days."

"Would he have told Lata?"

"I dinna, Laird. It was nay important to us."

Lorenz smiled at Liken. "If I don't pick up a trail I'll be back to talk with Lata." He mounted and rode out on the trail down towards the Valiant River on the theory that it was a larger body of water up towards the mountains and not near the Eastern Ocean. He had a hunch, Mandrin did not want to be seen near the ocean or out in the open. The second day he cut to the North to intercept them. If his theory was correct, he should find their trail.

It was the third morning when Lorenz picked up a fresh trail of two men on zarks going through the open prairie that was left on this side of the Skye Maist Mountains. They were descending towards the Valiant River and trying to hide their trail, but the prairie grass defeated any of their efforts. He knew he would find them by nightfall and urged his zark forward.

Before dusk, Lorenz had picked up the scent of a campfire and followed the trail to a clump of trees that always reminded him of the oaks on Earth. Like the Earth oak trees, they were near a creek or spring to nourish their root systems. The cold of the higher mountain elevations had traveled downward to join with the wind. It was enough to make any man seek the comfort of camp, a fire, and food.

Lorenz kept his zark moving forward and when he saw the camp set between two of the taller oak trees, he called out the Earth greeting one gave before riding in unannounced.

"Hello, the camp."

He saw the two men bolt upright as though ready to make for their zarks.

"I am no danger to ye. The Maca of Don sent me to assure ye that ye, your laddie, and the rest of your House are safe." Lorenz hoped they recognized his voice.

Mandril looked in his direction and asked, "Laird, tis that ye?"

"Aye, that tis what they call me. My fither wanted ye to ken that the Sisterhood on Ishner that sent the stinger has been arrested and their stinger operation destroyed. That should eliminate the Sisterhood on Ishner. Now he needs to ken why they were after ye."

"Laird, it tis better if we just disappear."

"The hell it is. Believe me, ye are safe and so tis your lassie, Lilith, or didn't that occur to ye?"

Mandrin stood silent for a moment. "Why would the Maca of Don go to so much trouble to help a Tri?"

"What difference would your being a Tri make to him? Ye have been in Don all these years and have seen what my fither has done to remake Don and Thalia. All of Thalia has speculated that ye, however, are more than a Tri if the Sisterhood was so anxious to see ye and yours dead. Ye are either the Lad of Ishner and descendant from the lost lassie of the Laird of Ishner or from the Lady of Ishner. Someone may know where the hell she is. I'm betting that ye just shortened your name by dropping the I and ye are somehow connected to the last Maca of Ishner."

Mandrin took a deep breath and looked at his son, Laramin, and then back to Lorenz before speaking. "This tis folly. They will say or whisper that Larmin tis Maca of Ishner when he tis nay."

Lorenz swung down from the zark. "Look, night tis coming. I'm going to call for a pickup and then we'll all go to the Maca of Don's Tower. He can sort out what is what. By the way, how do ye ken Larmin isn't the Maca?"

"All I have to do is touch ye with my hands and ye would ken that," said Larmin.

Lorenz grinned at him. "I wouldn't know one way or the other. I'm Earth and Justine, remember?"

"Laird, I do nay wish to endanger Don."

"How? With more attacks from Ishner? Ishmalisa is already screaming that Don has destroyed them. The Council is ignoring her. The next meeting of the Guardians Council of the Realm will appoint a Guardian for Ishner while an auditor goes through their finances to find out how and where they acquired the materials for building stingers."

"Part of that could have come from the materials for the trollers and submersibles, Laird."

"Maybe. That isn't what I do. By the way, did you have any other children, uh wee ones, if Larmin isn't the Maca?"

"Nay, Laird. I was quite young when I fled Ishner. My sib had warned me that the Sisters were coming."

"According to Jolene, your sister was Icatalin, but she disappeared shortly after the Sisterhood took over. It was assumed they did away with her."

"Laird, I dinna. She did warn me that I had to flee Ishner. My heart still weeps for her."

Lorenz nodded and called for a pickup by a carrier with space for four zarks.

Chapter 52

No Answer

Jolene, Guardian of the Realm, and JoAnne, Counselor of the Realm, were meeting with Llewellyn, Guardian of Flight, Pillar, Guardian of Army, and the newly appointed Guardian and Counselor of Ishner, Imandril and Ilarmin. Mandril had taken back his original name and Larmin had added the Ishner "I."

"I worry the Sisterhood has a hold on Ishner," said Imandril. "The populace there has nay reason to trust me or my House. If we or ye could locate Icatalin, then mayhap we would have a certain legitimacy."

"She may refuse to come forward." Pillar looked at them. "I ken all too well how we feared the Sisterhood, the Justines, and the Kreppies before ye arrived Guardian of Flight." Pillar could not address his superior as Llewellyn.

"If we appoint Warrior Troopers to guard ye and your House, the people will nay trust them or ye. They will feel like they are still under occupation. Ishmael has said the people of Ishner endured the Sisterhood being involved in the governance, but seemed reluctant to say more."

"Mayhap it would be better if the Council had appointed Ishmael and Issing as the Guardian and Counselor of Ishner." Imandril was not eager to take over Ishner. "I have been a farmer and small merchant in the area of the Town of LouElla. What do I ken of Ishner and fish any longer? It tis too many years away. I was but a youth of twenty-four when I fled."

"That tis nay excuse." Llewellyn disagreed with him. "I was but one and twenty when the Justines exiled me. I had nay seen Thalia or Don for nigh one hundred and fifty years. I just kenned that they needed me. Ishner needs ye and your House now. I suggest ye appoint Ishmael and Issing as Directors of the most important areas and listen to what they tell ye about Ishner."

"They will resent us," Imandril insisted. "Just as the rest of Ishner will resent us as interlopers."

"Then why did ye and your laddie agree to be Guardian and Counselor of Ishner?" Jolene demanded.

"I, uh we, were confused by all of the events."

The rest stared at Imandril. He was indeed a sorry specimen to lead if that was how he felt.

"Bah," snorted Jolene. "We will make clear that this tis but a temporary solution. Ye may discover there tis more about Ishner that draws ye to House and home more than ye are willing to admit."

"At least appoint some Troopers to finish cleaning out the area where the Sisterhood was located." Imandril was pleading.

"That has already been accomplished." Jolene looked at the two. "We are sifting through everything. If there tis anything hidden, we will find it. Jerome, Lad of Don, will be doing an audit with Issing"

"Guardian of the Realm, Ishmael, Lad of Ishner is here." The com interrupted their proceedings.

They all stood for the required Thalian greetings as Ishmael entered. The introduction to Imandril over, they all resumed their seats.

"We need your counsel on how to proceed with the introduction of Imandril's House. How tis it that ye and your sister did nay rise any higher in Ishner." Jolene felt it was best to resolve all problems before proceeding.

"If ye had checked (and I believe ye have), ye ken that our parents were but Directors of the Center in Iconda. They had been appointed by the Justines and the Sisterhood. Somehow their calculations went awry and our parents remained loyal to the original House."

Jolene nodded. "Aye, Ishmael, that much I ken and remembered."

"The Sisters thought Issing would be a ready recruit. When we both remained loyal, they condemned us as Abs. Then ye, Llewellyn and your mither, LouElla, freed us of the Justines and Kreppies."

Ishmael's voice was bitter as he continued. "The Sisters thought Issing too young to remember how they had somehow made our parents disappear in the far reaches of the Eastern Ocean. We did nay forget. We both remembered how they tossed us into the arms of the Abs because we would nay adopt their philosophy and accept that they had driven the rightful heirs to the House of Ishner into hiding or to death. I fear there are nay more remaining."

Silence filled the room and Ishmael swallowed before continuing. "The Justines and the Sisters had selected Ishmalisa and Illnor to be the Guardian and Counselor of Ishner till another Maca was born. They insisted that Ishmalisa was from House, but like us her parents had been but Directors and that was at Isling. As for Ilyan, she was so spoiled that they did nay teach her control or how to run Ishner. She was nay fit to be called Maca."

Ishmael looked at each one. "Now am I to leave or does this continue?"

Llewellyn eyes filled with amusement and a smile tugged at his lips. "I think ye should stay. Ishmael, ye have been a frequent visitor to Don. The Sisterhood could nay stop your friendship with my laddie. Why tis it ye did nay divulged any of this sooner?"

Ishmael took a deep breath. "Maca of Don, there was always the chance that our parents lived and the Sisterhood held them somewhere. I have given up on that hope now as ye have destroyed their headquarters and there were nay prisoners, but there are others. Like bawds, they emerge in darkness and gnaw at Ishner's soul."

"Do ye have an idea whether Icatalin lives or nay? She was older than I, but she was said to have been out in the fishing troller on the Eastern Ocean with your parents. All of us assumed she had gone down with them when the Kreppies sank it. The Kreppies did nay bother to look for survivors and they proceeded to blast more trollers to the bottom. They said that there were too many trollers for the number of Thalians left after the war."

Ishmael nodded and turned to Jolene. "Guardian of the Realm, I have nay proof, but I have seen someone at Port Issac during the height of our seasons. She acts and dresses as a Tri. I did nay approach her as I feared Ishmalisa would retaliate. Nay have I confided in any others. Who was there to dispute Ishmalisa's and Illnor's right to be Guardian and Counselor of Ishner? They were adequate in their dealings with all. Nay kenned how deep the Sisterhood had become entrenched till the last twenty years when they began to slowly squeeze out the male Directors. I feared for Issing. I have stayed mostly at Medicine with my counselor Melanie, but then I sensed something was wrong there also. It was like we were trapped again. There tis more. The Maca of Ishner had taken an Ab women and they were expecting a child. That child was born right after all left for the battle with the Justines. Nay kept track of her as she was an Ab. Somewhere though, there tis a Maca of Ishner."

"It seems we all missed that fact that the Sisterhood was spreading its tentacles." Llewellyn's voice was bitter. "Tis there any chance ye ken who this Maca tis?"

Ishmael looked at Llewellyn. "The Maca needs to come forward without being named. Ye should ken that."

"Do ye think the Thalian ye felt resembled Icatalin resides in Port Issac or was she there for the fish harvest and processing?" Jolene asked.

"I dinna. The sightings were too brief. I could nay tell if someone among those at the troller's side were with her or nay. I felt it best nay to linger." Ishmael answered.

"In that case, we will proceed with installing Imandril and Ilarmin as Guardian and Counselor of Ishner. We can then search for Icatalin in a discreet manner." Jolene smiled at them after her pronouncement. Imandrin's smile was brief. The man did nay look happy.

Chapter 53

Announcement

"Thalians of Ishner, some of ye may remember me, but most will
nay. I am Imandril, Lad of Ishner, and on my left tis my wedded
counselor, Lata. Next to her is our lassie, Lilith, who ye all ken
as the Kenning Woman. On my right tis our laddie, Ilarmin. My
fither was Iwilbur, Laird of Ishner and my mither, Izenia, was
his counselor. Both died in the battle with the Justines.

"I am nay Maca, nay are my laddie and lassie. Who and where
the True Maca of Ishner tis, we dinna, but we promise to search
diligently for Ishner's Maca. Our hope tis that the Maca will
come forward. Ye have heard the Guardian of the Realm make
the same request. All of us wish for a new beginning for Ishner
and for new prosperity now that nay are walking in fear of the
Sisterhood."

Imandrin took a deep breath as the scan ended. "Did that go
well?"

"Of course, it did," Lata answered.

All of them were a bit overwhelmed by their new lavish
accommodations of gyms, swimming pools, Ops room, extra
sleeping quarters, great rooms, kitchens and dining areas that
were all cared for by a staff of Directors and Keepers. They had
seen the homes, but the Council of the Realm had not made their
announcement to Ishner or the rest of Thalia. It was nay kenned

how many of Ishner's Directors and Tri Keepers had come under the influence of the Sisterhood or those that had benefited from the fishing and trade without a true Maca.

Jolene gambled that the broadcasts assuring the populace of Ishner that the Sisterhood nay longer ruled there. She fervently hoped that if there was a Maca, one would step forward. So far, none had. What kind of Maca would nay fight for control? If the Maca were in Ishner, how did one hide the Maca's hands?

After the broadcast was on the crystal, Jolene asked Imandrin to join her in her office to make certain he couldn't remember where his sib had spent time or was planning to go. Perhaps it would help her memory.

Imandrin remained bewildered and seemed to do nothing but shake his head.

"Guardian of the Realm, if I kenned where she had gone I would be the first to ask her if she had nay birthed a child before mine. Ilarmin does nay like fish. He likes kine, zarks, pigs, and the planting of the soil. He does nay wish to live on Ishner." the last was muttered under his breath, but Jolene had heard it and had heard something else in the timbre of the man's voice.

"How can ye be so certain if ye have nay seen your sib in all of these years?" Her voice was sharp and commanding.

Imandrin hid his face in his hands. "Because there might have been a laddie before Ilarmin." The words were muffled, but they brought Jolene straight out of her chair.

"And where tis this laddie?" She roared.

"Ye would have to ask the Handmaiden."

"What would my lassie have to do with a laddie from ye?" Jolene had charged around her desk and was looking at Imandrin who continued to hide his face.

Jolene removed his hands and continued to roar at him.

"Look at me! What have ye done? My younger tis married to your lassie. Are ye saying that they are sibs?"

"I am saying I dinna ken if they are or are nay." His voice was like that of dead leaves ruffling in the wind."

"Then ye must tell them."

"I canna. I promised the Handmaiden I would nay speak of our liaison if she would arrange a way for me to be far away from any that would remember me as the Lad of Ishner. She arranged for a sea Ab named Bi to bring me to the continent of Don. He pointed me in the direction of the Town of LouElla. If I tell, she will say I am the one who raped her."

By now Jolene was shaking him. "I ken nay raped her, and since it was so long ago, nay care." That she would need to tell her younger of this conversation tore at her heart.

"Go to your counselor and the rest of your House. Be ready to move in the morning. I must consult with others now."

Chapter 54

The Maca of Ayran

Jolene's words made Imandrin decide to confess to both Lilith and JayEll at their home. When he finished, JayEll swung on his heel and his powerful legs drove him out the door. He could not bear the sick look in Lilith's eyes or her moans of, "Nay, Fither, nay."

Once in his fliv, he headed for Lake Bliss. It seemed the proper place to mourn for a love that was lost forever into the maw of laws and Thalian taboos. He sat by the monument Lincoln, Lad of Don, had created for the Forgotten Warrior and wrapped his red cloak around himself. He could ignore the stench from Lake Bliss, but his body was still capable of feeling cold while his insides remained numb. How could he endure life without Lilith? And what if she were already expecting?

Mayhap, before he had Gar's Book and the knowledge that he was Martin, he might have been able to ignore the laws since all had been broken during the rule of the Justines and the Sisterhood, but as Martin, he could nay forget Gar's Commandments. He could nay wed one who was his sibling. The agony was deeper than just separation as they would nay be separated if he remained Martin. She was the Kenning Woman. She had to work with the Martin. He rocked back in forth in agony while the wind blew and the two white moons of early evening continued across the sullen, grey clouded sky.

* * *

Jolene marched into Jarvis's office. "Why are ye here at this hour when I need ye?"

Jarvis looked up. "Mither, there are the final reports on that last shipment from the Ayran 47 asteroid. It does contain the rare earth minerals that the Ayanas and Kreppies want. There is another element that we will have to name and keep for ourselves even if we are allowed to sell to our former enemies." He stood. "And why do ye berate me when for years ye complained I did nay work at being a Maca of Ayran?"

Jolene put her hands on her hips. "Ye have nay heard?"

"Mither, I have been busy with the crew here. I have heard nay of the gossip of Thalia."

"This tis nay gossip," she snapped. "Do ye ken what that fool that was once my lassie did?" Jolene did not wait for an answer.

"She bedded with Ilmandril and produced JayEll. He was so stricken that he has disappeared."

Jarvis sank back into his chair, his mouth open and shaking his head. "Dear Gar, where did he go? To lose your beloved like that, dear Gar."

It was Jolene's turn to stare. When had Jarvis ever shown such empathy? She took in air and continued.

"That tis why I am here. He tis deeply hurt and distressed. Lilith at least had her mither to comfort her. Who does JayEll have? Where would he go? Ye were laddies together as Abs. Did he have a favorite place then?"

Jarvis stood. "Mither, any favorite place we had as Abs tis gone or changed. And why did everyone panic and believe what Ilmandril said?"

It was Jolene's turn to shake her head. She and JayEll were the thinkers in this House. What did Jarvis mean? Why wouldn't they have believed Ilmandril?

"And as far as where JayEll tis, that tis simple if he were so distressed." Jarvis pulled out his com, pressed the circle for JayEll. It pinged and went silent, but it was time enough for Jarvis to record the coordinates.

Jarvis looked at his mither. "Do ye really care that much about my Elder?"

Jolene marched around the side of the desk and held onto her laddie. "I care that much about all three of ye. Bring him back to us, Jarvis."

"Aye, Mither, and if I do that can ye figure out a way to get Ilyan out of my mines? She disrupts everything and everyone with her crying, screams, and refusal to work."

"Deny her food."

"We have. She will then work one-half a shift before becoming a trouble maker again. Once we had to call in Medicine. The woman tis mad." He bid his Mither the Thalian farewell before grabbing his hat and cloak.

"I should be back within the hour, but I will be going to my home," he said as he went out the door.

He strode outside to his fliv and headed toward the most miserable place on Ayran. Would JayEll flee before he arrived or would he think that it was but a routine call that he had disabled? If it were the latter, JayEll would still be there at that miserable place where Lilith had found the Book. It took but two minutes to arrive.

JayEll was so sunk in his misery he did not move as Jarvis approached him. He was on the ground facing the fetid Lake Bliss, his arms locked around his knees as he swayed back and forth wondering how a Martin could break the rules of Gar and society?

In this heart he kenned that he and Lilith had already committed the sin of incest over and over. There was nay tolerance for such behavior. The genes of the Houses must always be protected. He would have to avoid her the rest of his days, yet there was nay way to do so as long as he were Martin and she was the Kenning Woman.

He continued to rock back and forth in misery. Where could he go? Where could he hide? If he ran from being the Martin of Gar, he would be committing another offense. The bleakness and darkness of life without Lilith was overwhelming and he moaned.

JayEll heard the boot fall of an approaching body and halfway turned his head to look up. To his surprise, Jarvis was beside him, reaching down, and pulling him upward into his arms. For a moment JayEll was ready to fight, but the contact of another Thalian offering solace through the embrace of his Maca overcame his first instinct. His sorrow over losing Lilith flowed into Jarvis and the answering wave of sorrow for losing a beloved flowed into him.

JayEll lifted his head and looked at Jarvis. "Ye too?"

Jarvis's eyes were hard and his mouth straight. "Aye, I am the one who has lost, but ye, my Elder, are nay thinking! Ye are acting like a bunghole!"

JayEll tried to pull away, but his Warrior Maca was too strong.

"Think, JayEll! Ye and Lilith were both at Medicine that day of discovering the Book. If there had been a reason that ye two could nay mate or wed, Medicine would have discreetly told ye both."

JayEll looked at Jarvis and shook his head. "I, I, I dinna. They may nay have checked for that. We were nay bleeding. They just scanned."

"Ye still are nay thinking. We do nay have to bleed. They scanned ye and they would have had to run the matches ere storing the information for Don and Ayran. That Ishner showed in Lilith tis a given, but so would the Don of her mither. Ye would have been Ayran from your mither, but what ye were from yere fither was nay Ishner or they would have examined their crystals and warned ye that ye should proceed with caution."

JayEll closed his eyes for a moment as his world came back into alignment. He laid his head first on Jarvis's right shoulder and then on the left. "Thank ye, my Maca. Ye are right. I was nay thinking. Like a true Warrior ye charged in to direct the battle."

He looked at Jarvis. "But now I must go to Medicine to verify that ye are right. Mayhap we should have done that at the beginning, but it was nay required." He started to turn away.

"I will take ye."

"That tis nay necessary, Jarvis. I am now back to normal, but there tis something I would like to ken. Who was your beloved? What did I miss?"

"It was Lillie, Lass of Don. Who else would have been a fit counselor for me?" The bitterness was in his voice. "I could nay even grieve correctly because I was spaced out. Ye canna imagine my horror when I realized that if I had been there, I could have stopped the murder."

JayEll leaned forward and the two embraced again, rocking back and forth as they had when laddies in a world of Abs; abandoned by House and empty of food and hope.

* * *

Melanie stood as the two announced Ayranians entered her office. They all greeted each other, and she motioned to the mugs of brew set out. She was wondering why both the Maca and the Lad of Ayran were here at this hour. She had checked and Jarvis was allowed brew again.

"Thank ye, Melanie, but this tis an official call. We wish to nip a rumor ere all Thalia has heard it."

Melanie's eyebrows rose. "Ye are a bit late if ye mean the one about Imandril being JayEll's fither."

"Damn." Jarvis took a chair and picked up a mug. "Ye had them both here nay long ago. Did ye see any matching of genes that meant that JayEll and Lilith could nay wed?"

"Jarvis, tis my place to ask." JayEll glared at him. "I need to ken." He stared at Melanie.

She touched a circle and an auxiliary screen appeared on her desk. "Bide a moment." She touched the circles for the Houses, then for Ayran, before locating the one for JayEll. "There tis nay need to pull up Lilith's as she will be Ishner and Don," she murmured.

She stared intently at information the crystal spewed across the screen, frowned, and pursued it backwards into the time when the Justines established the Sisterhood as the ruling House of Thalia. Then she looked up and gave JayEll a smile, her eye brimming with amusement.

"It seems JayEll, ye belong to the House of Ayran, Medicine, and the House of Don."

JayEll swallowed, picked up one of the mugs, set it down without touching it, and rose to look at Melanie. She held up her hand, palm forward to stay him.

"Ye may nay approach till I finish and make this screen vanish." She looked down and read the lines scrolling across the screen.

"Your fither was the Director of Scales for Medicine. When the Sisterhood took over they demoted him to Keeper. He objected and they sentenced him to be an Ab." She looked up at them. "That was a dangerous thing to do then. Nay could object to what the Sisters decreed."

She looked back down at the screen. The words had stopped, and she closed it before finishing. "He had wed and there had been a laddie, but he was grown. He and his mither later disappeared. I dinna if they went with the former Director or elsewhere. There was so much lost back then. We have nay discovered a match to either of them. I canna tell ye if your fither lives or nay. Nay can I tell ye what happened to that part of our House. The House of Don tis there as our Director's mither had been Don, but nay part of the ruling portion. Ye, however, are free to marry Lilith." She stood and held out her arms.

"Welcome to Medicine, JayEll."

When the Thalian hug was over, JayEll smiled at them. "Ye must excuse me, but I must now go to my Lilith."

He nodded at Jarvis. "I will be there in the morning if that tis all right."

"Aye, in the meantime, I have a meeting with the Director of Flight."

"He tis letting ye back on the ships?"

"Nay, but that last exploration may have been a break through. It will take years, but we may have found one of the elements needed for the new class of spaceships. I also intend to convince him that I should return as a Warrior and Trainer."

JayEll grinned at him and they bid each other goodbye.

* * *

JayEll landed at the back padport of the Don's Shrine of the Kenning Woman. He had not needed to try to track Lilith. He knew where she went when distressed. His eyes and palm print still opened the door and he stepped inside. The automatic lights diffused the darkness of night.

"Ye canna be here." Lilith's voice wailed over the com.

He pressed the audio by the doorcom. "Your fither was in error. I am nay Ishner. I am Medicine. I have just come from speaking with Melanie. We are nay related in any manner."

The com became silent. In a few seconds she burst into the kitchen, her dark eyes wide with wonder. Lilith stopped and looked at him, her tongue flicking at her lips. "Are ye sure? Why would your mither say such a thing if it were nay true?"

"Why would my mither say and do any of things she says and does? Lilith, according to Medicine, and the records they have, my fither tis a former Director of Scales that was forced out by the Sisterhood. He fled for his safety when he opposed their decisions. They have nay kenning of what happened to him other than he was condemned as an Ab."

She ran across the room and they held onto each other as though one might evaporate. "Thank, Gar," Lilith kept repeating.

"Aye, it was more than I could bear. I could nay have been Martin while ye were Kenning Woman. Even the thought of being away from ye day and night was like a knife dragging at my innards."

"JayEll, I, I, I cancelled your classes for tomorrow. I sorrow."

"Good, I'll alert them that it is studying time as usual the next day."

The com began beeping and her fither's voice rang out in the room. "Lilith, ye must come to the Guardian's home immediately. They say JayEll tis on his way to your house."

JayEll smiled at her. "I think ye best reassure him. The rumors fly easily in Thalia."

"Tis nay a rumor. Ye are here." She turned to the com.

"Fither, it tis all right. The other was nay true."

Silence and then she heard him roar, "I will be right there."

"Fither, he has been to Medicine. We are nay related."

Silence filled the room. "Why would the Handmaiden lie?" Imandrin's voice was low and puzzled.

"My Fither-by-marriage, nay ken why my Mither lies about so many things."

Chapter 55

The Sisterhood and the Maca

"Captain Issaric, they are sending Warrior Troopers to do full sweeps of the Maca's compound to make sure it tis safe for the new Guardian. Most of the sailing items have been removed to a compound here. Our records are at the Maca's Tower. I would prefer to move them to your troller." It was Ivana, a Director of Records. "We canna keep them from examining the Maca's Tower. Everything must be removed now and then to your troller this eve."

Captain Issaric almost choked on her swallow of beer before she looked up. Her sailing privileges had been revoked since it was discovered that Beauty and Belinda had sojourned on her vessel for weeks. So far her plea that the Maca had ordered it had kept her from being sent to Ayran, but the suspicion of treason remained.

They were seated at a bar in the Port of Issac, far from Iconda and the Maca's Tower. Ivana had entered and ordered a brew before sitting down. It had to look natural, but Ivana had kept her voice low.

"Ye may use the warecomplex as it tis empty now. I canna order supplies for sailing. My troller is anchored directly in front of the complex. Nay are allowed on board till the Council of the Realm permits it. Dinna try to do so. The sensors would alert the Council of the Realm."

"We shall use the warecomplex. As soon as it darkens, we will begin."

* * *

Isabelle hit the button for Idana. "They are moving something now. It tis taking carriers and they are headed for the waterfront. Gather our friends. We will stop them this time and Ishner will be free." She closed the line. She had no doubt that the Ishners of Port Issac would be there with their staffs and metal poles to fight the Enforcers with their stunners. They would not fail this time.

* * *

"Llewellyn, there has been an explosion at the Port of Issac on Ishner. These are the coordinates. I canna reach Ishmalisa. Send in your Troopers and let me ken." Jolene's orders were brief as usual.

Llewellyn hit the Warriors circle and the alert went out. "Captain Daniel, gather your troopers and Captain Pillar's. Stop the fighting at these coordinates. Captain Jarvis, ye and your troopers are to, bide a moment, tis another message." His instructions to Jarvis were interrupted.

"Guardian of Flight, I have heard from Issing. The Sisterhood has set a contingent around Ishmalisa and Illnor's home and taken her there. Issing had the com ripped away and a Sister's voice said they would all die if I reported this. They are apt to kill them anyway." Ishmael's words were rapid and his face white.

"Aye, we will attend." Llewellyn cut that com and went back to Jarvis.

"Did ye hear what Ishmael said?"

"Aye, Guardian of Flight. They are at the Guardian Home of Ishner."

Ye are to take Captain Aretha and her troopers and engage. Let me ken how it goes."

"Aye, Guardian."

* * *

Daniel and his Troopers had answered the call to arms without all wearing their Warrior black, but he did not delay. As the carrier landed, he ordered them to mass together. They had seen the fighting below and realized that Ishner was fighting Ishner and there was no way to distinguish who were the Sisters other than by the weapons or uniforms. They had not seen the flare of a stunner, but none doubted that one had or would be fired.

"If ye are fired upon fire back." Daniel ordered and led the way into the melee. He tossed one man, then a woman out of the way. The man gasped. "It canna be! We are fighting the Sisters. They are besting us."

An explosion sent blocks of stone hurtling through the air and people started to run in different directions. Instead of emptying the square by the building they ran into each other and knocked each other over while still trading blows. They became a mass of people yelling and throwing punches.

Someone in the crowd screamed and the stench of flesh being seared by a stunner filled the air. Anger surged through Daniel and he jumped up on a prow of a small boat and roared out to the crowd, his deep voice rolling into the night.

"Enough! Ye are killing Thalians. Have ye all gone mad? This stops now!"

For a moment there was silence. Then one of the women with a stunner stalked toward him. She had not raised it as Captain Pillar had his stunner trained on her.

"Ye have nay right here. Ye were nay given permission to land. Leave now!"

It looked as if Daniel grew and widened and the musk of a Thalian Warrior and Maca rolled out into the night. His arms and hands extended outward and he yelled again.

"I am Maca. Let any who deny me, challenge me now!"

Stunned Ishners and Troopers looked at him. He was the Lad of Don, Captain of Flight, and all kenned his part in the Draygon fight, but how could he be Maca of Ishner?

Ivana continued towards him. "Ye canna be Maca. That tis a lie of the Houses to keep their power. Your hands are any special."

Daniel's body seemed to swell larger and his grin was fierce. His arms looked ready to embrace her, stunner and all. The others watched. She marched up the walkway.

"I will prove to all what a lie this tis." She yelled and walked into his embrace.

The others watched as she stiffened and then let him lift her upward. She put her head on his right shoulder and made the "tsk" sound in his ear. Then she put her head on his left shoulder and made the "tsk" sound again. She collapsed against him as he set her on the boat.

"My Maca, forgive me. Forgive all of us. I believed that there were nay more Macas. I sorrow."

Ye will have to face the charges, but I will speak for all the beings of Ishner."

Ivana closed her eyes and nodded. Then she turned to the crowd and screamed. "He is our Maca. He tis the Maca of Ishner."

None in the crowd moved. Pillar started to move toward them, but saw Daniel's arm and hand go out in a staying motion. What, he wondered, tis the man doing?

Daniel had one arm over Ivanna's shoulder as he began to speak. "Captain Pillar, tell Medicine they are to land."

He looked out over the Ishners in front of him. "There will nay be anymore fighting. Whatever ye have in those boxes being carried will be confiscated. Those that still claim to be Sisters group together. Those that are from Ishner that were fighting them move into another group. Any that are injured remain where ye are. Medicine will attend."

Idana pushed himself forward and Isabelle paced beside him, her face twisted in puzzlement. They stopped in front of where Daniel stood and stared. No one in Ishner was large enough to challenge this man. Still words came from Idana's mouth.

"Ye claim to be Maca, but the only one that has acknowledge ye tis one of those that has stripped Ishner and trampled on all who wish to live here in peace."

Daniel eyed him and a tight smile came on his lips. "Then ye must lay your head on my shoulder and be certain." His arms opened wider.

Ivanna stepped aside and Idana stepped up, his lips in a tight line, and his face determined. He stood on tiptoes, but Daniel lifted him upward and the Thalian pattern of greeting and submission given. Daniel let Idana slide downward and Idana started to step backward and stumbled, falling towards the water.

Daniel caught him around the chest area and pulled him back. His brown eyes held amusement and a smile pulled at his lips. "I do nay wish to lose a loyal Ishner."

"My Maca, forgive my doubts." Like Ivanna, he turned to the crowd and yelled. "He tis our Maca."

The crowd started to surge forward, but stopped when they realized Captain Pillar and the troopers were barring their way. Medicine appeared and the crowd parted for them.

Daniel pulled up his com, but before he could use it, Isabella was in front of him. "They have taken Issing, Ishmalisa, and Illnor to the Guardian Home. They have threatened to kill them! Plus Captain Issaric tis still free. She tis the one that had given them access her troller's warecomplex.

"Where tis this Captain Issaric? Tis she still at the assigned home or has she gone into hiding?"

Isabella looked at Idana. "Tis he really our Maca?" She looked back at Daniel. "How can ye be? Ye are nay from our old Maca's line."

"He tis the Maca." Idana's voice was hoarse. "We put someone to guard Issaric's home. She should still be there."

"Who are ye two that ye can set up guards against the Sisterhood?"

The two looked at each other, and Idana spoke. "She tis still wary, but we have gathered our kin and friends over the years to thwart them. We kenned we had to attack this eve when they started to remove the stingers and the supplies to assemble more of them. That tis part of what tis in those teal boxes."

The message came over the com. "All clear. Guardian of Flight notified."

Daniel smiled. "I have a large group here that needs to go the Guardian of the Realm complex. Do ye have enough troopers to arrest Captain Issaric and bring her along?"

"Aye. We will see ye there," came the voice of Jarvis.

Daniel smiled and hit the com again. "Guardian of Flight, as a Captain I am ordering Captain Pillar to bring in all the Sisterhood detainees, but many are willing to ask for forgiveness. As the Maca of Ishner, I request that they nay be treated harshly."

"As what?" roared Llewellyn's voice.

"And as one Maca to the other, I thank ye for the example ye have given me. I will be in as the Warrior of Flight late tonight or early in the morning to add my report to Captain Pillar's."

He silenced that line and hit the com again. "Ishmael, where are ye? I need ye here. Meet me at the Maca's Tower of Ishner in Iconda."

Chapter 56

The Last Stronghold

"Captain Aretha, take six trooper and move to the front. I am taking the others and we will surround the house and scan for movement. When I give the signal, ye demand that they come out. Then duck low and scatter to a pre-selected spaces They may have a scanner."

"Captain Jarvis, as senior officer ye are in charge, but they will nay surrender." Aretha looked at him like he was mad.

"And I suggest ye all wear armor." He grinned at her. "They will nay come out, but it will distract them while we locate them with our scanners. Then we enter where they are."

"What of their prisoners?"

"Issing tis the only one I worry about." He turned to the troopers mobilized behind them. "Recorders, keep the scanners trained on the home. Highlight the area of those that change position. If they are in front of a window, fire. Move out."

Captain Aretha watched until Jarvis disappeared around the corner of the home. Then she used the amplifier on her com.

"All in the home. Come out now with your hands raised and surrender. Nay will be harmed."

She and the others ducked down and rolled over to the side as a blaze of light erupted through the front window pane and the door. They heard the door shattering, and the window crinkle.

Then sound of more windows crinkling as Ayran's metals shattered from the heat of a stunner blast. Someone inside screamed and the sound or a door going down echoed in the night.

Jarvis knew how the Guardian's Home was laid out as all were the same on Thalia. He vaulted through one of the destroyed side windows, rolled, and came up with his long stunner blazing. Two sisters went down to the floor, twisting in agony. Another who was approaching the doorway tried to duck back, but the small stunner in his left hand dropped her. Troopers poured into room, and began to fire away at the metal enforced walls.

The Sisters inside the locked office hit the home com. "We concede. Fire nay more as the Guardian, her counselor, and Director Issing are in here. Ye will be responsible for their deaths if ye dinna cease."

"Halt firing!" Jarvis yelled and the smoke from the wall shifted around the room and a piece of dislodged wall tumbled down.

Jarvis touched the wall com as Aretha entered from the front, her stunner held shoulder high.

"Ye will open that door, toss out your weapons, and permit Ishmalisa, Illnor, and Issing to walk out. Then ye will all follow them with your hands in the air. If those three dinna walk out alive and nay harmed, ye will nay have the chance to stand before the Guardians of the Realm."

The door open and three stunners sailed out and slid on the floor. Jarvis motioned to a trooper to pick them up as Issing, then Illnor and Ishmalisa entered the room. They moved over near Aretha when motioned to do so.

"How many Sisters are in there?"

There are four, Captain Jarvis," answered Issing. "There are more weapons and one is holding a hand stunner. Personally I would love to slug all of them."

Jarvis grinned and nodded. "Throw out the remaining weapons or we commence firing again."

Silence came from the room. Jarvis lifted his stunner when a lilac suited Tri walked out. "I have nay weapon," she began when a stun blast hit her back and she collapsed. More firing came from the room and another lilac clothed Tri rolled out and threw a long stunner spinning across the floor. "There tis one more and she has a small stunner." The woman stood and raised her hands. "We have been bested."

The flame came from the room and dropped her.

Jarvis, Aretha, and the Troopers began firing against the door, the walls, and the ceiling.

"No!" It was Ishmalisa. "Ye will destroy our Ops and Office." And the wall crashed inward.

"Do ye have a Maintenance ye can call?" Jarvis asked the three stunned Ishners.

"Aye," whispered Issing, "but it tis late."

"They need to be here to put out any ember and restore a certain stability. I am leaving five Troopers. They will gather the crystals and the secure the area till the Guardians of the Realm decide what measure to take."

"Captain Jarvis, they have buried more records below. I dinna if there are other material there or not."

"Thank ye, Issing. I shall alert the Guardian of Flight. Tis your home safe?"

"Aye, Captain Jarvis, they did nay trust me and they could nay control Ishmael if I was in too much danger."

Jarvis grinned at her. "Aye, that happened this eve. Ishmael called for your rescue." He pulled out his com and contacted Daniel.

"All secure here."

Chapter 57

The New Maca

Daniel and Ishmael landed at the walled padport of the Maca's Tower of Ishner within seconds of each other. Ishmael stood six-foot-three and had to stand on tip toes to lay his head on Daniels shoulders.

"What took ye so long, my Maca? Ye should have been here years ago."

"I was nay ready, Ishmael. Even now it tis strange to be giving orders to a man who was like my Elder when growing up." Daniel sounded perplexed. "And I ken damn little about fishing. Ye and Issing will be bearing that burden. I am a Warrior, but right now I need to get into this place and have ye change the identities in the Ops Room. Can ye still do so?"

"Aye, they did nay change that as they worried nay about what I would do as long as they controlled Issing." Ishmael led the way up the steps, and laid his hand on the side and looked into the eye screener. The door slid inward and they entered the back hall.

"If we go to the Ops Room, I can enter ye as the new Maca. Then we can go to the Maca's office and all the crystals will be available. I dinna think Ilyan used them."

* * *

Daniel frowned at the numbers going across the screen while Ishmael kept finding crystals stashed in drawers or containers shoved back in the closet rather than in storage compartments. Many of the crystals were blank.

Daniel inserted one of the crystals, and the screen showed several of the bedding scenes Lillie had recorded at her early parties. He tried another crystal with the same result. The third one showed Krepyons in their mating positions and Daniel tried to crush the crystal in his hands.

"Was there nay else but beddings on her mind?"

Ishmael had a sick look on his face. "I fear it was her favorite topic. Here, try one of these. It tis the shape and color for an account record."

Daniel pushed that one into the receptacle and the screen listed the shops along Port Issac's First Sector. The figures were there, but they were almost meaningless to Daniel. It had nay to do with the stars. He looked up at Ishmael. "Do ye ken what all that means?"

"Aye, it tis a list of the shops, their purchases of merchandise, the sales, and the credits given to the workers."

"All tis owned by the Maca of Ishner then?"

"Aye, like it tis in all of the Houses except Don."

Daniel nodded and frowned at the screen. "How would ye like to be in charge of all the recording and tracking of the shops?"

"I would nay like it. I am a troller Captain, and the sea and fishing are my duties. Issing has handled much of economics of Ishner, but she says the Sisters have brutalized the accounts and ferreted away the funds."

"In that case, Jerome has more to do than just audit here. He has managed to upset all of those that Andrew trained. His rambling words continue as he finds something to correct or update certain procedures."

"The other Houses will accuse ye of turning Ishner over to Don and your Elder Fither will rule both."

"I am Maca," roared Daniel. "I am hiring Jerome to do the work. He will nay be Ishner. Ye will find he tis far more honest than the Sisters, but ye or Issing will need to listen to him drone on about matters that ye dinna ken."

Ishmael looked doubtful.

Daniel stood. "I intend to spend the night here and leave early in the morning. Do ye ken if the Maca's bedroom here has been cleaned?"

Llewellyn's voice boomed over the com. "Captain Daniel, ye and Ishmael need to report to the Guardian of the Realm. She tis still at the Guardians Complex in Betron. Ishmalisa, Illnor, and Issing are being brought there. I shall meet ye there."

Daniel hit the com for Guardian of Flight. "Aye, Guardian, we are on our way." To Ishmael, he said, "My work as Maca tis delayed."

* * *

Daniel and Ishmael were ushered into the Guardian of the Realm's office. Daniel noted Llewellyn's fliv on the padport. After the greetings, Jolene indicated the seats.

"I dinna wish to have any more calls this eve. Ye, Daniel, have all the Houses in an uproar. How tis it that if ye are Maca, nay kenned it till now?'

Ishmael spoke first. "I kenned it when he had his Confirmation Rite, but he forbid me to say anything. He wished to be a Warrior. I could nay argue with my Maca."

"I kenned it once during a bedding when we were younger and I too was forbidden to alert anyone." Issing's face was almost stark, as though she wished to be elsewhere. "Tonight, I canna deny it."

Jolene looked at Ishmalisa and Illnor. "Did ye nay detect that he was Maca?"

Ishmalisa stood. "He tis lying! Our lassie tis the Maca!"

Illnor shook his head and tears filled his eyes. "Nay more, Ishmalisa. Look where our lies have put our lassie." He looked at Daniel and continued.

"Will ye forgive us, my Maca. We kenned years ago that ye were the Maca of Ishner when your hands touched us. Our lassie also kenned, but we kept the charade that the Justines and Sisterhood had instituted. Then we were threatened and ruled by the Sisterhood these last sixty-odd years. We have been punished, but our lassie needs help. She should nay be where she tis and it tis our fault for pushing her into a position she could nay handle. We should be in prison, nay her."

Ishmalisa was looking at him with horror in her eyes. "Ye have betrayed us."

Illnor hid his face, his body shaking.

Llewellyn noted with satisfaction that once again Jolene was speechless. Daniel stood.

"Guardian of the Realm, I need to complete my report and turn the crystal over to the Guardian of Flight. He will nay doubt share that with ye and with the Council. Tomorrow, I will visit Medicine to allay any doubts about my right to be Maca. Even if there is nay Ishner in my line, I am still Maca of Ishner and any that would dispose me, must challenge to the death. I will also inquire if Medicine can help Ilyan as part of her problem tis also my fault. Jarvis tis correct. That lassie tis ill."

Ishmalisa gasped and looked at him with eyes that filled with tears.

Daniel ignored the tears and gave the Thalian farewell to his elder father before closing the door behind him.

Chapter 58

Thalian Justice

The Guardians of the Realm Council was in an uproar. The seating for the audience filled and people stood or sat on the stone floor. Others were outside where the screens and audio enabled them to watch and hear the captured action

Jolene had tried to prevent a challenge to Daniel sitting as the Maca and Guardian of Ishner, but Troy and Rurhran objected and were clamoring for a vote.

Daniel stood and roared. "If ye wish to take down the Maca of Ishner, ye must challenge me. Elsewise, ye must take Medicine's word that I am a descendant of the Maca of Ishner through my mither, the Counselor of Don."

Marta, Lady of Medicine and Counselor of Troy, stood. Her face was flushed and her words harsh. "My sib and my lassie must have pulled up the wrong crystal. If true, his mither would be Maca. His mither was an Ab when she birthed him."

Both Melanie, Lass and Counselor of Medicine, and Marita, the young Maca of Medicine were angered by the accusation.

"That tis nay true." Melanie was shouting back. "We checked the one crystal of Ishner that we have with the blood lines of Imandril and his House. We also checked, Diana, Counselor of Don. Daniel tis who he says he tis. Why the Maca skipped to the next generation we canna say, but it maybe that Diana was destined to be the Kenning Woman."

Rocella, Lass and Counselor of Rurhran, stood. "There still needs to be a vote. This tis but a ploy of Don to gain more power."

"I dinna take orders from Don." Daniel stated.

Rocella smiled and started to speak when Raddan, Maca and Guardian of Rurhran, broke in. "I have had my Confirmation Rite, and I am Maca. Rocella, sit down. We are nay fighting Don or anyone else this eve."

Rocella glared at him, but sat. Why, she wondered, had the new Maca been male and not female?

Silence filled the hall. Marta licked her lips. "Guardian and Counselors of the Realm, I request time to redo what my younger, Melanie, and lassie did."

"Why," asked Jolene. "Has Melanie ever erred before?"

Troyner, Maca of Troy, stood. "We will withdraw our objection. Of course, Melanie and our lassie do nay err."

To Marta, Troyner whispered, "Ye ken that tis true. Ye canna stop what was put into motion by the Justines and Kreppies. Let it be. Most will forget that I am his fither. This tis but reminding them."

Marta stared straight ahead and clenched her fists. In her mind, she damned the old Kenning Woman into the Darkness. She had seen Daniel sitting in a relaxed position with the same type of amusement flickering in his eyes like his elder fither, Llewellyn, and the same type of slight smile. How was that possible? She wanted to cover her ears as Daniel continued speaking.

"Guardians and Counselors of the Realm, I have discovered that the former appointed Maca of Ishner was and tis ill. I fear I must take some of the blame for her condition and I would like to make it right. I did nay ken I was the Maca of Ishner when I was younger. That I kenned I was a Maca, tis true. Had I kenned I was Maca of Ishner, I would nay have dominated Ilyan as I did.

I would have ordered her to behave herself. Now that tis too late. Medicine can cure an addiction to brew if any indulge too deeply or too often. Why can they nay cure another type of mind illness? I submit that Ilyan should be imprisoned at Medicine while they work to make her whole again. It might be best even to let her parents visit at times."

They were all staring at him now. Some in the audience were muttering," Nay," loud enough for the Guardians to hear. Ishmalisa and Illnor held each other's hands as they sat in Ishner's Box. They feared there would be no help.

Jarvis recovered first. "I have been telling everyone that would listen that she tis ill. She does nay but scream. There are nay normal reactions to food or retaining her muscular build. She tis ill. Daniel tis right."

Brenda hit her audio. "Guardians, that woman helped the destroyer of my wee ones. She should nay walk free again. I dinna care if she screams or starves. Medicine can nay work on minds. It tis forbidden." She glared at Daniel who still had that slight smile on his face.

Llewellyn took a deep breath and spoke. "There tis a time for compassion. It canna be good that she tis below the ground and screaming, but what can Medicine do but sedate her?"

Lorenz interrupted. "My world tis far more primitive than here, but they have medicines, techniques, and, according to my younger, Gary, the ability to train the neurons in the brain to transmit messages or to process information has taken tremendous strides. Medicine here should be able to do what my world can do."

"We are nay allowed to invade the brain." It was Marita, Maca and Guardian of Medicine.

"I'm not talking about surgery." Lorenz responded.

"Nay am I." Marita continued. "We would need to use scans and inject minibots. The latter tis forbidden. Nay by the Justines, but by this Council. Even if we scanned it tis nay permissible to change the brain. We have nay seen such an illness on Thalia for centuries. I canna say why one has returned now."

"I'd say a lot has changed since the Justines and Krepyons disrupted your world and it is now showing up in the ones that were young when they conquered or ruled. Why else would a Thalian murder a Thalian? That too is a type of madness. I suggest y'all, ah, ye look for remedies now. When my younger tis here again, ask him about Earth's techniques."

Silence filled the hall. What the Laird of Don spoke true.

Jolene hit her audio. "Guardians and Counselors of Don, it seems that someone from another land has spoken true words. I suggest that Ilyan be moved to Medicine once we have constructed a secure residence. Medicine can determine if a visit from her parents would be beneficial. I also suggest that Medicine be allowed to proceed with a way to help Ilyan regain a sense of reality. Are there any that object?"

The Guardians and Counselors could be seen talking to each other and silence filled the hall.

"Who would build such a unit?" Marita asked.

Lincoln, Lad of Don, stood. He was seated in the compartment of Don to the left side of the Guardian rostrum. "I will gladly design and oversee the building of something that would be comfortable and secure. It would permit Medicine to observe when necessary. I have seen the facilities on my fither's world and I wondered why they were able to solve mind problems. Now I can use what I learned. It will benefit Medicine and their staff by being separated from the prisoner."

Lorenz touched his audio again. "Medicine, ye must have head scans from when people were injured. Ye took one of me when I first came here. Why can't ye compile all of those into one crystal base for comparison?"

"We could nay use yours, my friend." It was Melanie. "Ye are nay born Thalian, but ye are correct. We can build on those scans."

"Fine." It was Jolene. "We will proceed with those guidelines. Ilyan will be transferred as soon as it tis safe. Medicine can arrange for a visit with her parents to see if that brings a change in the scans. Any treatments, if possible, will be decided by Medicine and cleared by our Council." Jolene looked at the audience and the faces on screen. She hoped that Ilyan was the only one so deeply afflicted, and then remembered some of the odd behavior of the House members and Tris when the Justines and Kreppies were in control. She was grateful when she pounded the gavel down for the last time.

Jarvis rose and made his way to Daniel before descending the stairs. "I canna thank ye enough."

Daniel grinned, "Ye are welcome."

Illan and Ishmalisa surrounded Daniel the minute he and Ishmael were down the stairs. "When can we see her and bring her home?"

"That tis up to the Council and to Medicine. I have nay way of kenning."

Instead of thanks, Ishmalisa swung around and headed for the door. She paused long enough to look at Illan and motion towards the door with her head. Illan followed her, his heart breaking for his lassie.

Daniel shrugged and turned for the way to the Dining Arena when his way was blocked by a smiling JoAnne.

"Hello, my Maca of Ishner."

Daniel bent to pick her up. "I am nay your Maca."

"Oh, ye will be when we are wed. Ishner was the hold out for our Walking the Circle. Ye must give that approval at the dinner this eve. I, too, went to Medicine today. Our lassie will be here in ten months."

Epilog

Brenda had welcomed Tamar's request to Walk the Circle with Issing. The thought of another House wee one was enough for her to request the Claiming Rite for Tamar and name him Laird of Betron.

Lilith kept her Don name, but she and JayEll made their main home on Ishner and returned to the various Shrines of the Kenning Woman throughout the year. All seemed well for the friends, except for a lonely Jarvis.

Like the rest of Thalia, they were surprised when Jarvis and Aretha stood before the Guardians Council of the Realms and asked for permission to Walk the Circle.

"Dear, Gar, their laddies and lassies will be nay but Warriors," JayEll proclaimed.

Lilith had smiled at him. "I am the Kenning Woman, nay ye."

Now she was holding their wee one and standing at the edge of the mound looking out at the cold ocean. She was where she had stood in the long-ago vision just outside of the northern edge of Iconda. Her vision had been correct. She now lived here part of the year. The wind whipped her cape and she turned to walk back to their home of rounded teal. As she walked, she saw JayEll's red fliv land. It was followed by a blue lift from Don.

JayEll stepped out and walked towards her, pulling her and Ildora close for a hug before turning to greet their guests. At the sight of Leftan dressed in the brown garb of an Ab and accompanied by his mither, JayEll's eyes widened. The former disputer of every word from Gar's Book was dressed as an Ab, and in his right hand was the staff of a Martin. He stepped forward to meet them.

He wasn't sure his mither would give the proper greeting as her mouth was set in a tight, straight line as though she were clenching her teeth. As they came together, Leftan bowed and Jaylene put out here arms for the greeting. When JayEll and his mither broke apart, Leftan looked at Jaylene. "Now it tis your turn to speak."

Jaylene took a deep breath and bowed her head before looking at JayEll. Her eyes filled with tears as she spoke. "My laddie, I owe ye an apology and must ask your forgiveness. I deserted ye when ye were younger and helped bring those false charges of stealing against ye. Can ye ever forgive me?"

JayEll put out his arms to his mither and they stood there in the cold, wind of Ishner clinging to each other. Jaylene's body wracked with sobs. "I was so certain that he was the long, lived Martin that would bring a huge change to the thinking of Thalia, yet it was to be ye. That man deceived all of us over and over."

"Mither, I think ye will find that it was ye that was the most deceived. It tis over now, for he may be one that did go into the Darkness, but only Gar can determine that." He smiled down at her. "Come ye must meet our lassie, your younger, Ildora."

Jaylene put her hands out and grasped his biceps. "Nay, ye dinna ken. There tis more. I was nay forced. I kenned full well that Imandril was nay your fither. He was the ploy to hide who the true fither was."

"Mither, ye are nay thinking. We are wed as Medicine told me the man who was my fither had to be from Medicine."

Jaylene closed her eyes, swallowed, and nodded. "Aye, that tis true. He once was a Director of Scales for Medicine. When the Sisters made him a Keeper, he protested. They made him an Ab, but before they drove him out, he proposed that they proclaim him Martin. He had the education and ability to store and distribute the food and clothing items in a fair manner. They did make him Martin of the House of Abs. He would then be in charge of the employment meted out. His power over the Abs would have been complete except that he was lazy and let me coordinate the distribution and storing of the food allotments."

"That man was my fither? Mither, he denied me too. Why did ye nay tell me or report him?"

"JayEll, do ye really think the Sisterhood or the other Houses would have cared about Abs? They were too intent on retaining what little power they had been given by the Justines. The Kreppies did nay care about any Thalian, and as for that Martin, he did nay wish others to ken ye were his."

"Did he force ye to bed him, Mither?"

Once again, Jaylene closed her eyes and opened them before answering. "It was a mutual agreement. He had taught me what I ken about giving health care when there tis nay equipment or medicines. I thought I would prove to Di that I was woman enough to have a wee one and bring her back. I was consumed with grief when she left me and then took up with Rocella, then Troyner. I could nay ken how living in House would be such a draw for her." Her lips were taunt as though forcing the words through them.

"Ye still have nay said that ye forgive me."

"Of course, I forgive ye, Mither."

"Thank ye, my laddie. Now may I hold my younger?"

JayEll turned to Lilith and took Ildora and handed her to Jaylene. "This tis Ildora, Lass of Ishner and Lass of Ayran. She tis such a wee one for so many titles."

"We should go inside before ye remove the wrappings. The wind has a bite to it," said Lilith.

"There tis nay time," said Leftan. "We still need to go to Ayran. She has one more person to ask for forgiveness ere she tis right with Gar and receives His blessings of peace."

"And who would this person be?" asked JayEll.

"My Mither, JayEll. I have said harsh words against her over the years. I dinna think she will forgive me, but this Martin says it tis necessary that I ask her. Do ye disagree?" None missed the tinge of hope in her voice.

JayEll looked down at her. "I canna disagree as I have heard some of those harsh words. My Elder Mither has mellowed with age, and she may forgive ye, but dinna ask her if ye can return to House. She would nay supplant Jarvis with ye as Maca."

"I dinna with to be Maca. I am the Handmaiden till the day I die."

"Leftan tis wrong about one thing, Mither. Ere ye go. I as Martin, pronounce Gar's blessing and forgiveness on ye. We pray that your quest to repair the damage between ye and your Mither tis successful." He bent and wrapped his arm tighter around her.

"Return here when ye finish at Ayran." JayEll kissed her.

Jaylene turned and walked with Leftan to the waiting blue lift.

About the Author

Mari Collier was born on a farm in Iowa, and has lived in Arizona, Washington, and Southern California. She and her husband, Lanny, met in high school and were married for forty-five years. She is Co-Coordinator of the Desert Writers Guild of Twentynine Palms and serves on the Board of Directors for the Twentynine Palms Historical Society. She has worked as a collector, bookkeeper, receptionist, and Advanced Super Agent for Nintendo of America. Several of her short stories have appeared in print and electronically, plus three anthologies. Twisted Tales From The Desert, Twisted Tales From The Northwest, and Twisted Tales From The Universe.

Author Contact Information

http://www.maricollier.com/
https://twitter.com/child7mari

Lightning Source UK Ltd.
Milton Keynes UK
UKHW052130281220
376048UK00008B/434/J